THE WHOLE THING TOGETHER

ANN BRASHARES

DELACORTE PRESS

Text copyright © 2017 by Ann Brashares
Jacket art copyright © 2017 by Gallery Stock

randomhouseteens.com

Educators and librarians, for a variety of teaching tools, visit us at RHTeachersLibrarians.com

Library of Congress Cataloging-in-Publication Data
Names: Brashares, Ann, author.
Title: The whole thing together / Ann Brashares.
Description: New York : Delacorte Press, [2017]
Identifiers: LCCN 2016026996 | ISBN 978-0-385-73689-3 (hardcover : acid-free paper) | ISBN 978-0-385-90630-2 (glb : acid-free paper) | ISBN 978-0-399-55600-5 (ebook)
Subjects: LCSH: Interpersonal relations—Fiction. | Vacation homes—Fiction. | Families—Fiction. | Domestic fiction.
Classification: LCC PS3602.R385 W48 2017 | DDC 813/.6—dc23

The text of this book is set in 12-point Adobe Garamond Pro.
Interior design by Liz Dresner

Printed in the United States of America
10 9 8 7 6 5 4 3 2 1
First Edition

*With deep appreciation and love to dear friends
Nancy Easton, Bethany Millard, Janice Meyer, and
Elizabeth Schwarz, who helped me through this
story—and all my stories—over many miles
and many seasons in Central Park.*

THE THOMAS-HARRISON FAMILY, IN BRIEF

LILA HARRISON *married* ROBERT THOMAS.
Together they had three daughters:
EMMA, *now 22*
QUINN, *now 21*
MATTIE, *now 19*
Lila and Robert divorced.

LILA *married* ADAM RIGGS.
Together they have one son:
RAY, *now 17*
(Adam has two children from a previous marriage:
ESTHER *and* GEORGE, *both in their mid- to late twenties.)*

ROBERT *married* EVIE STONE.
Together they have one daughter:
SASHA THOMAS, *now 17*

SETTINGS
House on a pond in Wainscott, on the South Fork of Long Island
Lila and Adam's house in Brooklyn
Robert and Evie's house in Manhattan

1

THE HIGHS AND THE LOWS OF A RELATIONSHIP THAT DID NOT EXIST

The smell of home for him, more than anything else, was the smell of a girl he didn't know.

Home wasn't the creaking three-story brownstone on Carroll Street in Brooklyn where he lived most of the time, but this big house on a pond that let out into the ocean on the South Fork of Long Island in a town called Wainscott. He'd spent half the weeks of every summer here and half the weekends for most of every year of his life.

Ray sat on the floor of his bedroom amid piles of books, clothes, old toys, blankets, rain gear, fishing stuff, and sports equipment, and he breathed it in, seeking her part in all of his.

It was an old smell, habitual and nostalgic, associated with the happiness and freedom of summer, the outdoors coming in. It was also a new smell, recharged every other week, adding particles of new shampoo, a new dress, shiny stuff she put on her lips.

On the achy and full feeling of it, he got up and lay on his bed, where her smell was always the strongest. It instilled old comfort, the privacy of nighttime. He always had better dreams here, almost never nightmares. In his bed in Brooklyn he had nightmares.

He lay there in his shorts and T-shirt. He let his sandy, dirty bare feet dangle, out of deference. He used to never think about things like that.

Sleep in this bed, though sweet, had gotten fitful in the last year or so. Sweetly fitful. Sweetly frustrating. The smell, with its new and extra notes, got to be as stimulating as it was comforting. He didn't know exactly what those notes were, but they stirred his night thoughts in a new way.

"How's it going in there?"

He sat up. His mom's knock and entry were practically one motion.

"You're taking a nap already?" she asked.

"No, I was just—"

"Did you empty out the whole closet?"

He glanced back at the dark, walk-in closet. "Most of it. I tried to leave Sasha's stuff how it was. But some of it is mixed together. And some of the stuff I'm not sure of."

"It would be easier if there was a light in there," his mother pointed out.

He nodded. He probably hadn't replaced the bulb in two years. He hadn't cleaned the place out in a lot longer than that.

"Can I be done now?"

Lila gave him a look. "Seriously? You just threw everything on the floor. You have to deal with it."

"That's why I went back to bed."

She retied the bandana around her head. Her pants were covered in old paint and clay stains. "You should see the kitchen. You're lucky I'm not asking you to help with that."

He got up, not feeling lucky. "Why are we doing this again?"

"The girls organized it."

"The house looks fine."

"The other family is doing it too, next week."

"We should have gotten them to go first."

"Just get back to work, Ray. I left trash bags and boxes in the hall. Stuff you want to save put in boxes. You can bring them out to the storage room when you're done and stack them *neatly* on the shelves."

He surveyed the shelves along the bedroom wall. He and Sasha had had their unspoken agreements over the years about dividing up drawers, shelves, and closet space and their unspoken disagreements about dividing up drawers, shelves, and closet space.

Almost all the books were hers. Her entire Harry Potter collection still stood there, along with Narnia and His Dark Materials. He'd contributed *The Hobbit* to her Lord of the Rings set. He'd read almost all her books except the really girly ones, sometimes at the same time as her. He got indignant when he was reading one of her books, like the last Harry Potter, and she brought it back to the city.

He got out a recycling bag for his old comic books and his random piles of school papers. Among them he found one of her old science tests (91%) and her handwritten book report on *Charlotte's Web*. You would never mistake her rounded, regular script for the mess he made with a pencil.

The cabinet devoted to seashells, sea glass, smooth rocks, egg cases, and sharks' teeth was joint property. He couldn't begin to say who'd found what. They'd both been big hoarders on the beach. And all of it belonged to the sea, didn't it? He got rid of some crumbling coral and left the rest as it was.

He didn't bother with the bureau—since middle school he'd let her have the whole thing except one big drawer at the bottom with old sweaters and sweatshirts they both used. He kept his small and unimpressive wardrobe on two shelves and one hanging bar on the left side of the big closet. The medicine cabinet was at least ninety percent filled with her stuff. Granted, he had hardly any toiletries, in large part because he used her stuff. He was happy using her shampoo, taking a part of her smell around with him. He hadn't provided toothpaste or dental floss in years.

There was a lot of semibroken or useless crap to get rid of. He spent some time going through the fishing gear. He had to admit it took up more than his share of the closet, but she was welcome to use it if she took good care of it. They had one boogie board between them and he still took it out sometimes.

Did she? He didn't know. He found himself hoping so. He always imagined she loved this place, this pond, this beach, the weird house, this old camp bed under the skylight, as much as he did.

The surfboards they kept in the garage.

Though they slept in the same (comforting, fitful) bed, looked out the same skylight at the same moon, they didn't know each other. They shared three older half sisters, Emma, Quinn, and Mattie, but they weren't related. Sasha's father had once, long ago, been married to his mother.

He'd seen Sasha's face, very small, on the other side of Radio City Music Hall at their older sisters' graduations. He never saw her closer, because their two sets of parents choreographed the seating and the after-parties so they would never have to acknowledge each other. His sisters' birthday parties were like that too. Always separate, always two of them: the one with his family that involved homemade zucchini cake and craft-y presents around the Brooklyn kitchen table, and one with the other family that seemed to involve private rooms at trendy restaurants where a regular person couldn't get a reservation. He'd never been to one of those, of course.

He'd seen pictures of Sasha in the house from when she was little. He kept his eye out for new ones, but there hadn't been any in a long time.

He'd tried friending her on Facebook in eighth grade, and she'd declined. He'd been irritated at her for it, respected her for it, ultimately been relieved by it. He didn't really want to see her like that—another girl clustered with bikini-clad friends flashing braces and peace signs on Paradise Island or whatever. He wanted to keep alive the idea that she was different.

By tenth grade he'd deleted his Facebook account because he didn't want to see anyone else like that either. The projection of fake good times grated after a while. He had a tendency to harsh judgments, and Facebook made it worse. "You're such a curmudgeon," Mattie had told him. Which wasn't completely true. He used Snapchat and Rapchat as much as his friends.

He knew Sasha went to an all-girls' school on the Upper East Side where they wore uniforms. According to scoffing Mattie, there were a mere forty-two girls in Sasha's junior class. He pictured Sasha in a little pleated skirt. He tried not to do that too much.

Ray went to a public magnet school in Fort Greene, Brooklyn. There were 1,774 kids in his junior class and few pleated skirts.

The world of New York City private schools was like a club, insular, self-congratulatory, and pretty annoying, and Ray was not part of it. His sisters were part of it because their dad was rich. It was weird being from a different economic class than your own family.

So he didn't know Sasha through any of the normal channels. He felt like he knew her in an older and deeper way. He'd played with her toys, read her books, slept under her blankets, loved and fought with her sisters. He almost felt like she was part of him. She was his ideal friend in many ways: always with him, never disappointing. She never offered him the opportunity to judge her on surface things.

When he got to the pile of shoes, he began dividing, because dividing was what they did. He couldn't remember whose old beat-up and outgrown flip-flops were whose, so he tossed most of them into a garbage bag. He hoped she wouldn't mind. When he was in a good mood, he always gave her the benefit of the doubt. When he was in a bad mood, his opinion of her sometimes suffered. But even his most irascible moods, apt to ruin things, couldn't ruin anything with her.

Her old water shoes. His. When they were young their feet were approximately the same size and they could share stuff like that, and sometimes they did. But she often wore a special orthopedic shoe, which he wasn't supposed to touch, and that had given him an unexpectedly tender feeling toward her. Something about the way they stood, season after season, a little extra puffy and ready in the closet, you could picture exactly her stance when she wore them. In the last few years his feet had taken off in size, and hers, from what he could tell, had stayed pretty small.

Her sneakers, his.

Dividing was what they all did. As set down by their parents, they divided the house, divided the year, divided the holidays, divided the food, divided the paper products, divided the costs equally—well, supposedly equally. There was contention among the parents in nearly all the divisions: housework, lawn mowing, pool maintenance. In the case of his sisters, they got divided too.

His own parents seemed to enjoy a peaceful marriage, but it was the old dead marriage and bitter divorce between his mother, Lila, and Sasha's father, the semi-mythic Robert

Thomas, that shaped their lives. Besides their three daughters, this beach house was the one thing neither Lila nor Robert would give up and couldn't divide.

It was an uneasy truce, laced with the old poison. During the school year, changeover was Sunday at midnight, so the house had five empty weekdays to reset itself, to forget one family and remember the other. But in the summer, the house was in constant use. Changeover time moved to noon on Sunday, setting up that one witchy hour when the lives of two families bumped up against each other and strained the suppleness of the old house.

In summer there was the danger, the thrill, of seeing the other family, maybe catching a glimpse of their car on the way out. Every other Sunday, Ray imagined the house held on to their faint smells in the kitchen, wavelets in the swimming pool, maybe a little warmth in the bed. It was the ironclad rule in the summer that they never left the beach house later than quarter past eleven on Sunday morning, never arrived at it before quarter to one. They never risked a true encounter with the other family. And despite Ray's unspoken wish, they never had one. They maintained a half-life among half a family in half a house for half the year. If you put both sides together, it would kind of make a whole. But you never put both sides together.

In the closet was one row of distinctly girl shoes—flat sandals with straps, newer pairs with heels. No puffy orthopedic ones anymore. He wondered a little at those grown-up shoes, fleetingly sought to picture the now older girl who wore them, but didn't try for long, and didn't touch them. Because of the fitful bed problem, he'd become wary of letting his roommate become literal.

Brooklyn was his house, wholly, and his room there belonged to him alone, and yet he never felt as whole there.

He carried the first two boxes through the sliding-glass doors of the kitchen onto the flagstone path, through the fence that bordered the pool, and to the pool house. The front room, facing the pool, had regular pool-related stuff—a refrigerator, shelves, and hooks for cushions and towels—but the bigger, windowless room behind it was for the kind of storage you didn't visit too often.

He felt for the light. He hadn't been back here in a long time. It smelled of mold and mess.

He was struck right off by the old dusty crib. It had been his and also hers. He saw the plastic sheet that still covered the baby mattress to protect it from vomit. His vomit, to be precise.

What a history they had together, not together. Two babies who slept there, turned into people inside those bars. They used it equally but never at the same time.

Stashed under the crib were old toys. Why did they even have these anymore?

As he looked closer, he was glad they did. There was a wide plastic box full of Legos. One particularly rainy summer and fall they built a city, not together exactly, but sequentially, each adding to it week by week. He made the airport, she made the zoo. It had two amusement parks, four playgrounds, and a library, but no school, as he recalled, and not even any stores.

They were naturally harmonious as urban planners. And circumstances forbade his being imperious or bossy to her. He had no choice but to be patient, to let her take her full turn. He remembered the excitement of arriving at the house and tearing upstairs each week to see what she had added.

He loved that city. He ranted and raved when a cleaning service hired by the other family dismantled it just before Thanksgiving that year. Would she remember their city now?

There were balls, and light sabers with long-dead batteries. Another box contained the plastic animals they had jointly collected and shared over years' worth of birthdays and Christmases. There were the dusty stuffed animals she had loved gently and he had used for projectiles. There was the Barbie airplane he had publicly scorned but secretly played with a little during the long July they both had chicken pox.

He touched his fingers to the crib rail before he left.

One time when he was around nine or ten he stole one of the blankets from their bed and brought it to his regular bed in Brooklyn, hoping it would work its charm and ward off bad dreams there, too. But eventually her smell wore off and it just got to be another thing that smelled like him.

"My God, Quinn, I didn't see you. You're like a house fairy."

Quinn laughed from where she perched on her mother's bureau.

"How long have you been sitting there?"

"A few minutes. I watched you empty your sock drawer."

Lila cocked an eyebrow at her.

"And then put everything back."

"So you have been there a while."

Her mother wasn't very good at getting rid of things, Quinn observed. She wasn't a hoarder, but one thing suddenly represented everything and she got overwhelmed and closed the drawer.

"What about your room?"

"It's done."

"All of it?"

"I don't have that much stuff."

Her mother considered. "You don't. That's true."

What possessions Quinn had, she kept faithfully. She'd been the same size since she was fourteen, so that made it easy with clothes and shoes. She didn't judge Lila—Quinn didn't like to throw things away either. Not when they were still good to use.

Mattie loved shopping in stores, but Quinn did not. That was another reason she had few things. Indoor malls and big-box stores made her feel overlit and strangely dried out. Mattie dragged her to the Target in Patchogue, but Quinn knew herself well enough to wait outside.

There was a lot of grumbling about the cleanup project, but Quinn understood something the others didn't know yet. Emma, oldest and bossiest, was pushing it because Emma was falling in love. Emma saw through new and different eyes now, Quinn suspected, startled out of the regular blur of habit. Emma wanted everything to look better.

Emma hadn't confessed it yet. Quinn didn't know who it was, but she knew it was someone important.

"Why don't you tackle the den?" Lila suggested.

"Okay. I could do that."

Grandpa Harrison's mark was everywhere in the house, nowhere more than the den. It was all knotty pine walls and hunting decoys and pieces of driftwood attached to the wall by lengths of twisted wire. There was the wet bar in the corner with the 1970s ice maker, long broken. Most of the shelves bowed under hardbound books with titles like *Who's Who in America* and *The Social Register*.

Quinn never felt the living presence of Grandpa Harrison in this house. Because he was dead, for one thing, but that wasn't the main reason. He was repudiated, bankrupt, outmoded. It was just his stuff they contended with, and as stuff it was docile and easily ignored, holding out for a better time.

She turned to the cardboard file boxes piled in the corner behind the desk. Here were pictures, almost all negatives and prints. She took out the various envelopes and sat cross-legged with them on the ground.

The first box was mostly packed with photos of her grandparents at the country club with their friends. It was clear that what they loved was golf and cocktails. A few of them were heavily posed family pictures, where tiny Lila and her tinier brother Malcolm stood in stiff clothes looking uncomfortable.

Now Uncle Malcolm lived in the desert in New Mexico with his Vietnamese wife and their two-year-old son, Milo. Malcolm said he hated the East Coast and came back as little as possible.

You could see in the picture, from the tight top button of his shirt to the thick wool romper and dark boxy shoes, how that might have happened.

The next box had pictures of Quinn's own parents, the brief moment their life longings intersected. One photo taken on the lawn of this very house showed Lila with her straight blond hair down to her belly button and dark Robert, young as a boy, wearing jeans and a T-shirt. But they were heading in opposite directions, wanted different things. You could see it in the picture if you looked carefully—she is strident, he is eager. She wanted to use him—his Indian-ness—to shock her parents' system. He wanted to be part of the system he was supposed to shock.

A few months later Lila was pregnant and they got married, swooping into the next phase of life, where the big choices were made before they even meant to make them. Grandpa Harrison was predictably shocked and horrified that his daughter got pregnant by a brown-skinned young man with a presumably brown-skinned child when they weren't even married.

Years later, when Robert "saved his bacon," Grandpa Harrison came around to him. In fact, Grandpa came to treat Robert like a hero. Even after the divorce. Robert was the success in business Grandpa could never manage to be. "Robert thinks he can buy anyone" was what Lila said. Lila liked Robert better when her father hated him.

Once the shock wore off, the marriage faltered. Quinn had the feeling of it more than the facts. She was the wide-eyed, oddly patient kid who hung around beneath tables and in corners, taking the information back to her room or under her tree and sorting it out when she could. For a time there were accusations between them, cursing and shouting, three police officers at the house after dark, a custody war. There were no pictures in the box of any of that. Her sisters didn't seem to know or remember those parts, and she didn't want them to.

Then came remarriages, two new babies born in the same month, happiness on either side of the divide. The long, bitter silence set in between her parents. The fight raged on, but crooked and quiet.

There was one photo in the bottom of the box that seized Quinn's attention. It was small and square with a scalloped white border, of a different quality than the others.

The face was young, slightly turned away, almost too shy to smile. Quinn's hand began to shake as she held it. She'd never seen this before and yet it was something she had always imagined. The girl's dark hair was held back in a bun; her eyes were large and dark and deeply expressive. A dot glinted in the side of her nose; a bindi was pressed between her dark, strong eyebrows. She wore intricate earrings of worked gold.

Quinn ran upstairs as fast as she could. "Hey, Mom. Who is this?"

Lila studied it carefully. Turned it over looking for a date. "You found this in the den?"

"In the bottom of one of the photo boxes."

"Wow. I don't know what it was doing in there." Lila studied it closely. "That, as I understand it, is a picture of your biological grandmother. It came with your father's adoption papers."

"I knew it was. It had to be. Look at her face."

"God, she looks like you a bit, doesn't she? Those eyes?"

"A little Emma, too, in the proud mouth?" She was beautiful. She looked eerily like Sasha, but Quinn didn't say so.

"I see it. I really do."

"I've wished so many times I could see her. What a strange piece of luck. Do you know her name? Do you know anything about her?"

Lila's expression turned careful. "Of course you should be asking your father. He must have the papers from the agency in Canada that handled the babies from Bangladesh after the war. There wasn't much, but I do remember a few documents and that picture." She studied it again. "I haven't seen it since you girls were tiny. I didn't realize the resemblance. God, it almost makes me cry thinking of her."

Quinn was moved by the clutter of feelings she saw in her mother's face. It was hard keeping the love and hate separate in their family. Lila's love for her daughters and their origins, her desire for their happiness, could never quite be washed free of their father, whom Lila resented and avoided. For all the boundaries Quinn's parents had constructed between their lives, the really important ones couldn't always be held.

"I'll ask Dad," she said.

Lila had a warning look. "Well, it's not something your father likes to talk about. He didn't used to, at least."

"I know." Quinn held the picture protectively. "But I need to anyway."

2

A DEEPLY
CONSIDERED
STRANGER

There were times when Sasha felt particularly strange in this house. The place was beautiful—sea light and giant climbing trees, lush lawns, and the jewel of a pond pilfered from the ocean. She loved it beyond reason, waited impatiently through the long alternating weeks the other family had it, yearned for the first sight of the arched trees over the driveway when it was their turn again. But because it was a divided house, the faintest things could make her feel like an imposter, put her on the wrong side of family alliances.

Her father liked to remind her it was her and Evie's house as much as it was anyone's. She felt bad that he needed to say that, but he did. It was built by his ex-wife Lila Harrison's grandfather on land bought by Lila's great-grandfather. Lila's father rebuilt in the sixties to include lots of knotty pine paneling, decorative driftwood, and a bar in practically every room.

Lila was her father's first wife, before he met her mom, Evie. Lila was the mother of Sasha's sisters (fine, half sisters) and also the mother of Ray, who wasn't Sasha's half anything, but who was her agemate, her roommate, and (she might as well admit) her most deeply considered stranger. Lila was nothing to Sasha, besides descendent of the Harrisons and maker of weird craft projects.

When Sasha was old enough to begin wondering about these things, she'd asked her father why the house hadn't simply gone to Lila in the divorce, why she and her dad and her mom got it every other week.

"Because by the time we got divorced, Lila's father didn't own it anymore," her dad answered in his no-nonsense way. "Grandpa Harrison was an ass and a drunk, and if I hadn't paid off his debts and bought this place from him, he would have had to declare bankruptcy and move to a flophouse."

Sasha remembered wondering if he'd given that same account to her sisters.

Even though the property was still known as the Harrison place in town, her dad always made it sound like he was doing Lila a favor letting her have it even half the time. But Sasha also knew there were no favors, never favors, between her dad and Lila.

Grandpa Harrison might have been an ass and a drunk, but

Sasha's dad had made no effort to take down the portraits of Lila's more respectable ancestors that hung in the stairwell. Sasha considered this as she walked past the old men in suits and robes who signed things and judged things and founded things, and who reflected Sasha back to herself without comment. They belonged to Lila and Lila's daughters. They also belonged to Ray.

"Does it ever bug you to be judged by the men of the Harrison family every time you go down the stairs?" she asked her dad once.

Robert shrugged as though he'd never thought of it. "I like those pictures. They connect us with our history." He said it without any apparent irony.

She'd been too dumbfounded to respond. Had he actually convinced himself Lila's relations were also his? Even though they would have sooner cursed his brown face than shaken his hand? Robert took what he wanted from the world and left the rest. That was a gift of some sort. It had to be.

Sasha found her mother in the kitchen poking around gingerly in the cabinet under the sink, surrounded by contractor's bags. They were doing their part in "the Great Declutter," masterminded by her oldest sister, Emma, and begun by the other family the week before. Evie pulled out an object made of bent chicken wire, barely recognizable as a soap dish. "Do you think it's okay to throw this out?"

"Yes," Sasha said. She hated her mother's timidity sometimes. She hated her own timidity. The wrong side of family alliances mainly included her mother.

"What if Lila made it?"

Sasha laughed. She wasn't sure if her mom was trying to be funny. You could never be sure what odd crafty thing Lila had or hadn't made. "If she did, she should be especially eager for somebody to get rid of it."

"I don't know. . . ."

Sasha made a show of boldness, taking the thing from her mother's hand and throwing it into the nearest garbage bag.

Her mother went over to fish it out. "I think we should make a pile of stuff we aren't sure of and ask Emma."

"We are sure," Sasha said testily.

Sasha felt bad for the distinctions that made Emma and Quinn and Mattie—and even Ray—legitimate arbiters of bent chicken wire soap dishes and not her. That wasn't because she resented her sisters, but because she loved them. She didn't want to be on a different side than they were.

She spent a lot of time thinking about not belonging. She wondered if they spent any time thinking about belonging. She strongly suspected not. It was one of those negative identities— you imagined yourself in relation to what you didn't have.

Her father said to her once that Americans in the North didn't think much about the Civil War, barely identified themselves as Northerners because they had won it and moved past it. Sasha felt she was the South in this analogy.

That seemed a sad thing about human nature—how much more time we spend thinking about what we don't have, or have lost, than about what we have. Clearly Sasha had not inherited the peculiar gift of her father's.

She looked through the sliding-glass doors of the living room over the path down to the pond, shaded by enormous old linden trees. These were the days she would later be sorry not to have appreciated. She tried to induce appreciation, mentally get it firing like an outboard motor. It was a hard thing to will.

Was it even possible to see beauty in the present as it came at you? Or did it require a dose of time and loss and maybe a little pain?

"Have you finished in your room?" her mom asked.

Sasha poured herself a glass of water and drank it. "Ray did a surprisingly okay job. I just need to finish in the bathroom. I'm going back up. I've got nail polish in there from fifth grade."

"Not the lime-green."

"That and the Lip Smacker collection, including Cheetos and bacon."

Her mother shook her head.

In the bathroom she cleared out most of the medicine cabinet. She hesitated over the bacon lip gloss, but not for long. She almost wished she could take these and a lot of the other stuff they were getting rid of and have a yard sale. She remembered a really long time ago Emma setting up a table and selling her old stuff for a few bucks at their driveway entrance on Eel Cove Road. But it had barely been the kind of neighborhood where you could do that then, and it really wasn't now.

Standing there, she knew it wasn't the bad lip balm flavors that made her feel nostalgic. The stuff that wasn't hers evoked the deeper feelings: the capless, dried-out tube of athlete's foot cream, the crud on the shelves, the dots of whiskers in the white sink bowl.

Ray was not an ideal roommate. He was a famous vomiter. That was what they all said, anyway, and she'd slept in the evidence more than once. Later it was peeing on the toilet seat, a caked tube of toothpaste long-term missing its cap (why couldn't he ever screw a cap onto anything?), seaweed in the shower drain, and starting in the last year or so, the whiskers in the sink.

"It's weird to share a room with a boy," her friend Willa had said disapprovingly, standing at that sink when she'd slept over.

"I don't share my room with him. I've never even met him," Sasha explained in a canned way. Because though true, it wasn't quite honest. She did share a room with him. And a bathroom, for better and mostly worse. She did more than that. She shared a life with him, at least in her mind. Books and toys and sand in the sheets. A jointly collected menagerie of miniature plastic animals. Seashells, sisters, a view of the moon. She didn't know him, maybe, but how often did she think of him? How often did she live her life in this room, in this house, for both of them?

She used to want to meet him, fantasized about playing with him, made up games they might enjoy together. She was physically jealous that her sisters got to have him for their brother and she didn't.

But later, she began to think it was easier that she never did meet him. He had the best qualities of an imaginary friend. He was patient, sympathetic, and understanding, silently sharing

her things and spaces. He was never selfish or loud or bully-
ing. He never even disagreed with her. He was just what she
wanted, sometimes needed, him to be.

So in that way, he was an ideal roommate.

3

CORN AND MATTHEW

Emma was not the kind of person to have a secret. She liked to think it was because of her fine moral character, but it was also because she was kind of boring. She was an abider, an upholder, and a law-and-order kind of girl. The things she enjoyed doing were more or less the things she was supposed to be doing. She just wanted to make sure she was getting an A in the process.

"I'll meet you on the corner of MacDougal and Prince," she whispered into her phone. "If you leave the office in ten minutes, we should get there at the same time."

"Love you," Jamie said.

"Love you too."

"Em?" Her mother was standing in the dark hall of the Brooklyn house. Honestly, you could hear every word said in this place. Whispering hardly helped.

"Yeah?"

"Who was that?"

"Nobody. A friend." Emma grabbed her bag.

"Are you going out again?"

"Yeah. And then I'm going to stay over at Dad's." She started down the creaky stairs and her mom followed.

"Again? Why?" Her mom looked hurt.

"Because I'm going out in Manhattan and it's just easier."

"You never used to like to stay in the new house."

"Well, I've got a room there. And Dad really appreciates it."

Lila's face was getting complicated. "And you don't have your own room here anymore."

"I didn't say that."

Emma wasn't really staying at her dad's, but her mother would never know that. Lila would sooner call Donald Trump than her ex-husband. Emma hated to take advantage of her parents' hostility like Mattie was always doing, but sometimes it did come in handy.

"You're going back to Wainscott in the morning?"

"Yeah. I've got work starting at noon."

Her mom followed her all the way to the front door. It was kind of disconcerting.

"How come you keep coming back into the city?" Lila asked plaintively. "In the last few summers you never came back unless you had to."

"I'm an *adult*, Mom." She knew the way she said it undermined her point. "I'm a college graduate. I've got stuff to take care of." She reached out and gave her mom a hug. "I love you. See you out there on Monday, if not before."

Her mother held on to the hug for longer than usual. "Okay, okay." She stood at the door and kept watching Emma as she walked down the stoop and turned east toward the subway.

Emma looked back. "Mom, *what?*"

"Nothing. It's just . . . you're the child I count on NOT to be mysterious."

Mattie refilled the buckets of sunflowers on top of the long wooden counter at Reeses' Farm Stand, which stood under the shade of two giant oak trees at the edge of the Reese family's farm on Parsonage Road in Sagaponack, Long Island. She sprayed water on the lettuces arrayed on the shelves. June was big for lettuces. All morning her sister Quinn and Matthew Reese and Patsy hauled chard, kale, arugula, spinach, and butter lettuce from the fields onto the big tables under the shade of the tarpaulins behind the farm stand while Mattie divided them into bunches and bound them with red rubber bands.

The other big thing now was strawberries. Mattie picked through the bins and arranged them in green cardboard berry cartons. Between the stretch and snap of the rubber bands and the juice of the berries, her fingers were deep red by the time she switched places with Dana out front under the high sun at one o'clock.

"All yours," Dana sang, stealing a strawberry on her way out.

Mattie shot her with a rubber band in the back of the head.

People acted like Mattie was a ditz, but Dana made Mattie look like Albert Einstein. Dana used the calculator to add seven and two dollars. She posted pictures on Instagram of every semicool car that pulled up, preferably with some part of her dumb face barging into the frame. Half of the pictures were unidentifiably blurred because the car was moving.

"How's business, Matilda?"

Mattie squinted into the sunshine at Mrs. Reese. Matthew Reese was her grandson and, now in his early twenties, he was the manager of the farm, but Mrs. Reese, who was at least eighty, knew exactly what was going on at all times.

"Pretty good. We sold over two dozen cartons of strawberries in the last hour. Seems like the season is really getting started."

"I see we're running low. Does Matthew know?"

"Yes, ma'am. He's bringing more. Quinn and Patsy are picking right now."

"Nobody's buying sunflowers?"

"I just refilled them."

"How's your mother? Still delivering babies?"

"Yes, a few. But she tries not to take on many for the summer."

Mrs. Reese nodded. Her wrinkly face rarely changed expression. "That's fine," she pronounced obscurely.

Mrs. Reese always asked after Lila, but never asked about her dad or her stepdad, Adam. Mrs. Reese subtly disapproved of both of them for not being "local people," with the extra problem of not being white, in the case of her dad, or Christian, in the case of Adam.

Mattie saw Matthew and Quinn carrying the last two bins of berries up the hill. Matthew wore a faded blue bandana tied around his neck, which would have looked absurd on a regular person but looked distractingly good on him. His hair was sun bleached and his skin was already brown. His fame rang throughout the East End, and it wasn't for no reason. There was a joke in town: do the ladies stop at Reeses' for the corn or for Matthew?

Quinn wore old overalls and a tank top, her dark pixie-cut hair flattened by sweat against her neck. She and Matthew were talking a mile a minute, but Mattie couldn't hear the particulars.

"Did Dana go?" Matthew called to her.

"Yeah."

"Can you box these and keep an eye on the front?"

Mattie made a face. She hated when they tried to get her to do two jobs at once. "It's been pretty busy."

"There's nobody in the parking lot," Matthew pointed out.

"Well, there were a bunch of people a minute ago." She hated when she sounded like this, but it had been a long day.

"Okay, princess." Matt sighed. "I'll do the berries."

She wished it were flirtatious when he called her that, but she knew he was plain old irritated.

Quinn helped him, of course. The two of them expertly sorted and boxed while Quinn regaled Matthew with a story about a little kid she'd helped on Main Beach the day before. He'd hooked a three-and-a-half-foot striped bass on a Teenage Mutant Ninja Turtles toy rod and together they'd landed it.

Mattie sat sourly at the front while no cars pulled in, listening to Quinn the magical storyteller at work. She tried not to be interested, but she couldn't help it.

One problem was, it was impossible to be mad at Quinn, however much you wanted to. She was never boring, never predictable, never vain, never selfish.

Furthermore, you couldn't be jealous of her in any conventional way either. Quinn wasn't flirting with Matthew. Not even close. Her friendship with Mrs. Reese went just as deep, and her most abiding connection of all the family was to old Mr. Reese, who sat by the parlor window in his wheelchair.

Quinn kept her own hours, ate half the parsley in the greenhouse, rode her bike in circles inside the barn, and dressed like a gypsy. And yet the Reeses adored her and begged her to come back every summer. Quinn refused to work up front selling to customers, but the customers loved her. She watered and planted according to her own odd theology, but apparently the fruits and vegetables loved her too.

Mattie got to work on time every day. She never (hardly ever) talked on the phone and only texted if there were no customers. She wore her hair in two fetching blond braids and treated employees and customers alike to the view of her long legs in very short cutoffs. But the Reeses did not love her, except possibly Cameron, eighteen-year-old brother of Matthew, who happened to be a caveman.

Matt Reese, most importantly, did not love Mattie. He did not find it adorable that they had nearly the same name. He called her princess, without flirtation, and told her to quit working on her tan.

The self-same Matt huffed over, balancing a huge flat of berry cartons. He began arranging them on the display shelves.

"I can do that part, at least," Mattie allowed.

"What a model employee you are," he said.

Mattie shot him in the shoulder with a red rubber band. For good measure.

Emma was the one who put her finger on it: *Everyone loves Quinn the best, and she doesn't even try.*

4

ZERO-SUM

Emma's youngest brother and sister were born two weeks apart, a perfect duality. Here in Wainscott they'd slept in the same crib, gotten their diapers changed on the same table. Kind of like twins, except also kind of the opposite. They'd never even met. They existed for their big sisters in perpetual alternation, never gracing the same place at the same time.

"They don't know each other at all?" Jamie had asked over dinner in Manhattan the night before.

"No. I told you. My parents completely avoid each other." It didn't seem strange to Emma to love people who didn't love each other. She was used to it.

"And Ray and Sasha share a room in Wainscott?" Jamie persisted, eyebrows up.

"I'm not sure the word is *share*. They're never there at the same time, but I guess, yeah. They've always had the same room." When it came to your own family, it was hard to remember how weird they were. "When Sasha was born, my stepmom set up the complete nursery with all the fixings, and you know Lila. She didn't object to putting baby Ray in a crib festooned with pink and yellow if it meant she didn't have to buy a new one."

For Emma, her brother and sister were opposites who balanced each other out. Sasha was dark, Ray was light. Sasha was small, Ray was big. Sasha talked first, Ray walked first. Sasha had the problem with her foot. Ray couldn't make a hard "c" sound until he was five, so "cookie" was "tootie," "peacock" was "peatot." Rayspeak, they called it.

The two babies didn't have any parents or genes in common, so it was up to Emma to keep track of these things. Sasha had colic, but Ray was the throw-up king. (They called it spit-up for the first year.)

Mattie always favored Ray, because he was a brother and that was new and exciting. Emma and Quinn felt a responsibility to be more even-handed.

They didn't appreciate her for it, but Emma looked out for them. When Ray got grumpy or arrogant, she put him in line. When Sasha got timid and self-deprecating, Emma helped boost her up. She worried when they didn't get good grades (Ray) or try out for teams (Sasha). She worried when they didn't go out with anybody (Sasha) or went out with somebody too dumb for consideration (Ray + Violet).

That morning, as Emma packed her few things in Brooklyn to go back out to Wainscott, she heard Ray lumbering around in the kitchen below. It frustrated her that both he and Sasha were too lame to find jobs in Wainscott for the second summer in a row. Granted, it was harder for them than for their sisters. Emma, Quinn, and Mattie got to be out there full-time, while Sasha and Ray only came every other week.

Emma thought over the conversation she'd had with Jamie the night before, and in particular the word "share," which was how she got the idea.

"I had the most unbelievable brainstorm."

Ray looked up from his cereal and realized he was the only other person in their small Brooklyn kitchen. "Yeah?" he asked Emma after a long pause to see if maybe she did not need him to respond.

She did need him to. "And it is for you," she declared.

"Oh no."

Emma rolled her eyes. "Oh yes, is what you mean. Because I got you half a job."

He put his spoon down. "Really." It was not a question and did not hold hope.

"Really! You are a stock boy at the Black Horse Market in East Hampton earning $13.80 an hour."

He saw a problem right away. "Are you my boss?"

"No." She rolled her eyes again. "You are not cut out for baked goods. Not yet. Are you kidding?"

He was relieved enough to smile. "True. So what am I cut out for?"

"Dry goods. You can't mess it up."

"Huh." This time he meant it. "Really? $13.80 is good. The manager knows I can only work every other week?"

"That's the thing."

Of course there was a thing.

"The listing was for a stock boy or girl."

"I also have to be a girl?"

Emma laughed. "No, dumb-ass. I asked Francis, the manager, if you could do a job share. That was my brainstorm."

Ray pushed his bowl away. He was indebted enough not to slurp down the few teaspoons of milk remaining, because Emma hated that. "Which means?"

"Francis needs full-time, but he knows you can only do every other week."

"Okay."

"And there's another person I know looking for a job who can only do every other week."

Emma was always playing guessing games. And it was always boring, but before ten a.m. it was excruciating. He rested his head on his hand. "Can you please just tell me what you're talking about?"

"Sasha!"

"Sasha."

"Together you make full-time. Right?"

He sat up a little straighter, even though he hated to gratify Emma when she was already pleased with herself. "I guess. Yeah."

"You'd take the job together. You'd alternate weeks. Francis said okay."

"Have you told Sasha yet?"

"I'm just about to. What do you think?"

He thought. He breathed in all the smells of the kitchen. "He doesn't need us there together? Ever?"

"Exactly. That's the point. Together you make one employee."

Well. "What if she screws it up?" *What if I do?* "He can't exactly fire half an employee."

Emma lifted her shoulders in a dramatic shrug. "Let's be optimistic for now. Okay? Anyway, not even you two can mess up dry goods."

The Black Horse was precious, overpriced, and annoyingly located astride the perpetual summer traffic jam known as Montauk Highway. But $13.80 was pretty good. "Starting when?"

"Next week. Monday."

"Sasha goes first."

"Right. So?"

"If it's okay with her." An idea occurred to him. It seemed remarkable and a little wild. "Should I talk to her?" The mythical Sasha had a phone and a phone number, presumably. She was as close as ten digits, like anyone else. Right? She wasn't just an idea, a figment, a collection of possessions, a smell.

"You could, I guess." Emma's eyebrows confirmed the strangeness of this.

But why was it strange?

"If you want," Emma said. "Why, though?"

It seemed a natural thing, and yet he could come up with no reason. They were all trained to keep the households separate. It was a reflex. A matter of safety. Even for him. If you fell into the void between the two families, you might just keep falling.

"You don't need to worry about it," Emma assured him, crises averted, space-time continuum spared. "I'll talk to her."

Ray felt himself deflating a little, but he didn't want Emma to notice. "Okay, so now can you find me half a job in Brooklyn?"

"And Ray is good with it?" Sasha asked Emma over the phone, cutting half a brownie in half and then in half again.

"He is psyched," Emma assured her.

Sasha abandoned the brownie and sat down at the sun-soaked Wainscott kitchen table. She put her phone on speaker and set it down in front of her. "This Monday?"

"Yep."

"Wow. Okay. And your manager knows I don't have grocery store experience?"

"Yes. You'll be fine."

Sasha thought about it. It was remarkably perfect. She'd make some money, make her dad happy, get some space from her mother, and have a virtuous excuse for staying at the beach through the weekdays. The off weeks in New York she could study for SATs and volunteer again at the City Garden day camp.

"Em, thanks. This is amazing."

"No problemo."

Sasha got up and grabbed her phone and paced around the table. "Kind of weird to be sharing another thing with Ray."

"But genius, right?" It was hard to compliment Emma sufficiently, because she always outdid you. "And it's not like you and Ray have to hang out or anything," Emma went on. "The whole point is you don't have to be there at the same time."

Sasha sighed. She wanted to say that she had no issue with Ray. They weren't proxies for their parents. It wasn't her idea that the two sides of the family never touched. But she could think of no way to say it to Emma that didn't feel complicated.

"Can you get us an SAT tutor to share too?" Sasha joked instead.

"I bet I could," Emma said seriously.

"No, no. You don't need to do that."

"Oh, Matthew, you're a lonely young man."

"No, I'm not."

"Yes, you are. I can see it."

"I have my grandparents. I have you. I have the asparagus."

Quinn laughed, though she too counted the striving little spears of asparagus among her dearest.

Like Matthew, she had many loves at the Reeses' farm, and he was among her best and most trusted. There were Mr. and Mrs. Reese, the familiar fields of flowers and food; she knew every foot of every row by heart. There was the smell of the old falling-down barn. There was also Cameron, whom she did not care for.

For the last two summers she'd told herself she should try something more challenging. An organic farm growing heirloom vegetables and medicinal herbs in Northwest Harbor. A teaching garden for elementary school–age kids in the Springs. But she couldn't abandon her old perennials at Reeses': the asparagus, artichokes, rhubarb, spinach, strawberries, apricots, and plums were her dear old friends too. She couldn't help going over to check on them in late spring, and the next minute she found herself employed.

Every summer she and her sisters gravitated back here to the beach. Emma got fancy job offers from investment banks and tech companies, but instead spent her summer tying pastries in white boxes with red bakery string at the Black Horse. Mattie said she loved to travel but sat day after day in the dust of cars pulling in and out of Reeses' parking lot.

There was an unspoken feeling among them of needing to hold on to the old place. Because every time you looked, it changed. A new mansion sprouted up in place of field or forest. And around the mansion sprouted a hedge, so the streets became tunnels. It was changing so fast they worried that if they looked away it would be gone—a place they could no longer recognize.

"I'm happy you're back," Matt said.

"Me too."

She collected wild poppies at the edge of the melon patch for Myrna Chapman before she went in to find Mr. Reese.

He was sitting by the window, his usual spot.

"Quinn Hardy Thomas, I can tell it's you by your footsteps," he said without turning around. "Welcome home."

She went over and kissed him on the cheek. She dragged a chair close to him and sat. On the table next to him she left the brown paper bag of ramps she'd picked in the woods near her house. "Tell me about the farm," she said. She grasped his hands for a moment, orienting herself to him, to his particular warmth and pulse. He always liked to start with the farm. Other stories radiated from there.

As he talked about storms and snowmelt and local governance, Quinn felt the familiar sensation of floating above herself. She felt the strain and rub of his vocal cords, the soft ruffles of skin on his neck, the pent-up muscles in his arms, the nerve memories in the bottoms of his legs. She looked down at the map of the world stretching across the tops of his hands.

She'd done this since she could remember, did it more now. She became untethered from herself and sifted her way toward others. Through the cracks in their faces she found her way in. Not pushing or bursting, but just feeling and finding. Sometimes their sufferings overwhelmed her. Did she alleviate anything by her presence? She didn't know, but in some cases, she felt her peculiar kind of comfort was wanted.

Inside Mr. Reese whirled a dark pool you could fall into if

you weren't careful. Little sorrows circled down into the big ones. No sugar in his coffee, then no milk in his coffee, then no coffee. No feet to stand up to the sniveling accounts manager, no feet to stand up to his wife, no feet to stand up. Loss and loss and more loss.

But he was still here. He still sat at the window. Still smiled when she came. Why? She had to be careful to hold on to the edge. Not to fall in, but not to shy away either. That was her life's challenge. Not to shy away from the pain. Not to deny it, but rather to take it on. Give it a voice if it needed one. Accept that it had a right to be.

Mr. Reese had lost the first foot to diabetes and waited for the world to end. Until he lost his second leg from the knee down and the world spun stubbornly on.

He'd kept both feet, both eyes, his viscera, his nerves, and even his mind through the Second World War, then lost them all to sugar. "You learn to trust bitterness more than sweetness," he'd told her.

5

SUGGESTIONS FOR YOUR POSSIBLE HEART

The night it happened was in mid-April. The fourteenth, to be precise. Her father was throwing a fancy catered party at the house for the young analysts at his firm. They got lobster canapés in return for working a hundred hours a week fifty-two weeks a year.

Emma had come home from school for the weekend to do her housing application for NYU law in the fall. It was unusual for her to be staying at his house in Manhattan. Since he and Evie had sold the old apartment on Eighty-First Street, she felt more comfortable at her mom's in Brooklyn. But then, last year, her mom and Adam starting renting out the first floor of the house to a gay couple who celebrated their marriage in the tiny back garden. What little space they had in the Carroll Street house got smaller, so that the three sisters, now all in college, were left with one small room between them. Lila and Adam needed the money, she understood. Having tenants on the ground floor really helped.

As usual, her two families went in different directions. While her mom and Adam collected a modest rent from Andy and Hank, her dad and Evie bought a palatial town house on East Seventy-Fourth Street, where all four girls had their own rooms, but only Sasha lived in hers. It had temperature-controlled wine cellars, radiant-heated floors, intercoms, and mystifying state-of-the art HVAC and security systems nobody ever dared touch. It did not feel like home.

Her dad had begged her to come to the party. He was proud of the culture of his firm, his young, eager Ivy League brigade. He was proud of his young, eager Ivy League daughter. She'd resisted, because, well, who in their right mind wanted to go to that party?

Finally, out of guilt and a sense of daughterly duty, which she'd always felt a large share of, she put on a dress and carried her low expectations with her down the stairs.

For some reason there had been a young man standing in the doorway of her father's dressing room. She'd heard someone thumping around on her way down and went in to check.

"Sorry to interrupt, but what are you doing?"

He'd turned around fast. His shirt was partly unbuttoned, his suit jacket over one arm. He looked horrified. "Oh shit. You scared me." He'd looked down at his open shirt. His face was shiny. Guiltily he held up a stick of antiperspirant. "Just this. I shouldn't, I know."

He stood on the tall side of average, a little skinny, dark brown hair cut to please his elders. "I hope the boss won't mind." He laughed nervously. "Or find out, mainly. I hope he won't find out. Ever. Jesus."

Emma had smiled at him. She couldn't help it. His face was open and intent. She had meant to be annoyed, but she couldn't. "I won't tell him."

"It's hot in here, isn't it? Do you think he purposely turns up the heat to see who can take it?"

"Who?"

"Mr. Thomas."

Emma almost laughed because the truth was so much more innocent. Nobody could figure out how to work the insane HVAC.

"It's kind of nerve-racking to be in his house in the first place. I'm pretty junior still. I've never seen him outside the office before."

"I don't think he—"

"You look pretty cool. Did you just start?"

"Start?"

"At Califax, I mean. I don't think I've seen you at the office yet. Which floor?"

"Oh, I—"

He had sensed her discomfort and seemed to want to rush past whatever caused it. "I started last year. Sorry, closer to a year and a half ago. Or, well, what is it, April? So I graduated in January and started right after that. Califax doesn't usually hire midyear graduates, but they said—" He stopped. He put the antiperspirant down. "Sorry. I talk a lot when I'm nervous. Sorry. I say sorry a lot when I'm nervous."

"That's okay," she said.

"We should get back down there." He'd put his jacket on and turned to show her his back. "Can you see any sweat stains? My sister told me I'm supposed to have a summer jacket, like linen or something, but I just have two wool ones. Shit."

"No," she lied. "I can't." She'd followed him to the stairs.

"Can you believe this place? I've never seen an actual house in New York City. Where, you know, people live in the whole thing. Have you?"

"Well, uh . . . ," she'd said noncommittally.

"It's like, five floors. It's bigger than our house in Columbus. It's a lot bigger."

"Is that where you're from?"

"Columbus. Yes. Ohio. Shit. I can't even imagine how much a house like this would cost. Can you?"

"I don't really know."

"You could fit my entire apartment into this hallway." He'd glanced around the hallway. "Twice."

"Oh."

"It's not that they don't pay pretty well at Califax, you know? I'm not complaining. Well, sometimes I complain. Are you first year? I still have some student loans, so that's partly why I live in a—" He'd stopped and looked at her. "You are— That is—a beautiful dress—that you're wearing." He shook his head. "Sorry."

"Thanks."

"Do you want a drink? Are you drinking? My sister said not to drink, because it would be too easy to drink too much and make a total ass of yourself." He stopped. "Myself. Sorry. Myself, not yourself. I can tell you would never do that."

She laughed. She remembered so clearly that first feeling of her heart climbing out of her chest, up into her throat. "Right. I got it."

He took a long breath. "Sorry. I really wish I could stop talking."

"That's okay. I'm kind of enjoying it."

She had followed him down to the first floor, where most of the party was taking place.

Now she felt bad for being such a brat to her dad about coming to this party. It suddenly felt important.

She thought vaguely of making amends to her dad, and then she actually saw her dad, which was not what she wanted at all. He was large and in charge in his fancy linen jacket a few feet from the bottom of the stairs.

Oh, no. She didn't want to make amends yet. She did not want to see him right now. Should she dash back upstairs? Was there any way she could escape without him seeing her? *Shit.*

It was too late. He saw her. Her dad's face broke into a big smile. "You did come down! I hoped you would."

She remembered glancing at her sweaty new friend. Was there some way to finesse this?

He looked shinier than ever. *Shit.*

Her father's eyes went from her to her new friend and back. "Emma, have you met Jamie?" he boomed.

She and the young man had arrived at the bottom of the stairs together just as her father came toward them, wineglass in hand. Emma realized there was no way to stop this. Her father loved nothing if not a proper introduction.

"Emma, this is James Hurn, one of my very finest second years," he'd said proudly. "Princeton, class of 2013."

She looked at him. She stuck out her hand and shook it firmly, as she'd been taught from toddlerhood.

James Hurn had a slightly nauseated look, as though in anticipation. Or maybe she'd imagined that part.

"Jamie," Jamie had said weakly, trying to keep his face on this side of a grimace.

"Jamie, this is my oldest daughter, Emma," her father boomed even more proudly. "Princeton, class of 2016."

The look on Jamie's face as he dutifully shook her hand was so sweetly pained, so entirely crushed, she would have laughed had she not felt so suddenly, deeply attuned to his well-being. She winced apologetically.

"Sorry," he had mouthed to her.

"Sorry," she had mouthed back.

Emma had had a boyfriend senior year of high school. Kyle Bowen. He had a lot of chest hair. When he'd stopped calling after graduation she barely noticed. At Princeton she'd gone out off and on with the captain of the lacrosse team, Graham Cartwright. He looked great sitting at the dinner table. She remembered

Mattie's comment about him: "You know how people think you have to be smart to go to Princeton? Well, you don't."

Emma was always busy with school and sports and work. Boyfriends were a box she felt she needed to check. She'd never felt true empathy, tenderness, or vulnerability toward one until the night in mid-April. And then for some reason it happened all at once.

"The Reeses' land is worth millions of dollars," Mattie's father said at dinner in Wainscott Friday night, and not for the first time, as they started in on a dessert of strawberries Mattie had brought home from the farm. "Paula Reese is using some of the world's most sought-after real estate to grow spinach."

"And strawberries," Evie said with a perky look of gratitude at Mattie.

Sasha held up her spoon. "Better spinach than another giant mansion with fourteen bathrooms and a helicopter pad. Do you really want another one of those?"

Robert put on the half-bemused, half-eager look he got when Sasha sparred with him at the dinner table. "It's not my decision what people do with their money."

"No, it's not, but maybe Mrs. Reese is thinking about the community. Say another billionaire buys that land, which is exactly what would happen, and seals it off behind twelve-foot hedges. Then nobody else gets anything from it. Not even the billionaire, because he probably has five other houses. He'll spend a week a year there and not even rent it to anybody else, because he doesn't need the money. Another chunk of the East End . . ." Sasha snapped her fingers. "Gone."

"Sasha," Evie said, in her first-warning voice. Evie was always the silent referee. She never actually played.

Mattie got up to clear her plate. She got instantly bored with the Robert and Sasha show. She guessed they did some version of this every night, whether or not Mattie was there to be annoyed by it.

"Thanks to the Reeses," Sasha went on, "we get to drive along open fields growing food, and we get to buy the freshest corn and strawberries imaginable. And people like Mattie and Quinn get jobs."

Mattie rolled her eyes. "Leave me out of this. If I was Mrs. Reese I would take the cash in a heartbeat."

Robert pushed back from his plate and patted his belly. "Thank God I put money away for Sasha to go to law school," he said, his usual complain-brag.

When Mattie was really young—maybe five or six—she remembered asking her father if he loved Sasha the best because he loved Sasha's mother and not theirs anymore. *Of course not,* he'd said, as though this was a ridiculous idea. *I love you all the same.* But it sure hadn't seemed such a ridiculous idea to her. And he might have been more convincing if he'd taken even a second to think about it.

You always protect her, Mattie had accused.

Well, she's a lot littler, her father replied.

Now Mattie stopped halfway to the kitchen and turned around. "What did you put money away for me to do?" she asked.

Her father looked at her affectionately. "Buy a dress that covers your backside."

Both Evie and Sasha stayed quiet. Emma would have madly cackled and piled on if she had been here, but Evie and Sasha always had to be careful and Mattie knew it. They weren't even allowed to smile.

"Thanks a lot, Daddy," Mattie said, fake indignant. "And with what's left over between that and the cost of Sasha's law school, you can buy me a loft in Williamsburg."

"Can I?"

"You may."

Mattie stopped again at the kitchen door, a cheap impulse inside her still not quite satisfied. "What are you and Evie going to talk about when Sasha's at law school?"

"Ray? Over here."

Sasha turned around. Should she really answer to the name Ray? This seemed like a pretty big capitulation on her first day of employment at the market. But Francis, the manager, kept calling her that and she kept pretending she didn't hear him, which was not tenable long-term. Why did Emma have to put damned Ray's name first on the damned job application?

Sasha straggled over from the pile of pasta boxes. "Um. Well, actually it's Sasha," she pointed out again.

Francis shook his head. "Listen, I don't have time to get to know *two* employees. As far as I'm concerned, you two are one person."

"But—"

"Do you have a problem with that? . . . Ray?"

"Uh."

"Hey! Polly?" He bellowed at the first cashier. "Show Ray here how to do the restocking."

Polly yawned and pressed her temples throughout her explanation of what to do with the unbought stuff that accumulated at checkout.

Then there was Francis again. "Ray, get over here."

"Okay . . ."

"A few things."

She followed him out back to the dumpsters. The door nearly swung into her face.

"No sneakers. No shorts. Keep your Black Horse shirt clean. No jeans. No gum. I hate gum. No tattoos showing. This is a nice store. I don't like the piercings you kids have. Take out the hardware when you come to work. You understand what I mean? And a smile. A smile on your face at all times. Tell that to your brother or whatever it is."

She followed him back to the storeroom, nearly running to keep up. "My brother?"

"The other Ray. I don't want to have to say all this twice."

"Right. Well. You see, the thing is, he's not my brother."

Francis was doing something on his iPad. Was he even listening?

"'Cause. See. We're not related, actually. Actually, we've never even met."

Francis looked up at her impatiently. "He's Emma's brother."

"Yes—"

"Are you not Emma's sister?"

"Right. Yes, but—"

He was already halfway to the baked goods section. "I don't have time for this, Ray."

Sasha approached Francis casually a few hours later, near the end of her shift. The day's last shipment was shelved, the boxes removed. The muscles of her arms were shaky with fatigue, but she felt like she'd pulled off the stock girl act, at least for a day.

Francis was eating a cookie. He could often be found hanging around the bakery section. "How's it going, young Ray?"

She gave him a look. "Hey, Francis?

"Yeah?"

"I have an idea. How about if you get the real Ray to answer to the name Sasha. Then I, Sasha, will answer to the name Ray."

Francis chewed his cookie confusedly. When he finally realized what she was saying, he laughed.

6

I NEVER WONDERED.

"I always wondered if she was Muslim or Hindu. But I thought Hindu was more likely."

Quinn's father looked at the picture of the lovely Bengali girl, but he didn't really look at it. He handed it back to her. "Why did you wonder?"

"Didn't you?"

"I never did."

"She was your mother. How could you not?"

Her dad shook his head. "I'm not sure what Lila told you, but I don't know who that person is. I never knew that girl. My mother was Matilda Thomas of Califax, Ontario, God rest her soul. She was thoroughly Christian."

It wasn't the first time a conversation between them had led here.

"Do you have any other information about this girl? Do you know her name?"

Robert was back to his computer screen. "It was on the adoption papers, I think."

"Where are those?"

"Honestly, I don't know. I'm not sure I ever took them from the Brooklyn house. They were in the metal file cabinet in the basement, and I have no memory of moving them."

Quinn stared for another moment at the face of the girl who may or may not have ever held her baby.

Indeed, Quinn had wondered. As much as she admired the eloquence and beauty of the Quran and Hadith, images of the Hindu deities had sparked in her dreams since she could remember, as though passed along in her father's blood. He tuned out their enchantments, maybe, but Quinn felt them strongly. Now she felt almost sure she was Hindu. Because of the bindi.

"I wish I could have known Matilda," Quinn said, sensitive to his state. Robert's adoptive parents were a childless couple already in their fifties when he came to them, their miracle, their small life force. They were both gone before Robert turned twenty-six.

Her dad looked up, his expression changed. "I do too, my darling." For a powerful man, her father was quick to tears when it came to certain subjects, including his mother and his daughters. "You know she held you when you were a baby. I have a picture of that on my office wall. You've seen it."

Quinn nodded, withdrew from his study. She put the picture of his birth mother safely in her top drawer.

Her heart ached for her father sometimes, even though he did not ache for himself. His unspoken traumas roamed the house like orphans, and Quinn took them in.

She imagined that boy baby in the refugee camp. Was there someone to hold him? Was there milk to feed him? Who, if anyone, clapped when he took his first steps? In what language did he speak his first words?

Matilda Thomas might have held baby Emma and baby Quinn, but she never held her own child until he was over two years old.

Quinn once overheard Lila say to her brother, Malcolm, "He was so young when I first knew him, he still had terrors at night sometimes; I think his memory still reached back to the camp then."

At the time, Quinn had trembled with feeling, but she held back from barging in with all the questions she wanted to ask, because she knew she wasn't supposed to be listening. In so many quiet moments since then she'd taken out those words and turned them over in her mind.

Her parents first met at Andover summer school. Her mother was a sophomore in high school and her father a freshman. In the earliest letters, her mother called him Bobby.

At some point her father became Robert and he didn't have those dreams anymore. Lila was the last person left who had known him before the transformation was complete.

Maybe it was a relief for her dad to be with Evie, for whom he was never Bobby and never dreamed of the refugee camp in Bangladesh that was his first home.

Dear Ray,

I hope it's okay that I'm emailing you. Quinn gave me your address. I'm Sasha, your stranger-roommate (sorry about the thing with the screen last week), fellow sibling of our sisters, and co-employee at the Black Horse. It seems weird to write to you after all this time, I know, but Manager Francis had a few things for me to pass on to you, and Manager Francis is "not kidding around." So here it is: no sneakers, no shorts, keep your Black Horse shirt clean, no jeans, no gum, no visible tattoos or piercings. Oh, and "keep a smile on your face at all times." Even in the stockroom and out back by the dumpsters, apparently. I think that's everything.

So anyway, it's been an honor sharing a room and three sisters with you all these years.

Sasha

Dear Sasha,

I've been pretty much waiting my entire life to say

sorry about the vomit. Just, all of it. Every chunk. I am
sorry. I would hate to share a room with me.

I like to think that's all in the past. So looking toward
the future, sorry about the shaving scum. I'm trying to
be better, but I think I forgot last week.

I just needed to say that.

Thanks for the heads-up from Francis.

Ray

Also, thank you for trying to keep the shelves nice
and for watering the old kalanchoe plant (RIP) because
I never did and for having a lot of good books over the
years that I read without asking. And for writing a lot of
smart notes in your schoolbooks, which allowed me to
do better in English class. And for providing toothpaste
I've used literally for YEARS. And for having that silky
nightgown kind of thing you leave at the bottom of the
bed sometimes. And for making the sheets smell so
good that I can barely fall asleep at night.

Ray looked over the last paragraph he had written and erased
it all.

Francis eyed Ray as he stood by the storeroom door of the
Black Horse Market. "So you are the other half of my new
employee."

"Yes, sir."

Ray guessed Francis was studying him for possible tattoos and telltale piercing holes.

"You are large for just half," Francis concluded.

Ray shrugged. "But graceful."

"Not as graceful as the other half. Not as pretty, either. Not half as pretty."

Ray wasn't sure what to say. "I'll work on that."

"You heard about no jeans, no—"

"Yep, all of it."

"I am under orders to call you Sasha."

"From who?"

"From Ray."

"I'm Ray."

"The other Ray."

"There's another Ray?"

"Your sister."

"You mean Emma?"

"No, the other one."

"Quinn? Mattie?"

"You have a lot of sisters."

"Yeah, but none of them are named Ray, as far as I know."

"The small one. Pretty. Yellow eyes. Her name's Ray."

"My name's Ray. I think you mean Sasha. That one's not my sister."

Francis shook his head. "Hey, you know what, Sasha?"

Ray winced. "What?"

"Never fucking mind."

Dear Ray,

Could you please withdraw orders to call me Sasha?

Sasha

"God help us, Dad is mowing the lawn again." Emma stood by the sliding-glass doors in the Wainscott kitchen, phone in hand, watching the back-and-forth. "Where'd he get the mower?"

"I think he rented it." Mattie banged her breakfast things into the sink. "I'm guessing Mom stopped paying the bills again."

It was an old story. The lawyers split up the maintenance bills for the house; Robert paid his assiduously and Lila didn't. "I'm sorry, we don't have the money this month," Lila said freely to anyone who asked.

The feud was too bitter for Robert to just pay her share. The money hardly mattered to him; it was the capitulation he could not tolerate. Then he spent ten times the amount the lawn service cost on threatening letters to Lila from his expensive lawyers. Emma knew for a fact her mother swept up all the lawyer letters and threw them into the recycling bin.

Sasha turned from the toaster, a look of amusement on her face. "It's good for him. It gets him outside and moving. Otherwise he'd be at the computer or on the phone bothering the overworked guys at his office. Dad gets exercise, his employees get a break. It's really a win-win."

"Nobody tell Lila," Mattie said.

Emma glanced down at her phone. She'd prided herself on not being the person who looked at her phone every second. How many times had she rolled her eyes at Mattie? Now she was that person.

And of course Mattie was the one who busted her. "Oh, oh. Look who's sneaking away again."

Emma gave Mattie an imperious look on her slow, casual way out to the hall. Then she sped up the stairs and out of earshot. "Hi," she said. "Where are you?"

"Bridgehampton."

"I'm on my way. Meet me at Olive's. Have you had breakfast?"

"Just coffee. Isn't Olive's kind of public?"

"Don't worry. My dad's mowing the lawn."

"I hate sneaking around."

"I know."

"Do I feel worse about sleeping with his daughter or skipping out of the office today?"

"Hey, Matt."

Wave, smile.

"Yo, Mattie."

Smile, wave.

It was embarrassing how many people she knew at the Black Horse. How many people there she was now related to.

It was her day off from the farm stand, and she'd stopped in the big air-conditioned market to get sweet grape tomatoes.

They weren't in season locally yet and her mom wanted them for a recipe. She should have stopped at the Stop & Shop, where they cost half as much, but she couldn't resist getting a latte, a stale but free pastry from Emma, a glimpse of newly hired Ray haplessly stacking boxes of couscous, and the benefit of one of their employee discounts.

Ray was on break, it turned out, smoking a cigarette with Julio in back by the dumpsters.

"What are you doing? You don't smoke," Mattie said.

"I only smoke with Julio," Ray said.

She shook her head. "What time do you get off?"

"Seven."

"Mom says dinner at seven-thirty."

"Okay. I'll be home."

She returned through the back door. She spent some time considering tomatoes.

She felt a shadow over her that stayed a little too long. She turned.

"Are you Matilda Thomas?"

It was a nicely dressed man probably in his late fifties, light hair a mix of white and gray and leftover blond. He was a little uncertain and also familiar.

"Mattie. Yes . . . I'm—"

He put his hand out. "Jonathan Dawes. I'm a friend of your family from a long time ago, before . . ."

She waved her arm like a conductor both to cut him off and let him know the understanding already passed between them. So giant was the quake that ended her parents' marriage that everybody took sides or fell into the fracture. She was too young to remember much of the event itself, but her life felt like a series of aftershocks and rebuilding efforts.

Why did he look familiar? She tried to think. Suddenly she remembered something. A photograph. "You taught surfing, right?"

He smiled. "Yes. Exactly."

"You taught my mom?" She searched through her files for a very foggy memory.

"And you girls a few times." He was watching her face carefully. Maybe he was thinking she looked like her mother back then. People from long ago often said that.

"I'm sorry to tell you, it didn't really take in my case. I suck at surfing."

He laughed, but in a slightly abstracted way.

"My sister Quinn wouldn't shame you, though. She's actually good."

He was watching her face more than listening to what came out of it.

"I'm sorry," he said, maybe realizing this. "You remind me of . . ."

"My mother."

He paused a second before he nodded.

She liked how he looked. He had a fine face, square, tanned, alert, wrinkled in good places. He seemed the kind of person who didn't just say things to hear the sound of his voice.

"Is she still surfing?" He looked slightly pained but also eager, the way he leaned forward.

She liked his face; however, she also suddenly found she wanted to get away from him. "Who?"

"Your mother."

"Sometimes. Yes." She grabbed haphazardly at tomatoes. "I've got to get back home. My mom needs these for a recipe."

"Okay." He was still standing there, looking after her as she got in the cashier line. She pushed her hair behind her ears self-consciously, tried to act like she didn't know she was being watched. It was a game she'd played before. He wasn't watching her pervily, though. It wasn't that. She possessed a highly sensitive flirt detector, and she was pretty certain that wasn't what was going on. But there was something.

"I still surf every Saturday out at Ditch Plains," he said to her. She was half a store away, but his voice carried without him seeming to yell, kind of depositing itself in her ear. "If you ever want to come by."

Why would she ever want to come by? "Okay," she said noncommittally.

"Say hello to your mom from me." He sounded serious the way he said it.

She didn't look at him once as she paid and marched to her bike, but once on her seat and steering out of the parking lot, she did look back. He was still standing there by the tomatoes.

7

TROUBLE ME.

Business was slow at the market and the morning's deliveries were already unloaded and stocked. Emma flagged Sasha down on her way to register four.

"Dad said dinner at seven tonight. What time do you get off?"

"Seven. Can you tell them I'll be a few minutes late?"

"Sure."

Francis was making large slow circles around the bakery counter, as he often did.

"You want a day-old croissant?" Emma asked.

"No thanks. I should keep moving. Francis is giving me the stink eye."

Emma rolled her eyes and waited for him to disappear behind the deli counter. "Last year he was wearing a paper hat and scooping gelato from a cart out front."

"Power corrupts."

"Absolutely."

Sasha affected a serious voice. "But that was before he finished his MBA, Em. That would be Masters of Business Administration from Fordham."

Emma laughed. She put on her Francis face. "After I got my MBA, it gave me a new perspective on merchandising. . . ."

Francis appeared again and Sasha got moving.

Francis found her a few minutes later restacking cans of chickpeas.

"Emma is assistant *manager* for baked goods," he informed her. "She can't just be holding your hand all the time."

"Oh, I know. Definitely. You're right." Sasha loved the fact that Francis thought she and Emma always and only talked about work.

He watched her suspiciously. "You said you already finished the canned goods."

"I thought maybe I could do a neater job."

Francis nodded approvingly. "You look a bit like her, you know."

Sasha heard Julio fake coughing from a few shelving units over.

"Emma, you mean?" she asked. How could she make the bean-stacking fill up the next half hour? "Yeah, that's what people say."

"You don't look like your brother, though."

"Right," Sasha said. "He's not my brother, so that could partly explain it."

Francis had tuned her out by this point, as she knew he would.

Dear Other Sasha,
    The Regent of the Black Horse, Master of Markets, requests you take the early shift tomorrow.

Original Sasha

Other Ray:
    You are not permitted to leave your shoes or books in the cubby overnight.

Regards,
The Pharaoh of Fordham
(as dictated to original Ray)

"So I saw a guy at the Black Horse a couple days ago who said to say hello to you," Mattie mentioned, elbows on the kitchen counter, watching her mom wash the mounds of lettuce she'd brought home from the farm stand.

This was a perfectly regular kind of thing to say, such a multigenerational place it was for them, but Mattie had stopped and started three times. She was being oddly careful about when and how to lay it down.

Her mother was distracted. She kept squinting at her phone, unable to make it cough up some voice mail or other. "Oh yeah?" She put her hair behind her ear. "Who?"

"Jonathan Dawes."

Her mother stopped and turned. Her phone slid across the counter. Two handfuls of lettuce fell into the colander. Mattie looked for a trace of alarm in her mother's eyes and she saw it.

"You must remember him," Mattie added.

"Yes. Of course." Her voice almost came out casual, but her skin wasn't quite the normal color. "He used to teach surfing."

"Yeah, I can sort of picture that."

Her mother cleared her throat. "Did he recognize you?"

"Yeah, I guess he did. Or maybe he overheard someone say my name. I don't know."

Her mother retrieved the lettuce. She kept her face down.

He was an old boyfriend, maybe. Somebody who was important once.

"Did you grow up with him out here?" Mattie asked. Maybe he was a summer fling, a high school crush. She lifted herself up and sat on the counter. She wanted a better angle on her mother's face.

Her mother apparently wanted a worse angle. She abandoned the lettuce and went to the refrigerator. "Uh, no. I guess I met him later. He lived in LA. That's where he grew up." She gazed aimlessly at the dairy shelf. "He came to New York for a job. He worked in advertising, I think, and surfed out here on weekends."

"Is he married?"

Her mother didn't turn. "He was married when he was still in LA, but they split a long time ago, when he came here. I don't know anything about him now."

"What happened?"

"What do you mean?" her mother shot back, her body still turned away.

Mattie hopped down off the counter. She felt her heart fast and heavy. She didn't even know why. "I just mean, why don't you know anything about him anymore? Why didn't you stay friends?"

Her mother did turn now. She looked impatient. She grabbed her phone and started out of the kitchen, lettuce wet and wilting, refrigerator door hanging open.

"Mattie, why the interrogation? What does it matter?"

Mattie wanted to follow her, but she didn't.

"Plenty of people don't stay friends." Her mother's voice carried behind her. "You don't need a reason."

Down the hall Mattie heard one door open and another one close.

Ray looked up from the sandwich he was making and glared at his dad's cell phone erupting into "Ice, Ice Baby" on the kitchen counter in Wainscott. His dad must have left his phone when he'd gone for a run. Mattie had idly changed Adam's ringtone two years ago, correctly guessing he wouldn't figure out how to change it back.

It was yet another old-person kind of thing his dad did, Ray mused with some chagrin. When Ray went on a run he had music to play, of course, and a map app and a running app feeding into a fitness app. A run could barely be said to have happened without his phone.

Then the landline started ringing, so Ray picked it up like it was a prop on the stage set of a cooking show. "Hello?"

"Hey, this is George Riggs, is . . . ?"

"Oh, uh. George." Ray started to pace, regretted picking up the phone. "Hey. This is, uh . . . Ray . . . Riggs." Why did he add "Riggs"? What a weird thing to do.

"Great. Wow," George said, as sincerely as could be hoped. "How's it going, Ray?"

"It's good. So . . . How's everything . . . out there?" He felt the back of his T-shirt dampening with sweat. He realized he'd dropped his voice to sound older, and he was embarrassed for himself. Was it too late to change back?

"Great."

God. Awkward. For the life of him, Ray suddenly could not remember the name of the company where George worked or the name of his pretty red-haired girlfriend. He knew he would remember both as soon as he got off the phone.

If they just could have been strangers it would have been easy. "Okay, so you probably want to speak to . . ." Thousands of pointless calculations: *your dad, Adam, Dad* . . . "Dad?" He heard his voice rising with guilt and insecurity.

"Uh, yeah. Is he around? I tried his cell, but . . ."

"No, he went for a run. I'll tell him you called."

"Great. Thanks, Ray.

"Great."

"Okay, well, I'll see you soon, I hope."

"Okay, so . . . nice talking to you." Did he really say that?

He put the phone down and felt like crying. That was his brother.

"I'll be back on the four o'clock jitney."

"Okay. I miss you. Are you sure about this?"

"Yes. Just stop by the Brooklyn house tonight and we'll get the first meeting out of the way. Just super casual." Emma paced in front of the dumpster at the rear of the market, pretending she didn't see Francis checking on her from the back window. Her break was over, but he usually turned a blind eye for a few extra minutes. "I've been thinking about it, and I feel like if we make a presentation of it, she'll start asking a lot of questions."

"And otherwise?"

"Just a few questions."

"Now I'm nervous. If I start saying 'sorry' too much, will you kick me under the table?"

Emma laughed. "The thing is, I want my mom to glimpse what an awesome and lovable person you are, so that later when she finds out what you do and all, it won't be the only thing she can think about. She'll already like you before she can hate you."

"But what happens if she asks me what I do first thing when I meet her tonight?"

"I don't think she will. That's why we're going to be so in-credibly chill. She counts herself superior to parents who immediately ask their kids' friends what they do or what college they go to."

"That's weird. Okay. That's helpful, though."

"So come around nine. We'll say we're going to hang with some people in Prospect Park. We'll play it like we're recent friends, just practically acquaintances, right?"

"That is distant from the truth, Em. I'm a terrible actor."

She laughed again. "Just be friendly, okay? That takes no acting."

"Okay. Got it." She could hear him knocking his foot against his desk, and that was not a good sign.

"See you then." She paused. "I love you."

"God, I love you."

"I thought you were surf casting."

Ray turned to look behind him. The old dock stuck out into the pond like a crooked gray finger, and Quinn flickered along it, stepping expertly over the softest planks. He turned back to his line drooping in the still water of the pond. "I was going to. And then I came here instead."

"What's wrong?"

"Nothing. Why?"

She was suddenly sitting next to him, dangling her legs over the side. He had the weird sense that time elapsed in a special way for Quinn. Here she is standing, there she is sitting, now she is kneeling, suddenly she is flat. You never saw her in any of the bending poses in between.

"You fish in the pond when you're sad."

He turned to her. "That's not true." Was that true?

"And in the ocean when you're happy."

No, he didn't. Did he?

Quinn never tried to force a point. She just opened her hands and set it forth like a firefly. You caught it or you didn't. Even if you didn't, you tended to notice it blinking around, distracting you.

"Who called before?" she asked.

"What do you mean?"

"On the landline in the kitchen."

Had she overheard the whole business? She was a silent thing sometimes. She didn't spy exactly, just perched and absorbed. "Oh. Right. That was George." He studied the worm guts on his fingers.

"George Riggs?"

"Yep." He was glad she didn't say "your brother, George." "He was calling for Adam."

She reached into Ray's bucket and grasped its lone, wriggling occupant. She tossed it into the pond.

"Hey."

"You can't keep the little guy."

"Now I can't." He reeled in his line. He baited another hook.

"If you throw your line back in, you'll probably catch it again."

Ray laughed. Sometimes he did have the forlorn suspicion that he hooked the same poor bass over and over. That was enough to make a person sad if they weren't already.

"How's he doing?"

"George, you mean?"

"Yeah."

"I don't know. Fine."

"You didn't talk to him long."

Ray was quiet for a while. "No. Not really. No."

She was quiet too.

"I can never think of what to say to him," Ray heard himself saying. Sometimes when Quinn shut her mouth it caused his own mouth to open and issue unexpected sentiments. Why was that?

She nodded.

"He's a great guy. I know."

Quinn smiled.

He felt stupid, annoyed at himself. He wanted to clear away those words but they kept vibrating in the air. "You are friends with him, aren't you? I mean, outside of everything?"

"Everything," in this case, meant their strange, sprawling family. Quinn was related to George as a stepsibling, but not by blood. Not by the DNA of an inconstant father, as Ray was.

"Sure. Kind of." She pointed her toes through the skin of the pond. "I send him seeds sometimes."

"Seeds?"

"Yes. Like for turnips, sunchokes, yams. He has that community garden he works on in Oakland."

Of course George did that. He planted root vegetables at a community garden when he wasn't working a hundred hours a week at a software startup or saving dolphins from oil spills.

Ray suddenly felt too downcast to say the half-true things he usually said about how he wished he and George lived closer. "I don't really know him," he said instead. "I haven't seen the guy in, like, two years."

He looked at his sister, her stubby, dirty fingernails splayed on the dock, tanned legs melting into the planks. Her forearms were ropily veined like an older person's, but the haphazard hair tucked behind her ears made her seem more like a little kid. She was the only girl he knew with short hair, but did she ever get her hair cut?

"Sad," she said.

"Yeah, I guess." George's being his brother was a thing of some significance, because otherwise Ray had three sisters. Four sisters, because there was also Esther. Ray still kept a picture on his bulletin board from the time George took him to a Nets game when he was twelve. It was hokey to keep and impossible to throw away.

Quinn knocked her ankle against his. "It wasn't because of you, you know."

Ray acted at first like he didn't understand what she was saying, but he did understand.

"Adam left California before you were born," she said.

Ray shrugged.

"It was unfair to them. I know. But you didn't do anything wrong."

Ray didn't do anything right, either. He just hung around being a bratty kid while George went to Stanford and won some big engineering prize. If that guy didn't deserve a father who stuck around, who did? Certainly not Ray.

When Adam met Ray's mom, George and Esther were still in middle school. Adam was already divorced from Gina, their mother, but he lived a few minutes away from them in Sausalito and dutifully took them on weekends, from what Ray understood. Half a year later, Adam fell in love with Lila and moved across the continent to be with her. After that he only went back to California twice a year. George and Esther came to the Wainscott house for one week each summer until they finished high school, and then they didn't come at all. Ray could barely remember those times.

Adam and Lila got married in the back garden of the Brooklyn house when she was already visibly pregnant with Ray. He grew up pretty much knowing he was an accident. Why have another kid if you can't be bothered with the two you've already got?

Ray knew about the wedding only from the photographs. And he was admittedly kind of fascinated with those photos. Particularly he'd studied the graphic distress of his five half siblings. He'd even imagined the prelude: Gina grudgingly shipping George and Esther from California stuffed into their best clothes. At the wedding they look like captives in a hostage video. Lila's three little girls in their hippie hand-me-downs look like they turned up at the wrong party. Even Emma looks uncertain on that day. Quinn is large-eyed and serious. If you look closely you can see in every picture she's carefully holding Mattie's hand.

Why did parents ever make their kids watch them get re-married? Ray imagined a coffee-table book suited to a photographer like maybe Diane Arbus for publication around Halloween: *Children Watching Their Parents Marry People Who Aren't Their Parents.*

"I'm sorry, what was your name?" Emma overheard her mother asking at the front door of the Brooklyn house that evening.

It was 8:56, according to her phone, and there was Jamie framed in the doorway of their brownstone, a lanky, handsome, fidgeting portrait. She sped down the hallway and pulled up quickly behind her mother. Of course he wouldn't be on time. Of course he'd be early.

"It's James Hurn. Uh, Jamie." He shot his hand out like he was meeting the president. "I'm a friend of Emma's." He hit the word "friend" a little too hard.

"I'm Lila. Emma's mother," Lila said, giving him the once-over.

"Hi, Jamie," Emma piped up, probably too brightly. Her heart was pounding. "What's up?"

"Come on in," Lila invited, moving aside for him, shutting the door behind him. She was wearing jeans and slippers and a cardigan with a big moth hole above the hem in the back. She looked like she hadn't washed her hair in a week. Emma was so worried about what her mom would make of Jamie, she forgot to worry about what Jamie would make of her mom.

"I was just going to hang with some friends in Prospect Park and I came by to see if Emma wanted to come along." Oh Lord. He sounded like he was reading from a script. "This is an awesome house," he added in the least chill manner possible. This was the wrong kind of subterfuge for him. Was there any right kind of subterfuge for him?

Her mother had turned around by now. She was studying him carefully. "You want something to drink?"

Emma glanced at the living room, noticing how cramped the place felt with the dark wood and the billions of books. There wasn't a single surface that wasn't piled with stuff. Now she had to worry about that, too. She pictured Jamie's clean, airy suburban house with a big picture window looking onto a sunny lawn and a carport. What was a carport, anyway?

"Water? Club soda? Wine? Beer? You're of age, right? Are you hungry?" Lila was always friendly to their friends. She always liked to feed them and ask them about what they were reading and watching.

"Yes, ma'am," he answered quickly. He glanced at Emma for guidance.

Emma gave him a quick shrug in return, trying to telegraph that he should say whatever he wanted.

"I'm mean, yes, I'm of age. And no thanks, I'm not hungry, I just ate."

Lila looked from Jamie to Emma and back again with her perceptive eyes. The two of them stood stiff as boards, an unnatural distance apart. They looked like they were waiting for sentencing. This was not chill.

"Can't I get you a drink, at least?"

"Sorry. Uh. Just, uh. Water?" he answered.

"Sure," Lila said. "Sit down, why don't you? Unless you're in a hurry? Emma?"

"Uh, thank you, Mrs. Harrison," Jamie pitched into the brief silence that followed. "No, ma'am. I mean, yes, ma'am. No, I'm not in a hurry. Yes, I'd like to sit down." He gave a drowning look to Emma.

"Maybe we should get going," Emma called loud enough for her mother, who was pouring a glass of water in the kitchen. She sensed this was going downhill.

In a flash Emma had her shoes on her feet and her bag in her hand. But it was too late. Jamie had already perched woodenly on the sofa, across from her mother, with his glass of water.

"Emma, sit. Stay for a minute." Lila was on to a scent. Emma could just feel it.

Emma sat. It seemed the least controversial option. "Just for a minute," she said.

"So how do you know Emma?" Lila asked Jamie.

Emma clenched her fists. Downhill and off the cliff. This was a terrible idea. Whose terrible idea was this, anyway? God, she hated it when her idea was the terrible idea. She gave Jamie what she hoped was a reassuring look.

"We met at a . . . work function," Jamie said.

What could Emma really ask of him? Jamie was pathologically honest. It was one of the things she loved about him.

Lila looked perplexed, maybe owing to the fact that the Black Horse Market didn't put on a lot of "work functions." "And what is it you do?" Lila continued.

"Jamie works in business," Emma put in. She could tell immediately it didn't help.

"What kind of business?"

Emma let out the breath she'd been holding. Since when was her hippie-dippy mother the Gestapo? *"Mom."* She knew she sounded like she was twelve.

"What? Is it a secret? Are you a spy?"

"Investment business," Jamie said quietly.

This was not a great answer under any circumstances. Lila would be more open to him if he were a gas station attendant than a banker. "What firm?"

Jamie looked at Emma in abject misery and Emma just shook her head. Neither of them said anything.

"What is going on with you two?" Lila demanded.

"What do you mean?" Emma said weakly, unable to summon up any indignation. "Nothing."

"How long have you been seeing each other?"

Silence. They couldn't even look at each other.

"Nine weeks," Jamie finally answered, relieved to say something honest.

Lila looked at Emma carefully. "Okay. So that explains a lot about you, my dear one."

Emma returned her mother's gaze. "What are you talking about?"

Lila smiled. "I *knew* something was up. I knew you were involved with somebody. I just couldn't figure out who. But why are you both acting so weird? Why have you been so secretive?"

Emma and Jamie exchanged another set of plaintive looks.

"What? What? You're making me nervous now."

Emma cracked her knuckles. Jamie looked deeply queasy. Emma took a stabilizing breath. She opened her mouth and came out with nothing.

"My God, are you pregnant?" Lila asked.

"No!" Emma shot back. "How could you ask that?"

"Because I know something is up. Just tell me what it is."

Jamie couldn't take it anymore. "I'm an analyst at Califax Capital," he finally confessed, as though he'd murdered somebody. "For Mr. Thomas. Not directly for him. I mean, he's like my boss's boss."

Lila slumped back into her chair. "Seriously?" She looked more sickened than relieved.

"Yes." Jamie hung his head.

"And that's how you met? Through Robert, I'm guessing?"

"Sort of," Emma answered.

Lila looked deeply suspicious. "He didn't set this up, did he?"

"No," Emma said quickly. "Not at all. He doesn't even know."

Lila sighed. "I get it." She shook her head at Jamie. "You kids who work for Robert are worse than a cult."

Emma got up. "*Mom,* you don't get it. And that is a horrible thing to say." She grabbed her bag. Jamie got up too, looking between Emma and her mother uncertainly.

Lila sighed again. "I think I would rather you were pregnant," she said to Emma.

"Oh my God, Mom!"

Lila turned to Jamie. "But not by you," she snapped.

Dear Other Sasha,

A quote for the day from our fearless manager:

"It's weird. One week Ray is prettier and works harder. The next week he smiles a lot and carries heavier boxes."

I can't figure out who is who.

BTW, he's taken to calling me Little Ray.

Original Sasha

"We were not that chill," Jamie lamented as the two of them sat glumly in the window of a diner on Seventh Avenue.

Emma reached out and took his hand. "I'm thinking chill is not our best strategy. We're not very good at tricks."

"I can work on it," he offered.

"I don't even want you to." She took a sip of iced tea. "It's my mom's problem, not ours. She is insane. Both of my parents are insane. They make each other insane." She shrugged. "If not for each other, they might be okay people."

8

THIS IS HOW SHE APPEARED TO ME WHEN I DIDN'T KNOW WHO SHE WAS.

"What are we doing here?"

Ray hadn't penetrated much past the front door. He floated among the doorframes offered by the foyer, not pushing through any of them. Parker said the girls on the Upper East Side were hotter, and that might have been true, but between the tallness of the shoes and the shortness of the skirts, Ray was pretty sure he preferred the ones in Brooklyn.

What was he doing here? It was mostly kids from the kind of private-school scene he preferred to skip, but Parker knew somebody who knew somebody. Ray wasn't here to pick up girls. He thought of Violet in East Hampton. He and Mattie had come back into the city for the night to pick up some stuff and to give his mom a ride out to Wainscott in the morning. His shift at the market didn't start until one p.m. Violet had complained she wouldn't have any fun until he got back and encouraged him not to have any fun either. He looked around. Well, he was complying.

There was a girl standing alone outside the kitchen. He couldn't tell if she was waiting for a friend or the bathroom or what. She wasn't wearing a minuscule skirt or even leggings, but actual pants. She was small and her hair was long and dark. Her skin was also dark. She was maybe Hispanic, he thought. He didn't mean to be leering, but when she turned to put her plastic cup down on the hall table, he noticed the generous shape of her hips in relation to her waist. And then after that, even though her shirt wasn't particularly tight or low-cut, it was hard not to notice that though her frame was small, her breasts were large and round. Parker always went for tall, athletic girls, but this girl had the kind of feminine body Ray was madly attracted to.

She didn't look impatient and he didn't see an indication of a bathroom around. He could only see her from the side and her hair was obscuring most of her face, but he could tell she was pretty. She wasn't doing anything with her hands. That was another thing that got him.

When you're alone, look at your phone. It was a tenet central and unquestioned. Why wasn't she looking at her phone? She looked up at him. He suddenly realized he was alone and not looking at his phone either. He was looking at her. He was worried he was staring at her like a cartoon character with his eyes bouncing out on springs.

Now what? He was clearly caught. He waved. She smiled and waved back, a little awkwardly. She looked kind of familiar. Did he know her from somewhere? Or maybe he just liked the kind of face she had.

He felt he needed to look somewhere else. Should he say something? It would be painfully awkward, he suspected, but had they passed the point where it was even more awkward not to? He wasn't usually an overthinker like this.

A friend of hers came out of the kitchen. A member of the blond, tiny-skirted tribe. He took the opportunity to keep looking at the girl a little longer. Did he know her? She cast one glance back at him as her friend drew her down the hallway. Caught again.

She had an idiosyncratic, shuffling way with her feet. A couple of sparks flared in his memory, but they burned out before he could think of what they meant. She was a dark, humble contrast to her towering, spike-heeled friend. He saw boys' heads swivel and gawk at the friend as the pair went by, but his shuffly girl was the actual beauty, her lovely body hidden under modest clothes. She was the kind of pretty only someone as deep as him understood. He laughed at himself for this thought and continued to think it anyway, as though her loveliness was something he'd invented.

You're not here to pick up girls, he reminded himself, struck and a little disoriented as she walked away.

Parker, in the dining room, looked lost in his own way. The

phone was out and glowing in his face. He looked up. "Dude, let's go."

Which meant Parker didn't know anybody or that they'd run out of beer. Ten minutes before, Ray would have happily sailed out the door, but now he held back. "There's beer in the kitchen," he pointed out.

"I had three. The girls got cuter but not any friendlier."

"There's beer pong in one of the bedrooms."

"Like ten guys are waiting."

"Fine. I'll pee and then we'll go," Ray said.

Ray started a slow circuit around the apartment. He knew who he was looking for, but he wasn't sure what he would do if he found her. He went from room to room, trying not to be creepy or obvious. He held his breath slightly as he turned every corner. What was the matter with him?

But the girl wasn't in any of the rooms. He even waited for turnover from the bathrooms, but she didn't come out of any of them.

She must have left. He felt a puzzling, slow-moving ache, and behind that, a small gust of relief. He knew it the way you just know things: In that shuffle of hers was the potential for a lot of complicated feelings. The kind he'd never felt for a girl before. Now he wouldn't get to feel them. He wouldn't have to feel them.

Mattie and Ray had come back to Brooklyn together in the late afternoon, she to pick up clothes and go to the dentist.

Now he'd gone to some girl's party in Manhattan while she stayed home and snooped around the house until she found the photograph in a filing cabinet in the basement.

She had an almost eerie sense of where to look for it among the relics: piles of curling prints, slippery negatives featuring black teeth of ghostly relatives.

It was in a pile of prints, bound by a rubber band and marked with a slip of paper that said "1997" in her mother's writing. They were beach pictures, nothing notable there, but the cast was different. Instead of her sweating, ageless, subtly out-of-place father in his flowered swim trunks and signature Ray-Ban sunglasses there was a blond man in faded wetsuit bottoms holding up a surfboard who looked like he'd been born right out of the sand. There he was leading Emma out on a miniature board. There he was holding tiny Quinn's hand as she found her balance at the front of his longboard. There he was standing with her mother, her very young mother, their four feet melted into sand and surf. She imagined it was her mother who took the other pictures, so who took this one? Mattie suspected, somehow, that the subjects were unaware of the camera.

The question, always, was how did this relate to the sequence of their lives? How did it relate to the Great Upheaval? It was after, but not by much. Maybe a few months. So near the moment of devastation, and yet so peaceful-seeming.

But the particular photo she seized on, the one she couldn't stop looking at, showed this same blond Jonathan Dawes, lately of the Black Horse Market, holding baby Mattie up by her feet. In it, she's standing on his open hands teetering high above the sand, a balance of fear and delight in her face. Could she possibly remember this? Seeking purchase in the air on a pair of flat hands, anticipating the plunge into soft sand? No, she was too young. She probably just remembered seeing the picture.

She studied his squinting face looking up at her. He was smiling broadly; he was all about thrills. Maybe not all about thrills. He looked a little bit careful, too.

Leaving the party, Ray's mind was full and his eyes were absent. The elevator doors opened, a cluster of people pushed in, and suddenly he was standing behind her, less than a foot away. He smelled her hair before he saw her. The smell made him dizzy. It took a shortcut to a part of his brain that didn't deal in words. He didn't mean to look down at her chest, but what could he do? He was suddenly electrified and uneasy.

Next to her was a friend, a different friend, a girl with black hair piled high on top of her head.

"Are you Parker Murray?" her friend turned to ask his friend.

Parker looked up from his phone. "Yeah."

"You're Zach Kaplan's friend."

"Yeah. I thought he was gonna show up tonight," Parker said. "Do you go to Trinity?"

"No. Sacred Heart. I know Zach from the beach."

The two were having a normal conversation, and the elevator was beeping downward, and Ray was deep inside his brain, struggling to surface, feeling drugged and slightly panicked at the same time. He stared at the part in her dark hair, which wasn't quite straight. He was caught in something he didn't understand.

Without warning she turned her head and looked up at him. She had a small, delicate face, a pointy chin, and large eyes, which in this light looked yellow-bronze. He was caught for sure, bare and bewildered, unable to close up his face in time.

She didn't look annoyed; he didn't look away. She was caught too. She was bewildered too. She turned her head to face forward again and kept it that way.

His heart was thumping so hard he wondered if it could be seen from outside his shirt, if maybe she could detect the vibration in the few inches of air between them.

Again the question: did he know her from somewhere?

Numbly he followed them through the lobby. They were all standing kind of awkwardly on the sidewalk under the awning of the apartment building when the girl with the black piled hair turned directly to him and said, "I'm Chloe Neil. Have we met?"

"I don't know. I don't think so. I'm Ray."

The dark-haired girl made a sound, an audible in or out of breath. It was quiet, but it shook him. He could feel her eyes on him. He looked at her, instinctively alert.

Afterward it seemed to him like he was experiencing what was happening, predicting what would happen, and remembering what had happened at the same time.

Chloe looked expectantly, impatiently at her friend. She kind of bumped the girl with her hip. "Hello? Do you speak?"

"I'm Sasha," she said to Ray, clamping strange, lovely eyes on his eyes.

It took a while for the outlandish possibility to reveal itself. He was thinking in very slow motion, through thousands of feet of air and liquid, cloud water sloshing in his ears. *Did that mean . . . ? Could she be?*

No. Other people were Sasha. There were plenty of Rays. At least, there were a few other Rays. But the way she looked at him and the way she said it . . .

She thought it too, didn't she? And if she thought it too, then didn't it have to be so?

"You're not . . . Sasha Thomas," he said. He had to ask. He felt pinned under the possibility.

"You know each other?" Chloe asked, attentive to the strange air.

Chloe and Parker uneasily watched them watching each other.

Sasha stared at him unguardedly. "You're . . . you're not. Are you really Ray?"

He was sort of Ray. Not quite Ray. He didn't know who the fuck he was right now. His mouth was moving forward without him. "Occasionally I go by Sasha."

A laugh burst out of her, unexpected by either of them. Each of them sort of looked around to see where it had come from. His heart puffed up, exalted at the sound.

She was still laughing. She had an absolutely beautiful smile. "And I've been called Ray," she said.

"Obviously you know each other," he heard Chloe say somewhere in the background. Apparently Chloe took a sour view of inside jokes.

"No," Sasha finally said, muffled.

He felt himself straining toward her. "No," he echoed. "We've never even met."

Chloe had called an Uber. She was checking her phone, calling the driver, pulling Sasha toward the corner.

Sasha was barely on her feet, barely aware of her feet. Ray (Ray!) was receding from her on the sidewalk.

"The stupid driver is waiting on Eighty-Eighth Street," Chloe declared. "I told him Lex, and he's the one yelling at me."

Ray stood there looking at her. His friend was already ambling away down the sidewalk in the opposite direction.

Sasha wanted to say something, but she didn't know what. There were too many things to say for her to say any one of them. No small talk, no big talk, and nothing in between could possibly touch her feelings.

He wanted to say something too. She could tell. She wished she weren't being pulled away so forcibly by deranged Uber customer Chloe.

She felt a little bit desperate. Thoughts bounced and ricocheted and didn't quite link up. What if she never saw him again? What if this was the only time?

And she hadn't even managed to say anything.

She waved awkwardly to him as her steps bent around the corner. She felt like crying, hating to break off the sight of him. She could have wrenched herself away from Chloe, but what would she do then? Run back to him and stand in front of him and say more nothing?

She had known what he looked like in a general way. That

his hair was light and straight like Mattie's. That he was tall and athletic like Emma. She'd seen a few pictures over the years. Not enough to recognize him out of context, just enough to fit the pieces together.

But she didn't know how he really was, moving, talking, and breathing, in three dimensions. That his body was warm and magnetic, even three feet away from her. She wasn't prepared for that.

She had so many points of reference and extrapolations, but he was different when he was right there. This Ray was her Ray. This was the Ray who read her books and slept in her bed. Her Ray was the same person as this person. This person was Ray and he belonged to himself. She didn't really have a Ray.

"Sash, come on!"

The driver honked at them. Chloe was already in the car before Sasha knew what was happening.

Sasha sensed that once she got in the car and shut the door, this bewildering moment would crash to a close, so completely over it might as well not have happened at all.

"Sasha! I've got four minutes to make my curfew. You've already blown yours."

Had she?

"And you were the one who made a deal about leaving."

Sasha got in heavily and heavily shut the door. She cast a look at the window as they pulled into the street, driving away from him.

Chloe turned on her. "What was that about? I thought you said you didn't know him."

Sasha wasn't ready to open up to Chloe. She wanted to hold on to the last images of Ray. There had been so much imagined Ray, such a minuscule amount of real Ray. She didn't want Chloe's perspective sewn into the experience, a further distortion.

She didn't even want the confusion of her own perspective. She just wanted to hold on to him, how he was. The particular force of him in his laugh, posture, smile. His hands, his eyes, the way his feet stood in his shoes. Not any specific trait or part, but the feeling of them, the feeling of him as a real, solid person.

She had the ache of tears in her throat. She wished she were still near him, feeling that strange warmth emanating from his body. Had she imagined that?

"He sure made it seem like he knew you." Chloe kept staring at her expectantly.

Sasha shrugged numbly. "It's just that we know people in common."

"He's super cute, don't you think? We should have gotten his number. We can message him on Facebook. His friend was decent too." Chloe rooted around in her bag for a piece of gum to cover the beer and smoke.

Ray was not on Facebook, Sasha could have informed her, but didn't. She knew this because he'd tried to friend her back in middle school and she'd shied away. A year and a half later she'd regretted the decision, but by the time she'd mustered the courage to reach out to him, he wasn't there anymore. "He deleted his account," Mattie mentioned, by the by, leaving Sasha hungry, as always, to know even one thing more.

"I think he might have gone out with Piper Greenlow," Chloe rattled on. "You know her? From Chapin? She was bragging that this super-cute friend of Zach Kaplan's friend from Brooklyn was calling her."

Sasha could not answer that one. She stared at the lights on Park Avenue and willed them not to turn yellow yet. She was relieved when the car pulled over at Seventy-Fourth Street.

"Bye. Thanks for the ride," she called as she slammed the door. She wasn't thinking about Chloe. Or she was only to the extent that she wished she hadn't let Chloe drag her away from Ray. (*Ray?*)

But it was useless, she thought mechanically as she punched in the code and walked into her house. It was time to check herself, her own stupidity. She didn't like how her thoughts were traveling. She needed to shake herself out of it.

Ray wasn't her friend. He wasn't her boyfriend. He wasn't her Ray in any way. They had no relationship and never would. Even though they shared a room and she pretended they had some special bond, they didn't. That existed in her needy mind and nowhere else. They lived on opposite sides of a chasm created by two people who actively loathed each other.

That was how it was and would ever be. There was no point, nothing gained by trying to cross it. It was sheer perversity to demand to know the one person in the world who was structurally off-limits to her.

What if she had stayed standing with him on the sidewalk? What was it that needed to be said or done? She could think of nothing.

* * *

Ray told Parker to go ahead. He wanted to walk. Parker didn't want to leave him alone. He kept walking alongside him all the way to the express trains at Fifty-Ninth Street.

"Why are you acting spooky? Do you know that girl or not?"

Ray didn't feel like answering. He was too preoccupied, too freaked out. He kept replaying her face, her laugh, trying to make sense of it, to hold on to her. But once they were rattling downtown on the number 4 train, he answered anyway.

"Yes and no. I don't know her, but our parents used to be married. My mom and her dad."

"You're joking."

"No." He looked at the ceiling of the subway car. He pushed his fingers through his hair, making it all stand up. Emma hated when he did that. She would pat it all back down as though it was her hair to be in charge of.

"Geeee-zus." Parker let out a long, sincere breath through his nose. "So she's that kid. The one who leaves her crap around your room."

Ray appreciated Parker's consideration. "As a roommate, she's had a lot more to complain about than I have," he muttered numbly.

"She seemed cool. Very pretty."

"The thing that's really fucked up is, I had *no* idea." His face was hot at the thought of her body, the force of his attraction. "I probably should have recognized her, but I didn't. I was looking at her like she was . . . you know . . . a girl."

Parker seemed to understand what he meant. "She is a girl."

"She's not. Not to me."

"How can you say what she is to you? You just said you don't even know her."

"I don't get to." The lights in the subway car blinked off and on again. "To know her."

"Why not? It's not like you're related to her. You're not."

Ray almost laughed a little. "If you have to say that, maybe that's not good."

9

GETTING STRONG BY GIVING THINGS AWAY

Emma intercepted Jamie at the front door of the Wainscott house. He looked so handsome in his jacket and khakis. His hair was combed. She knew he was doing his best.

"No strategy this time, I promise," Emma said to him in a low voice, kissing him on the cheekbone. "No secrets anymore. I told them everything this morning. My dad is so excited he might jump into your arms."

Jamie was too nervous to laugh, but he looked encouraged and hopeful, his strings taut and vibrating in tune with hers.

She'd come to anticipate his cues: fingers going like windmills and tappy feet when he was anxious, hum of contentment low in his throat when it was just her, thumb pressed to his temple when he concentrated on work, open and honest gaze in all conditions.

For some reason she'd had the idea that in choosing a man she was supposed to look for strength and opacity. But it was seeing Jamie's rough seams up close that brought him into the soft part of her heart.

She squeezed his hand. "It's the best possible thing. You just get to be you."

"This is one of the most beautiful places I have ever seen in my life," Jamie said, as if on cue, staring from the terrace over the lawn and down to the pond.

The rest of them stood around approvingly. Quinn almost had to laugh at their bobbing heads.

It was the quickest way to their communal heart. Maybe because of everything it took to be here, to hold on to it. All the compromises and stalemates. And because it was beautiful.

Back in the house, the big table was set. Quinn had watched Emma oversee the angle of every spoon and fork like she was the butler on *Downton Abbey*. And Evie, in her way, had been wise enough to step back.

Evie was supposed to be the reigning queen of this dominion, but who was reliably and completely on her side? Not Emma or Mattie. They'd met her within a few years of meeting their own mother but remained as skeptical as though she'd arrived yesterday. Sasha was the center of Evie's life, but Quinn knew Sasha was desperate to identify with her older sisters. Robert loved Evie but felt the desires and rules of his powerful older daughters. Quinn could understand how her father's mind worked: *The girls were the victims here, right? Just kids. None of this was their fault.* Gus, the guinea pig, was on Evie's side, unless someone else remembered to feed him. Based on Evie's luck with the dishwasher, not even the dishes totally trusted her.

It seemed unfair that Evie had to play the overdog, when she took all the knocks of the underdog and got none of the sympathy. Evie was generous in hundreds of quiet ways. She never tried to take credit for having dinner on the table, food in the fridge, gas in the car. She never sat back in a chair but perched momentarily, like she'd taken a priority seat at the front of the bus and was waiting for a more deserving person to come along.

Tonight Emma had allowed Evie to set out some cheese and crackers and grapes under her watchful eye. Now the assembled party sat around the coffee table stiffly eating, and Quinn had that butterfly feeling in her chest. Her spirit needed to visit each one of them. She couldn't help it. The mix of hope and fear pulled her like pollen.

Jamie had a benumbed look, and yet a great eagerness ran right under it. He was handsome and well-made, but with no sense of entitlement. It was no wonder her father looked so supremely happy sitting in his wing chair.

"Now, Sasha, you are the youngest? Is that right?"

"Right. Except for Ray. On the other side. He's seventeen, too." Quinn saw Sasha's effort to sound casual.

Jamie nodded. Did he know what "on the other side" meant?

Quinn could see his gallantry in wanting to get everybody straight, not wanting to step into anything.

"Ray is Lila and Adam's son," Evie filled in bright and quick, before Robert could get involved. Quinn saw the familiar look of all-purpose apology forming on Evie's face. "We're a complicated family, aren't we?"

"This is barely the half of it," Mattie said wryly.

Jamie looked highly unsure of what to say. Quinn could imagine the delicate calculus taking place, his wish to be kind to Evie undermined by Emma's impatience toward her. "It looks like a great family to me," he ventured, a little quietly.

Quinn saw Emma's fervor, her inchoate anxiety lighting on little things, like whether the sofa had spots on it and whether the crackers were stale. This was different for her from just parading around with the photogenic lacrosse guy. Did Emma even know how much more vulnerable she had suddenly become?

And there was Sasha, trapped in the elbow of the sectional sofa, staring at the grapes, internally begging her mother not to say anything embarrassing. Quinn could practically see the old war-weary soldiers battling it out in Sasha's brain. Sasha wanted to defend her mother and also be on the same team as Emma.

Sasha, like Ray, was a dear and loyal person but had little reward for it. Her loyalty was rejected by Mattie and patronized by Emma. Ironically, of all the people in her two-part family, it was Ray, a world apart from Sasha, who could prize what she had to give.

The only way Sasha found to please Mattie was failing to

shine in any of the ways Mattie shone. Mattie was the baby; she was Daddy's girl, the beauty, the head-turner, the flirt. Sasha gracefully ceded all these and more, chose other areas to make her case. Sasha got strong by giving things away, and Mattie got weak by indulgence.

Sasha was born knowing she had to be careful because she had parents who loved each other. She had their father all the time. She was raised by a vigilant mother/stepmother but had no stepparents herself to resent or feel resented by.

Dinner began, a torrent of clanging dishes and passing bowls and things tasting good enough to inspire wordy praise. Quinn observed Emma's keen, flushed face, practically willing the deliciousness into the strip steaks.

After dinner there was a lot of hectic cleanup on the part of Jamie and a good blueberry crumble. Then came a long walk on the beach for Emma and Jamie. And the rest of them standing around like five versions of the nurse in *Romeo and Juliet*.

Emma's hopes were so visible, Quinn longed to fulfill them. She wanted the wind to blow the right amount, the moon to reveal itself from behind the clouds. She wished she could make it exactly right. But more than that, she wanted to protect her sister from the hopes themselves. *Do you really want this? The drunk kind of love always wears off.*

Quinn challenged herself to embrace pain, but she realized she'd been less capable at embracing hope, the very mother of pain. Hope was the thing she was scared of.

It was a familiar weakness, not wanting the people she loved to want things too badly. Her protection could only extend so far.

"You think I'm hopeless," Mattie told her once, and it stuck in her head.

"I just don't want you to hope too much," Quinn had blurted out, and regretted it thousands of times.

"I think she really likes him," Evie said with a sigh.

This was so unmistakably true, not even Mattie could find a way to argue with her.

"I think she's got good taste," her dad said, smiling like a fool.

Hope was tricky with the people you loved most. It was more dangerous than speeding cars and biting dogs. Quinn could see why parents around the world let their kids sit on soft surfaces and stare into screens all day.

Dear Other Ray,
    So how fucking weird was that?
    Sorry if I was kind of speechless. I was . . .

Ray sat at his keyboard staring at his screen for a long time. What? What was he?

    Surprised. And kind of disturbed because I didn't
    realize you were you. And I thought . . .

His fingers stopped again. He thought what?

What if he was honest?

> *you are really beautiful, which is why I wandered*
> *around for the whole party (loser/stalker) trying to see*
> *you again. I am guilty of looking at you in THAT WAY*
> *and thinking of you in THAT WAY, which seems pervy*
> *and inappropriate under the circumstances.*
> *And BTW, it was scientifically confirmed in the*
> *elevator that you smell better than anything in the world.*
> *How am I supposed to fall asleep in our bed now?*

He deleted the whole thing quickly so he wouldn't do some
moronic thing like send it.

Matthew was going around the farm with the dreaded clip-
board.

"I already logged in my hours this week," Mattie said. She
stretched her legs onto the overturned washbasin.

"I know. I'm making the schedule for the rest of the summer.
When do you need to go back to school?"

She lifted her face to the sun, let out a long breath. "I don't
know. I don't know if I'm going back." She was in a reckless
mood.

"Why not?"

She sat up. Usually she'd lost Matthew's interest by this point
in a conversation. No cleverness, mischief, or flirtation managed to hold it. For three years she'd tried.

He was actually looking at her seriously.

She might as well keep being honest. "I don't know what I'm doing there. I don't really care much about my classes. . . . You know, my sister Emma is all high-achieving Princeton this and that. Now she's got this boyfriend, and I wouldn't be surprised if they got married. Quinn is, well . . . she's Quinn."

Matthew smiled. She didn't need to explain. He sat down on the chair across from her. She wasn't sure she'd ever seen him sit down before.

"I don't know who I am or what I'm supposed to do with my life. Why waste everybody's time and money on going back to college?" She was halfway stunned at herself. Everything she'd said was true, but she hadn't quite known she felt that way.

Matthew looked at her levelly. "Makes sense to me. I didn't go to college. Not yet, anyway. Maybe I'll find a reason to one day. But I don't want to be one of those people who go to college because they can't think of anything better to do. I always have plenty to do here."

Mattie almost looked around to see if somebody would pop out of the storeroom with a camera, pranking her. This was so unusual.

She nodded sympathetically. "I don't want to be one of those people either. And I'm worried I am. It's not like anyone expects anything of me. My dad thinks Syracuse is for nitwits and party girls. I know he loves me, but he doesn't take me seriously."

Matthew scuffed his work boot on the dusty floor. "That's a shame. I mean, it's a shame if you want him to take you seriously." He looked at her straight on. "Do you?"

Had someone put a truth serum in the cider today? She felt a little dizzy. She was as quick as anyone to lie, but she didn't want to in this case. She considered the question honestly.

"Do I want him to take me seriously?" She shook her head slowly. She sighed. "I don't even know."

He shrugged, mildly self-conscious. "As my grandfather always says, you start with yourself."

"What does that mean?"

"It's Howard's favorite line. I make fun of him, but it's true. If you want to be taken seriously, be serious. Take yourself seriously."

She stared at him, eyes large and slightly afraid. "Okay," she said.

He stood up. "Anyway, you can work here straight through October if you want. Apples, late corn, squash, pumpkins, cider keep us busy into fall, but then we shut down for the winter. I can't offer you anything after that."

Riding her bike home an hour later, Mattie was still in a daze. She felt like she'd been given a gift, but she wasn't quite sure of the nature of it.

Heartthrob farmer Matthew Reese had uttered words so wise he'd punctured holes in her ordinary tricks and manners. She felt air blowing in where there wasn't any before. Like somebody opened the windows in a musty, neglected house.

Do I want to be taken seriously?

Maybe she did.

And all at once she understood precisely the nature of Matthew's gift. He'd taken her seriously.

* * *

For Sasha it felt different to be in her Wainscott bedroom now. It felt different to sit, let alone lie down, on the bed. It felt different to brush her teeth. It felt embarrassingly different to take off her clothes.

She couldn't look at the bookshelves in the same way, couldn't look out the window, couldn't glance in the mirror. His bed, his books, his view, his face. For all the years they'd shared the room, she'd always felt him in it. But not like this.

Ray. Actual Ray. Who was Ray, really? What was Ray? A flat, winged fish. A unit of sunlight or hope.

He had always been her version of him. Suddenly he was his own version of him, and it was entirely different. He had taken himself back. It seemed kind of selfish of him to overwhelm her carefully nurtured version just like that, in just one meeting.

Sasha remembered when they got the new house on Seventy-Fourth Street, Con Ed couldn't get access to the electric meter, so for six months their bill had been based on estimated usage. The seventh bill was a lot higher, and when her dad asked why the difference, her mom said, "Well, Con Ed finally read the meter."

Now that Ray was actual, he was different to her and she was different to herself. She had a straining kind of feeling about him she'd never experienced before. She wanted to hold on to her estimate of him, but again and again she tried to summon him the way he was: shoulders, eyebrows, hair that curled a little behind his ears. She wished she could have imaginary Ray back. She wished she could breathe the real Ray in, feel his warmth again.

I'm not sure I want to feel any of this.

In eighth grade, they'd both been assigned *To Kill a Mockingbird*. She'd left her copy at home in Manhattan the weekend she had an essay to write, and she got into a panic over it. She'd already gotten an extension. She jawboned Emma into driving her to the library, which was closed, and the bookstore in East Hampton, which didn't have it. You couldn't get it on Kindle back then. By Sunday midday she was in tears and even suggested going back to the city early, which she never wanted to do.

Then, as she lay in bed, a mirage floated before her on her very own nightstand. There it was, facedown, *To Kill a Mockingbird*. His copy, her salvation. She opened it gingerly, afraid the title and words would change if she tried to read any of them. On the inside cover, she saw Ray's name in his writing. There were his underlines, his scrawly annotations, his notes inside the back cover.

She found herself following his thoughts, nearly crawling into his brain.

We live in the same place, but never together.

By six p.m. the essay was done. She'd gotten so carried off, she'd added her own underlines, her own notes. She'd forgotten she probably shouldn't do that in his book. But when she came back two weeks later, she saw he'd added more, words winding through her words, picking up on ideas she'd written.

Now she fished the old copy from their common shelf.

She remembered times when she'd separate their books, but they always ended up mixed together again. She stared at the old handwriting, his in blue ballpoint, hers in black, woven together.

She got out a piece of blank paper and stared at it for a while.

Nice to meet you, Ray, she finally wrote, folded it, and stuck it inside the front cover.

Ray lay on his bed. He missed her when he was in Brooklyn. How could he miss her? He did not know her. He'd seen her once.

He did, though. He missed being in her bed. He missed the smell and the feeling of her. He remembered, with some chagrin, the blanket that was supposed to fend off nightmares. What if he brought her silky nightgown thing back here? He had to laugh at himself for the outrageousness of it. How pervy would that be?

He had no hope of being with her in any bed, of course, but in Wainscott he felt like he could. He imagined he had. It wasn't even sexual. Or not totally sexual. Okay, so there were aspects of it other than just sexual.

There had been no contact, no email, between them in over a week. Not since the incident on Lexington Avenue. He missed that, too. Now that he'd seen her in person and smelled her in person, he wasn't sure what to write to her anymore.

He loved when he saw her name pop up when he checked his mail on his phone. He felt a little empty each time he opened it and didn't see her name, which was pretty much every time.

Did she think of him a millionth as much as he thought of her?

Even one millionth would be encouraging.

He needed to get back in contact with her in a way that wasn't creepy or overwrought. They didn't even need to talk about what happened. He picked up his phone. He poked his finger around until he came up with a short message:

> *Dear Other Ray,*
>
> *Is Francis trying to get with Emma or what?*
>
> *Other Sasha*

He pressed send.

He checked his mail plus or minus one thousand times over the next twenty minutes. And then he saw her name.

> Dear Other Sasha,
>
> 100% he is.
>
> I'm hoping it's your week when he finds out about Jamie.
>
> Other Ray

And there was joy.

How long did he have to wait to write her back so he didn't seem creepy or overwrought?

10

OR/AND

Emma looked around at the other tables. Was she dressed-up enough? Jamie hadn't warned her he was taking her to the fanciest restaurant in Southampton. Suddenly she wished she'd done her hair better and worn mascara.

"Is this a special occasion or something?" she asked him. "It can't be our anniversary yet."

His fingers started going. "It is sort of. Three months."

The waiter delivered two glasses of champagne she didn't remember ordering. "Wow, nice," she said.

Were they going to be one of those couples who celebrated a

lot of extra milestones? Was Jamie secretly a half birthday kind of person? She wasn't sure how she felt about that.

"Did you get a raise?"

He laughed, but his face looked slightly dyspeptic. "No."

His feet were getting tappy. Hmmm.

Two bowls of light green soup appeared. "Sweet pea and mint," the waiter announced.

She looked at Jamie questioningly. Was he doing some kind of telepathic ordering? "I love sweet pea soup," she said.

"I know," he said. "You always order it."

She dipped her spoon in and tasted it. "Delicious."

She ate contentedly. He was oddly quiet.

"So I saw the funniest thing on YouTube," she said, not exactly sure why it popped into her mind. "This guy took his girlfriend out to a restaurant with a secret plan of proposing to her. He thought he was being super clever and romantic putting the ring in the bottom of her piece of cheesecake. So anyway the girl gets going on her cheesecake, and you can see she's really psyched about it. She's kind of a big girl actually and she's plowing into it—who can blame her—and then all of a sudden she starts choking and—"

Emma could not ignore the look of panic on Jamie's face.

"Jamie, what?"

She'd never seen his face turn completely red before. This was new.

"What?" Did he not like that story? Did he not like cheesecake? Did he know the person in the video?

He stared with horror at her bowl.

She looked down at her soup bowl. She held her spoon aloft. "Jamie?"

He reached across and took her soup bowl from her.

"Hey . . . Jamie?"

He squeezed his eyes shut. He had both hands on her soup bowl like she was going to wrestle him for it.

The wheels were turning slowly in her mind. "Jamie . . . You didn't . . ."

He kept his eyes shut. He nodded.

"Not really?"

He nodded again.

"Seriously?"

She started laughing. She couldn't help it. She took the soup bowl back, though he tried to keep it.

"No way, no way. Just no way." She spooned around until she felt a little clink and an extra weight in her spoon. She brought it up to her mouth. "Yum."

"Emma!"

She put it in her mouth, sucked off the soup, and pulled it out again, clean and shiny.

Jamie was caught between laughing and crying. He grabbed the ring from her hand, but she had it long enough to see it was a beautiful flat bezel setting, platinum, just what she would have picked. The diamond was too big for him to be able to afford in any comfortable way.

He dropped onto one knee in front of her chair. Most of the

other diners were staring at them by this point. "Em, can we just erase the whole last episode? Pretend it never happened? Restart? Please?"

She was still laughing, a nervousness and buoyancy launching her heart into a new state of possible joy. "Never."

"Yes. I'm restarting now." He cleared his throat. "Emma Thomas?"

"Yes."

"Even though I'm an idiot and terrible at playing tricks and always manage to embarrass myself around you, will you marry me anyway?"

Her face got quivery and full. She pretended to consider.

"I know we're really young—you especially—and I know I should probably wait, but I can't."

She nodded tearfully.

"You don't have to say anything yet. You can wait a year or five years or even ten years if you want. I just have to lay my cards on the table. I want you to know my intentions and not hold anything back from you."

Emma started to cry in earnest.

"I want to be with you forever. I want to make a home and a family and do everything together. I know I'm always falling off balance with you, but you make me feel safer and happier than I've ever felt."

She wiped her eyes. "Okay, I will." She didn't actually need to consider.

She'd thought, before she met Jamie, that deciding to get married would be an agonizing decision. How do you know?

How can you possibly know? How can you be sure? Especially with her parents in the background. And now she didn't think at all. She just felt sure.

"Really?"

"Yes." She stuck her hand out and he put the ring on her finger. They were a little shaky on both sides. It fit fine. It was pure platinum and diamond loveliness.

"Really?" He came over and lifted her out of her chair.

"Yes."

He spun her around. "Just like that?"

"Yes."

He kissed her. "You sure?"

"Yes, Jamie."

"I can't believe it."

She put her mouth to his ear. "I'd rather go make out on the beach than stay here with every single person watching us."

"Oh my God, me too."

Jamie paid and zipped them out of that place at lightning speed. They walked onto the darkening beach, toward the empty part.

He slipped his arm around her. She held up her hand for him to see the ring and he kissed it. "Shit, that completely backfired, and I'm still happier than I've ever been in my life."

She nodded, that happy too.

"Yes, it was a surprise. Completely."

Sasha could hear Emma on the phone in the living room from where she sat on the patio. She could see the back of Emma's dark head, her shoulders tense and high as she sat on the sofa. She could feel Emma's excitement, overexcitement, anxiety, certainty, uncertainty rising and filling the room, pushing through the screens. She imagined what an aerial view of the house would look like if you could pick up Emma's energy as a color, like infrared, on film.

That combined with the wind off the pond raised goose bumps on Sasha's skin. She tucked up her knees and stretched her sweatshirt over her bare legs and even her feet. The fabric would remember itself but wouldn't go all the way back.

"I know, I know."

It was Emma's mom, of course. Lila would be the first call.

Sasha felt a queasy strain for Lila that an event this big happened on Not Her Weekend, but she trusted Emma to talk over it.

"We're thinking next June. Almost a year . . . Yeah, at the house."

Sasha had no experience of Lila at all, but she often imagined her. It was embarrassing how she sometimes had to remind herself that Lila was not her mother, and that in fact she'd never met her. It shamed her how quick she was to see through her sisters' eyes, to respect Lila's authority, to see her own mother through judgmental stepdaughter eyes.

"Not that huge. I guess we could get a tent."

Emma was quiet while Lila talked for a while. Sasha wished she could eavesdrop on both sides of the conversation while she criticized herself for listening to the one.

"I'll be twenty-three by then," she heard Emma say a little huffily.

Emma was quiet for another couple of minutes. Sasha could practically feel her sister's spirits deflating. She couldn't overhear, but she could imagine some reasons why Lila would be less than jubilant.

"Can't you just say congratulations? Can't you just be happy if I'm happy?"

Sasha got up to sneak away through the other door.

"Yeah, is he there? Can I talk to him?"

Sasha stopped.

"Hey, small bro." Emma's voice was softer now.

Sasha moved closer to the screen. There was no way she could leave now.

"I know. I know. Thanks. Crazy, huh?" Emma sounded different when she talked to Ray from when she talked to anyone else. She didn't sound like that when she talked to Sasha, did she?

There it was again. The heave and the ho. The zero-sum game of her and Ray. It summoned the old feelings and insecurities. They had a brother and she didn't have one, and he lived with them in a cool place like Brooklyn, the place they went when they left where she could never go, and he was funny and he was annoying, and he made gross sounds when he ate cereal and his friends were also boys, and what was she but just another girl?

But now she had her own access to Ray, limited though it was; her own private thoughts, her zinging heart when she saw his name pop up on her email list.

Emma's voice changed again. "What do you mean?" She was quiet for an unusually long time.

"I guess everyone." Brief uncertainty. Pause. "Yes, *everyone* everyone. Neither of them can skip it, can they? They'll just have to deal."

It was never great to eavesdrop on Emma's side of a conversation. She almost always said what you thought she'd say, but an ominous notion was beginning to seep through in spite of Emma.

"*Everyone* everyone" was actually two people.

You could sit on opposite sides of an auditorium at a graduation. You could attend different nights of a play. You could split the sports seasons in half. You could have two birthday celebrations and two graduation parties, but you couldn't really require two weddings.

Sasha listened through Emma and understood Ray exactly. "*Everyone* everyone" was Emma's two parents, who had barely exchanged words since before Sasha was born.

"All of 'em. Why not?" Emma had bustled quickly past uncertainty and settled on stridency. "It's my wedding. Everyone." She laughed, but her voice was tight.

And stranger, more ominous, more thrilling, "*everyone* everyone" was also actually everyone: her *and* Ray. Lila *and* Evie. Robert *and* Adam. Even George and Esther from California, probably.

In this one instance, they would go from an "or" to an "and."

"Anyway, it's not until June. They have a year to get themselves figured out."

Whatever Ray said in reply, Emma wasn't happy with it. She was fed up.

Quinn said Ray often told the truth you didn't want to hear.

Emma stood from the couch so fast she sent a couple of throw pillows to the floor. "Don't be such a downer, Ray," she snapped. "Don't act like it can't happen just because it never has."

Big Sasha,
> Have you met Jamie yet?

Little Ray

LR,
> *Yes, Em brought him to Brooklyn end of last month. Lila didn't even wait until he left to start complaining.*

BS

BS,
> Robert acts like he's the second coming, so Lila probably likes him in inverse relation to that.

LR

> *Ha! Lila did say something kind of like "Emma's probably seeing him because Robert put her up to it. It'll be over as soon as she meets a guy she actually likes."*

Ouch.

I know. In every way.

How did Lila take the news about the engagement?

She said to Emma "I don't see what the hurry is"
and put me on the phone.

For some reason, they always celebrated Adam's birthday dinner at the Lemongrass on Seventh Avenue. As far as Mattie was concerned, it wasn't the greatest food, and it was always pretty noisy. It was the kind of place you got takeout from on a Tuesday night on the way home from the subway, not a place you went for your birthday. The servers were happy to give you gross red bean ice cream for free but in too big a hurry to sing anything to anyone. Maybe that was the point.

Adam never ordered the whole fish, because it was expensive. He gave Ray a look if he got the shrimp.

Whereas her father would have ordered two of the whole fish and ten pounds of the lobster, if they had any, because at some point he'd gotten the idea that lobster = success. Robert wouldn't have looked at the prices. That is, if he went to this restaurant, which he wouldn't, because it was the kind of place you got takeout from on the way home from the subway.

Mattie wondered if her mom cared about this difference. Her mother had always professed to loathe their father's money and his showiness, and Mattie believed her. Her mom loved that Adam was scholarly and modest without a hint of materialism in him. But Mattie also wondered, not for the first time, how much her mom enjoyed the absence of money.

"Adam's not poor, he's just cheap," Emma had said once, in her offhand way, as if that made anything better.

Mattie studied her mother across the table. Her mother capably chopsticked individual peanuts from her plate and nodded encouragingly at things Ray said, even though Mattie doubted she could hear half of it. You couldn't have a conversation in this place. Maybe that was the point. When her mother caught Mattie's gaze, she quickly looked away.

Since Mattie had spoken the flammable name of Jonathan Dawes, she couldn't get her mother to meet her eyes, much less allow her a minute alone together.

Straggling home after dinner along Seventh Avenue, her mother kept her arm through Adam's. Emma shot ahead, talking on the phone, while Ray kept appearing at Mattie's side, no matter how many texts she sent or store windows she stopped to look in.

"What's your problem?" she finally asked him, in a friendly way.

"What do you mean?"

"Do you want to tell me something?"

"No."

"Yes, you do."

"Not particularly."

"Girlfriend advice?"

"God, no."

"Violet won't leave you alone?"

He shrugged one dismissive shoulder.

"Okay, what?"

He zipped the zipper of his hoodie up and down a few times. "Did I tell you that I met Sasha?"

Mattie ditched her phone in her pocket. "My sister Sasha? No. What do you mean?"

"I met her at a party in Manhattan. I didn't even know it was her for most of it."

"What are you talking about? You've *met* Sasha before."

He shrugged. "I saw her face as a dot across Radio City Music Hall at your graduation. I've seen pictures of her from when she was younger. Obviously I've shared a room with her for seventeen years. But no, I had never met her."

Mattie was struck by this, and not just because of Ray's uncharacteristic intensity. "That can't be true."

"Of course it's true."

Of course it *was* true. When would her parents have allowed themselves within shouting distance in the last seventeen years? "Now I can't decide if it's weirder that you hadn't met or that you did meet." She picked at her thumbnail. "I'm trying to picture it." Her mind recoiled a little at the picture. She was pretty used to keeping the two families separate. "Did she know it was you?"

"We only figured it out at the very end when we were all leaving. One of her friends knows one of my friends' friends, et cetera. That kind of thing."

She nodded. "I guess it was bound to happen sooner or later. What did you say? What did she say?" Mattie wanted to keep the goodwill flowing. But some old, shadowy feelings were peeping over and around her shoulder that she'd never felt with Ray before.

Was Sasha just one more person Ray could think was smarter and more serious than Mattie? It had always given her a small sense of liberty not to have to worry about Sasha on this side of the East River. Her fingers were already itching to call Sasha and get her side of things. Why hadn't Sasha told her?

"I don't remember. I think we were both too surprised to say much. I guess it was kind of awkward."

Ray looked young and confused and sadly honest, the way he said it. He was clearly struck by Sasha.

The shadowy feelings were hovering in Mattie's ears, reminding her that Ray might have noticed, if he got past Sasha's dark, slumpy clothes, her bowed head, and her turned foot, that she had an exceptionally curvy little body and the prettiest face of all four sisters. Mattie felt like an evil stepsister sometimes, wanting people not to notice Sasha's buried charms in the presence of her own flashy ones. And the shallow fact was, they usually didn't.

Mattie remembered once confiding her insecurities about Sasha to her friend Sophie Marlow. "Seriously? Mattie, you are way prettier, way funnier, way cooler, and way, way more popular than her," Sophie had said, interpreting Mattie's concerns in the basest possible way. Mattie never hung out with Sophie anymore, actually, because Sophie was more viper than friend and had the habit of telling you what you thought you wanted to hear but actually just confused you and made you a worse person.

Ray and Mattie walked in silence for a block, both of them preoccupied and a little stifled. She felt frustrated that they weren't getting to any of the real things.

"So how's your boyfriend?" Ray asked. "The tall fellow?"

Mattie jabbed an elbow into his rib. "Shut up," she said laughing.

Mattie did hang out with John Harman sometimes, but he was not her boyfriend and he was notably not tall. It was a sore point that he was at least three inches shorter than her.

"I saw him on Eighth Avenue and he was wearing heels."

"Ray! He does not wear heels, he wears boots."

"Boots with heels, then."

"You don't know what you're talking about."

They admired the chocolate éclairs in the window of the President Street bakery and then lapsed into silence again.

"So what did you think?" Mattie finally asked.

"Of what?"

"Of Sasha?"

"Oh. Right. I don't know." Up and down went the hoodie zipper. "She seemed familiar. She looked familiar." He considered. "It seemed strange that we're strangers."

She considered too. "Familiar how? You mean she looks like us?"

"Like Emma and Quinn, for sure." He laughed and pretended to step on her foot. "You don't look like anybody."

11

IT'S A WEIRD WAY
TO HAVE A FAMILY.

Sasha sat aimlessly on a chair at the kitchen table in Wainscott, watching the family go by. She was agitated by Ray feelings, so she needed to get out of her room. Granted, it was his kitchen too, but not in so powerful a way.

She let her mother and Mattie come and go. When Quinn walked in she opened her mouth.

"Can I tell you something strange?"

Quinn stopped with a carton of milk in her hand and turned around. "Yes."

She idolized Emma and she admired and feared Mattie, but Quinn was the one she craved, for whom she felt the fearful hope in her mouth whenever she called Quinn her sister, always warding off that ghost word "half." "I met Ray last Saturday night."

Quinn's eyebrows shot upward. "My brother Ray?"

Sasha felt nicked by the wording. She nodded.

"What do you mean?"

"I was at a party. He was at the same party. I didn't realize it was him until we were standing outside on the sidewalk with a couple of friends."

Quinn looked at Sasha's face carefully, nodding.

"I've never been close to him before." Sasha had to push herself to explain. She resisted talking about Ray head-on, even saying his name, for fear of giving away too much. "I only ever saw pictures from when he was young or saw him on the opposite side of an auditorium."

Quinn got a glass out of the cabinet, a pensive look on her face. She poured milk. "I guess that's true. 'And never the twain shall meet.'"

"The twain did meet, though. On the corner of Eighty-Eighth and Lexington."

Later Quinn came out to the patio and sat at the foot of her creaky chaise, turning it into a seesaw. Sasha scooted up to make the balance.

"I guess it's easier for everyone to keep you and Ray in separate worlds."

"That's how we've always done it," Sasha said philosophically.

"Because of Lila and Dad."

Even that everyday locution was hard. Quinn always referred to her parents from Sasha's point of view instead of her own. Emma, ever precise, said "my mom and our dad." Mattie said "Mom and Dad," though the mom she meant was not Sasha's mom. There was something wrong about each of the ways. These were two people who could no longer be captured in a sentence together.

"Of all of us, you and Ray are the only two who aren't siblings or steps or related at all. You aren't anything to each other, but you are my brother and sister." Quinn pressed her thumb to her mouth, thinking. "It's a weird way to have a family."

Sasha was quiet for a long time. "Do you think we would like each other? If we knew each other?"

"I love you. I love him," Quinn said simply. "I think you would love each other. But that math has failed me before."

Sasha nodded.

Quinn's sad face was never intentional like Mattie or her mother's, but it was the most distressing. Quinn bore a child's love for her parents no matter how they hated each other, how ugly the scar they made down the center of her life.

Kids come first. Both adult halves of the family shared the mantra. It was one of the few agreements, and neither of them meant it.

"When Ray was little I would stand with him at the edge of the pond," Quinn finally said. "He would spend hours catching tadpoles and frogs with his hands. The next week you would come and we would collect things in the woods. You would make these beautiful little terrariums. There were so many times like that when I wished I could be with the two of you together."

For some reason Sasha felt like crying.

Quinn lowered her gaze to Sasha's face. "I think I would love it if you and Ray knew each other. You two are opposites in most ways, but you make two halves of a whole. It scares me a little. I'm not allowed to want the two halves to come together. But I always do."

"You want to what?"

Mattie looked dangerously pleased with herself, standing in her tank top and Pink Floyd pajama shorts in the middle of Quinn's bedroom.

Quinn sat up in her bed. "You're talking about next month? This coming August?"

"Everybody has an engagement party. Why are you looking at me like that?"

Quinn's eyes opened directly onto her thoughts, mostly because she didn't think to shutter them.

Mattie came and sat cross-legged at the end of her bed. "I think the best method is jumping in, you know? Because why let everybody build it up for a whole year? Why not start breaking down the barriers now? Get some of the drama out of the way. Give us all a little practice before the actual wedding?"

One nice thing about Mattie was she tended to answer her own questions in case you didn't. She was happy to carry on a conversation without your assistance.

"Here at the house?"

"Yes. Come on. Will you help me?"

Quinn pushed the covers off, folded her legs under her. "Have you asked Emma?"

"No, I want it to be a surprise."

Quinn looked at her seriously. "I think that is one of the worst ideas you've ever had."

Mattie smiled. "And that's saying something." She jumped off the bed and walked to face the mirror over the dresser. She cocked her head and made her mirror face before she turned back around. "Okay, fine. So we'll tell them. We don't know Jamie that well. And we don't want to scare him away forever."

It hadn't escaped Quinn that she and Mattie had just become "we" in this enterprise.

Mattie paced and considered. "Do we want to scare him away? Maybe we do?" she mused. "No. If Emma hasn't scared him away all on her own, then maybe we should keep him. Anyway, I think I like him." She opened Quinn's closet and stepped in. "Well, I'm glad that's decided, then," Mattie continued from inside the closet.

"What are you doing in there?"

"Nothing. You have nothing I want." She came back out. "Except storage space. Can you ask Mom?"

"Ask her what?"

"Or tell her. Can you tell Mom about the party?"

Quinn sat at the edge of her bed. "Why?"

"Because she can't say no to you."

"Sure she can."

"Well, she can't say yes to me."

"And Dad?"

"Can you tell him too?"

"Seriously?"

Mattie looked sheepish, but it wasn't sincere. She was reckless.

"I don't think I want to."

"I know." For the first time Mattie allowed Quinn to see the intensity under the request. "But will you anyway?"

Quinn watched Mattie flounce confidently from her room, knowing her sister would do what she asked.

It was precisely because of what it would cost that Mattie wanted her to do it. Because her parents would understand that, too, and on the strength of that, maybe they wouldn't say no.

"This August? One month from now? Are you serious?" Emma looked around to make sure Francis wouldn't catch her talking on the phone while at the bakery counter.

"Yes. It gives us enough time to plan the party, but not enough time for them to dig the trenches and plant the explosives," Mattie explained.

Emma shook her head. It was one thing to imagine her parents in the same room next summer. This had a terrifying nearness.

"Mom and Dad will never agree to it."

"They will. Quinn is asking them. She never asks them for anything."

"Does Quinn think it's a good idea?"

"She said as long as nobody gets surprised."

"I'd have to ask Jamie right away. His parents would need to come from Ohio."

"Ask him."

Emma considered for a moment. "Listen. I'm flattered and honored you guys want to do this. But . . . why do you want to do this?"

"Because we love you. We want to celebrate. Everybody has an engagement party."

"Not with our family."

"Well, maybe it's time to get them on board. Maybe it's time for them to get over themselves and put their kids first."

Emma smiled ruefully. "Matt, that's crazy talk, and you know it."

"But it shouldn't be! That's the thing!"

Emma laughed and then got serious again. "I don't know."

"Here's another way to look at it: we get the worst of it out of the way before the wedding."

This made a certain kind of sense. "Okay. I'll talk to Jamie. I gotta go."

"Do you remember a guy named Jonathan Dawes?"

Mattie had made her way into her father's study unobtrusively.

His back was to her. His laptop was open; one phone was in his hand, another on the desk. One earphone was stuck against one ear, a newspaper on his lap, a cup of coffee a few inches from his elbow. Two wide screens mounted just above eye level showed the changing prices of commodities, mostly in red.

Her father barely registered her. His gaze ricocheted from screen to screen. He always left the door to his study open, but people didn't usually step through it.

It had taken a lot to get the question out the first time. She couldn't relax until she'd asked him, but she didn't really want to ask him. In fact, she was relieved that he wasn't paying attention. She didn't want him to pay attention. It would be a big relief to turn around and walk back out. But then how was she supposed to get any peace?

Suddenly he was looking at her. Her silence always caught him as her voice did not. "Matilda. Did you say something?"

She pulled at a string trailing from the hem of her cutoffs. "Nothing important. I just . . ."

"What?" Now he was curious. Once he was curious, you were stuck.

She could make up some dumb thing about her debit card, or she could ask again. "I ran into this guy at the Black Horse. He was kind of familiar, and I wondered if you knew him."

"Who?"

She yanked at the string until it made a groove across her palm. She had to say it now. She felt like a bomb disposer, but she had to. Clippers out, wires in hand.

"Mattie?"

"His name is Jonathan Dawes." *Snip.*

His face showed nothing.

"I guess . . . he's big into . . . surfing." Her volume descended with each word.

Bomb disposers didn't always know right away whether they had succeeded or failed. She didn't know. She didn't even know what constituted success or failure in this case. She remembered Emma's old policy: "Don't ask Dad a question unless you already know the answer."

His eyebrows rose. His mouth compressed a bit. He cleared his throat but said nothing.

"I think he taught us to surf when we were small. Do you remember that at all?"

His body was still. Absolutely. Phone still poised in hand. Commodity prices fell behind his head. Was he thinking? Was he remembering? Was he distracted? Was he mad at her?

"No."

"You don't remember him?"

"No."

"You don't remember us learning how to surf?"

"No." Was he glaring at her? Was she being paranoid?

She snapped the string from the hem of her shorts. "Okay."

He rotated back toward his screens, hardly seeming to move.

"Dad?"

Nothing. Phone down. Head bent.

"Okay." Now she knew which wire she cut: the one that caused the explosion. Slow and quiet maybe, but now unmistakable. And in some terrible way, maybe that was success. Because now she also knew she hadn't come in here to fix anything.

His posture was strange to her. She didn't know what to say. He never turned his back on her. She felt like she should say something, but she didn't know what. Her face felt hot and her palms were wet, and she wished she could put the wire back together and rewind the detonation.

She was his pink girl, his yellow-haired baby. She rode on his shoulders. She climbed on his head. She'd never been around him and not known how to be.

She walked out of his study.

"Close the door, please," he said. It was the voice he used with the pool cleaner when there was scum on the surface. It wasn't the voice he used with her.

She closed the door, but she couldn't make her legs walk her away from it. She stood there trembling.

She heard something roll and then crash. Something involving glass. She put her hand on the knob and listened to quiet. She could feel them both breathing on either side of the door, but far apart. Her heart was racing, but she didn't dare go through the door again.

12

BOXES (AND CANS)

On Sunday afternoon Quinn brought Myrna Chapman a brown bag of yellow Saturn peaches. She liked to stop by there once or twice a week after she finished in the Reeses' orchard, bringing some of whatever the trees had best to offer that day.

Myrna had been her grandma Hardy's babysitter growing up and later her friend. She lived in a Victorian house near the road in the village and had once kept the most beautiful garden Quinn had ever seen.

Quinn was always turning up at Myrna's when she was small, when her own house got loud. Myrna would give her chessmen cookies and grown-up black tea and teach her about flowers.

Quinn was a pest when she was tiny, a student when she was a little older, and a real help by the time she was about twelve. Myrna won the village award for her garden one year "hands down," as everyone liked to say at the time, and she had insisted on sharing it with Quinn at the presentation.

"Mattie is throwing an engagement party at the house for Emma and Jamie this August," Quinn announced, cutting up two of the peaches and putting them in a bowl in the middle of Myrna's small kitchen table. "I got the job of asking my parents."

Myrna looked amused. "And what did they say?"

Quinn sat down across from her. "They both said maybe, but they will both say yes."

"How do you know?"

"Because Mattie decided we're going ahead with it anyway, and Jamie's parents agreed to come all the way from Ohio. Jamie is my dad's star employee. My dad has to be there to greet the Hurns as father, boss, and host. And once my dad and Evie agree to be there, then my mom has to too. She will hate it, but you know her. She has to represent her side of things. She couldn't abide my dad acting like it's his party and his house and his daughter."

Myrna nodded. "Right you are."

"Same old," Quinn said.

Myrna's fingers were twisted and thick-knuckled now as she reached for a slice of peach, but her pleasure was pure in the taste of it.

"Will you come?" Quinn asked.

"Of course," Myrna said.

Myrna hadn't been invited to their house for many years because it was presided over by Grandma Hardy, and Grandma Hardy had judged Myrna for getting divorced when people at the club didn't get divorced yet. Twenty years later Grandma Hardy herself was divorced and remarried and living in Oyster Bay, saying things like, "Why in God's name did I wait so long?"

"I've never seen my parents in a room together," Quinn said. "Not that I can remember."

"I have."

"How were they?"

Myrna tipped her head, remembering. "Hard to say. Your grandfather was drunk and acting like a lout—the housekeeper had burnt the roast, I think. A truck from the volunteer fire department rushed in because the fire alarm went off, and your parents tried to keep Emma quiet."

Quinn smiled. "They weren't always the source of trouble."

Myrna smiled. "It's generational."

They savored the peaches for a few moments in silence. "I think I'm going to make a flower cake for the party," Quinn said.

"Lovely. I still have dianthus and borage. Those are wonderful in a cake."

As Myrna got older, her garden got smaller and closer to the kitchen door, until now it was a small patch of hardy perennials hugging the back wall of the house.

At first Quinn was pained by this march of diminishment.

"I could keep it going for you," she'd offered ardently, almost in tears. "The whole thing."

Myrna was moved by her offer, but firm. "A garden should reflect what you yourself can and want to do."

As Quinn rode home from Myrna's, it occurred to her she'd said something that wasn't quite true. When she was eleven, she'd come down with a mysterious illness that lasted for days. Finally the fever got so bad they put her in the hospital. She was in and out of consciousness, hallucinating and dreaming. Which was a mercy, really, because she just hated the sounds and smells of the place.

She remembered one moment of rough clarity when she woke up in the dark hospital room. She looked through the open door to the hallway and believed she saw her parents framed in the doorway, both of them. She remembered their heads bent together, talking in low voices.

She might have been hallucinating, but she thought she saw her father reach for her mother's hand and grasp it for one moment before they turned in different directions and walked away.

Violet looked pretty. Ray liked the sparkly stuff on her eyelids. He didn't mind the way her knee kept touching his under the table. But he really hated that question.

"Nothing. Why?"

Violet put her hair behind her ears. She shook her iced coffee. "You just seem very distracted."

That was fair. He was so distracted it took him a few seconds

134

to process that she'd just accused him of being distracted. "Yeah. Maybe. I don't know."

That wasn't totally fair. He didn't know, but he had a pretty good idea. He was comparing a girl he'd touched nearly every part of—hooked up with, hung out with off and on for two years—to a girl he'd met for less than five minutes outside a party.

With Violet it was always casual, never really intimate. But she was eager and ready and always around. Whereas the *other* girl was totally off-limits.

He knew them in completely different ways. Violet he knew from the outside—how she looked and dressed and how she felt in his hands. And though he'd barely seen (let alone touched) the other girl, he only knew her from what she did and wrote and read and made.

It was a flaw of character, his father told him once, to favor what you didn't have over what you did. What you couldn't have over what you could.

But would *she* ask him so often what he was thinking?

He stood. He took his overpriced Hamptons coffee cup from the table. "I have to be at work in a couple minutes," he told her.

Violet stood too. As they walked toward the door, she slid toward him. She kissed him on the jaw and he breathed in a flower smell.

"Are you going to Frasier's tonight?"

Violet smelled different every time. Always good and strong and girly, like the makeup aisle, but never the same.

She was looking at him impatiently out on the sidewalk.

"Sorry . . . Frasier's? No, I already told him I couldn't make it." Frasier was an old Wainscott friend. Ray was happy to go surfing or fishing with him but couldn't stand his parties. "I'm home tonight. Family dinner."

"Then back in the city?"

"Yeah. I'll see you the next week, I guess."

"I might come in for a night."

"Okay," he said.

"It gets boring out here without you."

Violet got bored quickly, he knew. He kissed her and turned to walk to the Black Horse, happy for his thoughts to be free from anyone wanting to get at them for a while.

Would *she* get bored quickly?

For some reason he thought of the Lego city. He couldn't really imagine Violet, not middle-school Violet or any Violet, working for five months on a Lego city with six parks and no school or even any shopping.

He tried to re-create *her* face in his mind, but it was already blurry less than two weeks after seeing it. In fact, it had grown blurry that very night as he tried to fall asleep, superimposed as it was with memory and expectation. He had no problem picturing Violet's face.

He'd had those few minutes of clarity, before he knew she was *her*, when he really saw her. That was the moment he kept trying to go back to, meeting eyes in the hallway outside the kitchen. That was the part that churned into an odd brew of confusion, shame, and excitement.

He had enough clarity to know he thought she was beautiful. As beautiful as Violet. More beautiful. Maybe other guys would disagree with him. Violet was tall and glamorous and head-turning. But he agreed with himself.

Why was he doing this?

He went into the Black Horse through the back door. He checked in with Julio and got to work in the storeroom.

He started unloading boxes of fancy Italian spaghetti from cartons onto storeroom shelves.

He peered around the aisle at the back of the last set of shelves to look for more cartons. Instead he found a faultless rendition of the three pyramids of Giza in cans and boxes.

He smiled. He leaned against the old fire door. His heart was full. He proceeded to spend the next hour stacking miniature tomato paste cans into the Great Sphinx.

No, she wouldn't get bored easily. And he had a flaw of character.

Question of the day for Little Ray:
Did Quinn ever take you to see the narwhals at the
Coney Island aquarium?

Big Sasha

BS,

Yes! She loved that place and she hated it. She cried over the ancient walrus. "He can see the open ocean from his tank!" So I cried too, naturally.

Did she used to take you under the blue whale at
the Natural History museum?

LR

LR,

*Many times. She had stories for each one of the
scary undersea dioramas.*

*She was the only one in the family who took me
anywhere. If not for Quinn, I would have turned out
like Cameron Reese.*

BS

Please.

"Do you think it's possible that Mom had an affair when she
was married to Dad?" Mattie chose a moment when Quinn
was wrestling the deep-rooted weeds in a patch of summer
squash.

Mattie decided to burden Quinn with this in its totality. She
knew Quinn would take most or all of the weight, and it was
just as well. She was tired of carrying it alone.

Quinn stood up. "Why do you ask?" She looked neither surprised nor hungry for information, as other people might.

"Because I keep thinking about it. That guy in the Black
Horse I told you about?"

"Uh-huh." She was back to the weeds.

"I asked Mom about him and she shut down completely. She hasn't looked me in the eye since."

"What did she say?"

"Nothing remarkable. She said he was a surfer. He taught her and us for a bit. I knew all that. It was how she looked and acted."

"Right."

Mattie took a breath. "And then I asked Dad." Mattie picked at her fingernails violently. "He was so weird, Quinn. He hardly said anything. Silent but cold. I've never seen him act like that."

Quinn nodded, but her face, even from the side, was pained.

"It was Sunday afternoon and he was in his study. After I asked him he told me to close the door and right after that I heard something crash on the ground." She felt shaky as she told it. "What does that mean, do you think?"

"Something fell."

Mattie let out her breath. "Quinn."

"Do you want to know what it means?"

"I don't know if I do, but I keep pushing, and I can't seem to let it go." She cracked all her knuckles. She closed her eyes. "None of us knows what happened. Don't you kind of want to know?"

"They don't want us to know."

"Obviously they don't. Why not? What happened?" Mattie felt itchy and reckless, and even though her recklessness always seemed to cause Quinn the most trouble, it didn't stop her. "Are you not curious?"

Quinn wiped the dirt off on her pants. "I don't think there's any piece of information that would change the things we know are true," she said slowly.

Mattie was barely listening. She opened her hands. "Other people divorce amicably. They stay friends. They have dinner together. They share holidays, go on vacations. I know plenty of people like that. Our parents haven't stood within a hundred feet of each other in almost twenty years. *What happened to them?* And why can't they tell us?"

"They want to protect us."

"From what? Maybe they want to protect themselves. Maybe it's the one thing they've agreed on in all this time."

"Maybe even that amount of agreement is good."

"When we were little kids maybe. But at a certain point, they don't get to decide anymore."

At last Quinn's large eyes turned on her with all their force. "Please be careful, Matt."

No, that was not what she would be doing. She would trample, lurch, and careen. "Maybe I get to decide. Maybe even Jonathan fucking Dawes gets a chance to decide."

13

AND ON TO THE NEXT WORRY

Sasha spent two days trying to think of what she could write to Ray about, and then she saw the sphinx behind the back shelves in the storeroom of the market alongside her pyramids and she almost cried.

She almost cried with appreciation of it. In her heart surged a tidal wave that started to trickle out of her eyeballs. That was weird.

But it brought such a rush of the old feelings. The Lego feelings and *To Kill a Mockingbird* feelings and the little plastic animal feelings. It was nostalgia, but something new and momentous, too: the synthesis of her old Ray and the bewildering stranger Ray she'd met outside Samantha Rubin's apartment building. Here was a beautiful rendition of nearly the whole of Giza made of cans and boxes stretching across the poorly lit aisle behind the last wall of shelves that led to the defunct fire door.

It brought back an old version of herself that she'd missed, hadn't really known was gone.

And then Francis came around in back of the shelves and found her.

"What the hell is this?"

She let out her breath. Shit. With her eyes she memorized the last moments of box-and-can Giza.

"Are those pyramids?"

"Yeah."

"Did you make this?" She couldn't quite read his voice. If Francis was even a little impressed she wanted to include Ray, but if he was purely annoyed she didn't.

"Um."

"Have I been paying you to make a play world out of dry goods?"

She tried to look contrite and not just put out. "I'm sorry. I had a bit of extra time after I finished with the morning shipments and restocking. I thought maybe we could use the images on social media."

That was complete bullshit, but Francis talked about the value of social media almost as much as he talked about his MBA.

She could see the wheels turning. "You mean, we could post it on Facebook."

"Sure. Maybe create an Instagram account."

"Okay." He nodded, eyebrows raised. "That's good thinking. You know, that's why I like to hire you kids."

"Ray did it too. He really deserves credit." She smiled. She couldn't help feeling proud.

"You're Ray."

"I mean the other Ray." Now she knew exactly what she would write to Ray as soon as she got off work. Her heart began thumping irrationally. Her fingers tingled with anticipation.

"He did?"

"Yeah."

He laughed. "Here I was imagining Ray was an adult. I mean, you've seen that gorgeous girlfriend who picks him up after his shift every day."

Sasha swallowed hard. Her heart kept up, but its rhythm changed. Her smile dangled uncertainly on her face, then fell off. Gone was her triumph. She could barely speak. She felt a little dizzy. She wouldn't have thought Francis had the power to injure her, but there were so many things to feel bad about in that one sentence of his she couldn't sort through them.

Ray was an adult. She was a child. Ray had a girlfriend. His girlfriend was gorgeous. His girlfriend was devoted. Sasha had in fact not seen the gorgeous girlfriend. Not at all. Sasha had not even fathomed her. Sasha had no person, gorgeous or otherwise, picking her up after her shift. Not every day. Not any day.

Now she looked at the dumb can pyramids and just felt stupid. Was Ray making fun of her when he added the sphinx?

Francis turned to go. "It's cute." He gestured to the spread. "Really. Did you get pictures already?"

She felt stricken. She tried not to. "No. I will."

"Good. And then take the whole thing down and put all that stuff back where it goes."

She nodded, miserable.

"Tonight."

"I think we should call before we go to Lexi's," Jamie suggested.

Now that Jamie's parents had agreed to fly east for the engagement party, he and Emma had decided it would be good to call them and stage a preliminary introduction before the hubbub in August.

Emma pushed her phone against her ear so she could hear better. "Can you get out of work early?"

"I'll try. I'll go back to the office after the dinner if I have to."

His voice sounded tight. She wished she could see him so she could read his mood.

"Let's meet at my place at six."

"That early?" She'd never known him to leave the office before eight on a weeknight.

"Yeah. I think so."

She arrived in front of his apartment building in Long Island City just as he did. He kissed her like he meant it, but his face was anxious. His feet were tip-tapping the whole ride up in the elevator.

"It's just a phone call," she said. "Your folks are the easy ones, right?"

He shrugged. "I don't know. Whose parents are easy?"

She was trying to understand. He didn't talk about his family much. His parents were married. He had one sister who was fifteen and prematurely capable. His dad worked in sales for a chemical company. They lived in a nice airy house in a nice subdivision with a carport.

Was it her he was worried about? She had thought of this before. "They won't be able to tell I'm Indian over the phone," she said as he let them into his tiny apartment.

He looked aghast. "What do you mean?"

"I was just worrying that when they meet me, they might be surprised I'm not a bit . . . whiter."

He grabbed her and hugged her hard. "Oh, Em, you are so perfectly perfect. I hate that you're worried about that." He let her go. "Anyway, I told them all about you—I think I used your description: half-Bengali, half-hippie. They met your dad once for about a tenth of a second when they came to see the office last year."

So that wasn't it.

"I'm calling," he said.

They caught all three Hurns at home. Everyone was warm, polite, full of congratulations, a little awkward. Jamie's mother effused about the case of champagne Robert had sent.

"I am touched that you are all coming here for the engagement party," Emma said at the end. "I can't wait to meet you."

"See, that wasn't so bad," she said after they'd all chimed in about how much they were looking forward to it and hung up.

Jamie nodded.

"They all sound great, in fact."

Jamie's eyes looked more guarded than she'd seen them. "My mom is easier sometimes than others," he said.

"Well, she sounded like a picnic compared to mine."

Mattie was the only one around, so Mattie was the one Sasha had to ask. Not ideal, but it had to be done.

"Who is the gorgeous girl who picks Ray up from his shift every day?" It was none of Sasha's business, and not objectively relevant to any aspect of her life, but there it was.

Mattie was painting her toenails on a lounge chair by the pool. Mattie was so distracted these days, Sasha hoped she could excise the information she wanted, like a surgeon in a hurry, without a lot of curiosity or haranguing in return. "You mean Violet?"

Shit. She had to have a cool name like Violet. "I don't know. Do I?" Were there a lot of these girls?

"I guess you must mean Violet. She's always turning up. I don't know about gorgeous." Mattie considered. "Yeah, maybe she is. Do you know her or something?"

"Manager Francis told me about her."

Mattie rolled her eyes. "Francis is lascivious. What is he, thirty? Violet is in *high school*."

Sasha really did have to wonder about herself. Why was she surprised there was a Violet? Of course there was a Violet. Why did she feel betrayed? Was she completely bananas? What kinds of ideas was she harboring? And yet, her mouth opened again. "Are they serious?"

146

Mattie was occupied with fixing up a botched toenail and didn't appear to judge her for asking. That, at least, was nice. "Serious? They're kids," Mattie said, as though she herself were a senior citizen. "It's hard to use 'serious' and 'Violet' in the same sentence."

Meanly, Sasha was happy to hear this. "Is that right?" She craved more.

"Violet's been hanging around Ray since they were in middle school. She goes to Nightingale, I think, where no boy has ever stepped, so Ray's like the white rhino. You know how that is. She's your classic bratty East Hampton kid who hangs around Main Street wearing a lot of makeup and trying to spot celebrities." Mattie raised an eyebrow like she was a justice of the Supreme Court or something.

The pleasure of that damnation was short-lived. Now Sasha was on to the next worry. Was Ray like that? Was that really the kind of girl he went for? That didn't square with what she imagined. But then again, when it came to Ray, imagination was mostly all she had. "And Ray is into that?" She didn't even try to stop herself from asking.

Mattie waved the bottle of nail polish around. "I don't know how much of it is Ray being into her and how much is Ray putting up with her."

That didn't sound very romantic, did it?

"Emma calls her 'Just Violet.'"

"Why?" Sasha asked, perhaps a little too eagerly.

"Because whenever she turns up at the house, we all go, 'Oh, it's just Violet.'"

Sasha laughed. She wondered if it sounded as diabolical outside her brain as it did inside.

Mattie finished the second and final coat on her second and final pinky toe and finally came out with the inevitable. "Anyway, what does it matter to you?"

14

TALK ABOUT GETTING
MORE THAN YOU CAME FOR

I still surf every Saturday out at Ditch Plains.

Had he somehow known Mattie would come to this?

At the time it had struck her as a laughably extraneous piece of information. And yet she'd remembered it. And here she was driving Adam's crummy Honda out to Ditch Plains early on a Saturday morning.

Mattie's mother did not want to talk. Her father most certainly did not want to talk, but she somehow got the sense that Jonathan Dawes did.

The towel and the book felt like props to her as she picked along the sand. This beach was only a few miles down from Georgica but belonged to a wilder world. The break was long and rugged and already dotted with surfers. The height of the cliffs and the speed of the wind gave it an edge-of-the-earth quality. Jonathan Dawes must have come over to their world, to the flat water of Georgica Pond, when he balanced little girls on the water.

Mattie felt self-conscious as she made her way toward the water. This beach was run by notoriously cranky locals. If you hadn't surfed here for a decade or two, if you couldn't acquit yourself on a board, you were not welcome. And yet she noticed more nods than scowls. Maybe blond girls in bikinis got a pass here, just as they did in most circumstances.

She recognized him from the back a couple hundred yards down the beach. He was wearing wetsuit pants so supremely faded they might have been the same ones from the picture seventeen years ago. His hair had a strawlike texture from years of salt and sun. He was holding a respectably beat-up longboard, standing with two other surfers. He was one of the locals, not cranky, maybe; if anything, he was the kind of institution the cranky ones were protecting.

She was moved by him, in a strange way. How well he belonged, how relaxed his body looked. How much he was part of this exact place. And how he was still part of that old time, when nothing else from then felt the same.

It seemed a credit to her that her life might overlap with his. This was an intoxicating thought and a treasonous one.

She was frozen there, clutching her book and towel, when he turned and saw her. He cocked his head, and then smiled and came toward her.

She was almost surprised that he registered her. She forgot she was visible and part of this scene. She had lulled herself into the idea that she was watching him as though on a screen, a pair of abstract eyes gazing at him in his natural environment. She'd forgotten she'd come here to interact. She wasn't sure she wanted to anymore.

There was something momentous about his walking toward her. Because of the raking sunlight and shadows and his look of question and expectation. Now she knew she was choosing something.

Had she meant to?

She must have meant to. She didn't get here by accident.

He got close and put his arms out to give her a hug. She was awkward, clutching her things. He was not awkward, sort of hugging around them.

"Nice to see you, Mattie. I was hoping you would come."

That spooked her. Her mind ran back over the things he'd said, the things she'd said. She was another stupid Hamptons kid at the Black Horse. What was he hoping for?

I look like my mom. That was why he was looking at her like that. By this she reoriented herself.

"I wanted to ask you something," she said boldly.

He nodded as though this, too, was what he expected.

Now that she was here she wasn't sure how to put it.

Was she mad at her mom? Did she want to catch her? Prove something? What good would that do?

No good. And yet she wouldn't let it go.

"Did you . . ." She trailed off.

He didn't prompt her or seem to want to rush her.

"Were you and my mom . . ."

He cocked his head again. He didn't seem nervous at all. Not in the way she was nervous.

". . . involved with each other?"

He didn't look surprised or mad. He didn't say anything.

But already she was wanting to retreat. "I know it's not my business to ask personal questions. You don't know me."

At this he laughed.

"What?" she said, self-conscious, embarrassed.

"You're right. I don't know you." She could tell he wanted to put her at ease. He laughed again, less joyful this time. "I almost feel like I do." He caught her eye for less than a second. Was it she who looked away or was it him?

"Because I look like my mom."

He shrugged. "You do."

"Everyone says that."

He nodded. "Right. I can imagine."

She regrouped again. "Did you know her well back then?"

"For a time." He was strangely peaceful.

She waited for him to say more, but he didn't. "We have some pictures. With you. From then."

He didn't look skittish or scared, like her mother did. "I have a few too," he said.

He'd been in love with her mom. That seemed almost certain to her now.

He walked a little way up the beach to where the sand perched over the surf and sat down. He gestured for her to join him. They were quiet for a while. "Have you asked your mother about this?"

"I tried."

"She didn't want to talk."

Mattie snorted a little. "At the sound of your name she shut down. I think she's pretty much been avoiding me since."

He looked wistful, but he didn't look hurt. "It was a complicated time. You probably know that."

"The divorce, you mean?" This was territory where she got reckless.

For the first time a look of trouble passed over his face. He sighed again. "I respectfully defer to your mom in this case."

Was he the reason for the divorce? Was it that obvious? Her mom cheated and her dad threw her out? Was it as simple and tawdry as that?

He pushed the sand around with his hands. "I am delighted to see you here, Mattie. I really would enjoy getting to know you again. If you ever want to take up surfing, please look no further. I am available almost any time and my rates are quite reasonable." He smiled at her. She figured he was probably joking about the rates part.

"But if your mom doesn't want to talk to you about this, then I don't feel comfortable talking to you about it."

About it. So there was an "it." He wasn't denying that. "About you and my mom?" she asked, wanting to eke out a little more.

His voice was less certain, more measured when he spoke again. "About me and her. And you."

"And *me*?" she fired back indignantly without even thinking. "What does it have to do with me?"

She wished she'd stopped herself from saying this, especially thinking on it so many times afterward. She would probably feel this memory like a kick in the neck for the rest of her life.

She'd fired back without listening or understanding because of the old child-of-divorce catechism: *It has nothing to do with you. Never blame yourself for what happened.* She'd heard that from every adult in the land—even virtual strangers—and recited it to herself on a thousand different occasions. It was a reflex in her child-brain. It flared in her eyes and blinded her from seeing what he was really getting at.

He didn't answer. He couldn't, it seemed, and that gave her a dizzying and painful stretch of time to think.

And you. She couldn't let it in. But it came in anyway, in sharp little jabs, each one injuring and disorienting.

She was just a baby back then. The jabs got, slower, duller, more bruising. What could a baby have done? *Thud.* Except the notorious thing a baby can do to wreck a marriage.

But that couldn't be her. She couldn't be that. She found herself looking down at his feet.

When she looked back at his face she saw deep discomfort. He thought she knew. Or at least suspected. He thought that was what she had come here to investigate, maybe something she was open to. Now she felt bad for him. She felt worse for herself.

He pressed sand down under both hands, hard. He looked up at her and dusted them together. "I'm sorry, Mattie." He looked genuinely sorry. "You need to talk to your mom."

*　*　*

Half the time, when Evie went to Wainscott early for the weekend, Robert arranged for the firm's car service to drive him out
so he could get work done. Usually Sasha went with her mom,
but now and then she went with her dad.

Here was a conversation Sasha had heard before: Back of a
spotless black car, maybe a Mercedes or a Town Car. Today it
was a Suburban. Her dad tapping on his phone. And then the
driver, usually polite and well-meaning: "If I may ask, where
are you from, sir?"

Her dad looks up, already impatient. "Canada. Outside
Toronto." Back to his phone.

"Before that? Your family?"

When this happens, they all know what the driver means.
The driver himself is Indian or Pakistani or Southeast Asian.
He sees potential kinship here. *You're not one of them,* the driver
is thinking, maybe with some pride. *You are one of us, aren't
you? Who are you really?*

Her dad will have none of it. "All Southern Ontario. That's
it." Nothing to see here, folks. Keep moving.

The driver invariably looks skeptical, maybe even hurt.
Maybe he looks to Sasha's Bengali eyes for help. If so, she gives
a fleeting look of compassion mixed with warning.

She's always tempted to say more: My dad is Bangladeshi.
You can tell, can't you? His biological mother was, in any case.
He never talks about it, but something terrible happened to
her in the war in '71. He's a war baby, but he'll never say that.

155

He was sent to Canada at two years old to be raised by white parents. He's tall now. They fed him milk.

Her dad grew up skating on homemade ice rinks in backyards, just like all the other kids in Ontario. From what she could understand, he wasn't particularly sensitive about the fact that he looked different from the other kids—that he was visibly a different race. He wasn't defiant about it. He wasn't very interested in it. "I like to stay busy with the things I can do something about," he'd told her once.

To hear her dad tell it, he's Canadian through and through. He had the best parents in the world. He'd sing you all four verses of "O Canada" and a dozen Anglican hymns before he'd tell you he was the unwanted baby of a teenage rape victim born in a refugee camp in Bangladesh. He played ice hockey at Princeton. He's the founder of Califax Capital. He has four beautiful daughters. That's all you or anyone needs to know.

Her dad was back giving orders on his phone. Nobody, not even strangers, could tell anything about him on the phone.

Quinn had passed the Body Arts tattoo and piercing store in Hampton Bays dozens of times and never thought of going in. A few of those times she'd noticed the middle-aged woman with the black-red hair and the many tattoos smoking out front. Impulsively Quinn pulled her bike into the parking lot.

The woman was inside. She introduced herself as Raven.

"Do you pierce noses?" Quinn asked.

"Yes."

"Can you pierce my nose?"

"How old are you?"

"Twenty-one."

Raven made a face. "Are you really? I would have guessed sixteen. Who rides their bike along Montauk Highway? You have ID?"

"Yes."

"Sure thing. You want to do it now?"

"Can you?"

Raven looked around. "I don't see any other customers, do you?"

Quinn shook her head. The place was darkly lit and the walls were covered with potential tattoo designs. There were a lot of serpents and dragons on first glance.

"You'll need to fill out a form and pick your jewelry, and we're good to go."

"Okay." It seemed that Raven favored tattoos involving wings. Butterflies, angels, dark birds of prey, an owl, a winged lion, a dragon, a bat or two.

Quinn filled out the paper, gave her ID, and picked a tiny titanium half circle to start with.

"Is your name really Quinn?" Raven led her to the room in the back, where the atmosphere was less mystical but the light was better for piercing holes in people.

"Yes. It was my father's mother's maiden name." Raven pointed to a reclining chair like at the dentist's. "Is your name really Raven?"

"No. My mother named me Barbara."

"Oh."

Raven had a leather corset kind of thing strapped tightly across her wide bosom, stretchy pants, and high-heeled black boots. Under all the wings, her skin looked crepey and tired. She had many rings jammed onto her short fingers. It was hard to tell if any one of them meant she was married. She had a scar on her neck and another on her forearm. Quinn's mind floated over, beginning to imagine her as the girl her mother named Barbara.

Everyone had a mother. That was the thing. The week before, Emma had dragged her to a movie set during World War I. Quinn sat balled up in her seat as soldiers fell in droves, and for every one, Quinn thought of his mother. Mr. Reese had a mother once. It was one of nature's many mercies that people didn't usually get old enough to watch their kids get old.

Quinn sat back in the piercing chair.

Was Raven someone's mother? Quinn floated out a bit further. For some reason she didn't think so.

"Which was your first tattoo?" Quinn asked.

Pop went the piercing gun, and for that moment Quinn was entirely in her own body.

An hour and a half later, the redness had gone down, and Quinn had a jot of titanium in her left nostril. She also knew the story of every one of Raven's thirty-one tattoos, and thus had a nearly complete story of her life, from the first at fourteen to the most recent ("not the last") for her sixtieth birthday in April. Her first boyfriend chose the first, a lamb sitting nestled in her cleavage, and she'd chosen herself wings for every one after.

Quinn hugged Raven after she'd given her fifty-eight dollars, including tip, and also a bag of sweet yellow Shiro plums she'd retrieved from her bike basket. Raven squeezed her for a few extra seconds. "You're a soul gazer, you know that?"

"What does that mean?" Quinn asked into her shoulder.

"You've got those eyes—you take in a person's soul."

Quinn thought this was only partly true. She did take people in, but it was her own soul that did most of the traveling.

Riding home on her bike in the dark, Quinn wondered why she didn't stick in her own body more. It was a perfectly fine body; she had no complaints about it. It actually worked quite well—people used to say she was the most gifted athlete in the family, but that unlike Emma, she had no feeling for hierarchy or competition. So why did she slip out of it so easily? Why wasn't her obligation to it more binding?

What if she slipped out of her body one time and forgot to come back? Like Ping the duckling, when the door of the wise-eyed boat closed, and he was left to bob down the Yangtze River. Would that be a tragedy, really, or some kind of apotheosis?

Quinn pedaled past the Reeses' farm and got the itchy feeling of the lettuces being dry, so she stopped and leaned her bike quietly against the side of the barn. The moon rose as she tended to the greens.

Quinn knew time passed differently for her. That was another thing. She didn't orient herself to hours of the day or days of the week. She'd tried to for a long time to honor the units, but they didn't hold for her, didn't feel consistent or sequential as they did for most other people. Time tightened or bagged, ambled forward or doubled back, depending on the light and the season and her mood.

Sometimes she imagined the days of the calendar were a series of doorframes leading from one chamber to the next. Quinn wasn't walking through the doorframes. She wasn't even in the building.

In the care of plants, the work was her clock. The plants set the time.

So she realized when she got home that dinner was well under way, and she was meant to be there at the beginning of it.

Her father stood up to greet her. She'd forgotten about her nose, but he noticed it instantly.

"What in the world have you done to your beautiful nose?"

He wasn't kidding around. He was pained, she could see.

She touched it, remembering. "I think it makes my ordinary nose look more beautiful," she answered honestly.

"Let me see," Mattie called, getting up. "Wow."

Sasha came over too.

"Why would you do that, Quinn?" her father demanded. "You know how I feel about piercing. If you take the thing out, will it close over?" His voice went unusually high and turned brittle.

"I think it's cool," Mattie pronounced. "When did Quinn ever try to be cool before?"

"Most Indian women pierce their noses when they come of age," Quinn said.

"You are not an Indian woman," he shot back.

Quinn was sorry now. She was sorry that her father was troubled by it. She was sorry that Sasha had to see her get scolded, because she knew Sasha minded it and was her staunchest defender.

"By blood I am partly a Bengali woman," she said carefully. She felt Sasha's warmth and distress at her elbow.

Evie came over, knowing she couldn't hold the table or the evening together at this point. She put a hand on Quinn's shoulder. "Promise your father you won't get anything else pierced," she said lightly, champion of neatening.

Quinn turned to him. "I promise," she said solemnly. "Not even my ears."

"Your ears would be fine," he muttered.

Quinn's mother arrived at changeover on Sunday, but it was half a day before Lila stopped Quinn in the kitchen. "Hey, wait. Stop. Something's different."

Quinn nodded.

Lila held Quinn's face between her two hands.

Quinn pointed to her nose.

Her mother squinted at it, dotted it lightly with the tip of her finger. "It looks nice. I like it."

Little Ray,
 Did Quinn ever tell you stories about the Indians of Eel Cove? I had a dream about them last night.
         Big Sasha

BS,

Oh my God, yes. I loved the mother/chief/witch doctor with the sea-glass beads. I still think about her potions. (To forget your name, to share your mind, to hear things people say on the other side of the world.) Do you remember how the kids in the white family would go to the regular doctor and they'd just get more twisted up and needy, and then one of them would sneak off to the chief for a real cure?

LR

LR,

That was when Quinn was sick. I never put it together back then. We were only six or seven, I guess. I remember visiting her in the hospital. I remember the night she got home, she got out of bed and walked into the pond in her pajamas.

My memory of her in the hospital is so dark and strange I wasn't sure it actually happened. But if you remember it too, I guess it did. I snuck into her bed with her. She said, "I've got to get out of here, because there's no way to get better in this place."

BS

15

WHAT IT COSTS

"Just tell me he didn't go to Princeton."

"He went to Princeton," Emma said flatly.

A trip to the farmers' market on her morning off had sounded like a good idea when her mom suggested it. Now Emma was trailing her mother with a net shopping bag full of weird root vegetables and wanting to cry. One minute her mother was examining heirloom tomatoes and the next she turned on her.

"I just don't understand what the rush is. Why barrel into this? You're twenty-two years old! You just met him."

"You got married at twenty-two."

"Exactly, and look what that got me!"

Emma shook her head in disbelief. "Thanks a lot, Mom. It got you me and Quinn and Mattie."

Lila dropped the tomatoes into the bin and put her arm around Emma. She kissed the side of Emma's head. "Darling, of course. I would never ever change that. But you know what I mean."

Emma pushed her fingers against the spiny husk of a pineapple. What kind of farmers' market sold pineapples? "I seriously doubt any farmer around here grew this."

"And this party Mattie and Quinn keep talking about," Lila muttered. "My God! This August? Is that really necessary?"

"I think it's sweet," Emma said tersely.

Lila huffed out a breath and turned to a bin of tangled string beans. "The thing I don't understand is, what do you gain by getting married? You can do all the things you want without getting married."

"You got married. Twice."

"Because I had children. Don't tell me you're ready to have children."

Perversely, Emma wished she could produce a few children right then and there. "I want to get married because I love him. We want to live together."

"Emma, you have your whole life for that. Now is when you're free. You can travel. You can experience how you feel with lots of different people."

"I don't want to experience lots of different people. I like how I feel with him."

Her mother put down her bag. "Now you do. But how do you know what you'll want in five years? Or ten? Or twenty?"

Emma didn't like where they were and she didn't like where they were going. She didn't like the dark judgment stirring in her chest. "Well, maybe the idea is that you commit to somebody you love and you stick with them, regardless of what happens in five or ten or twenty or a hundred years, because they're your family and that's what marriage is and because you made a vow."

Lila turned away. She picked up her shopping bag and moved along to the berries. They paid for their groceries in silence and walked to the car in silence.

Emma hated the way her mother's car smelled after baking on the hot street. She hated how much crap there always was in it: the pottery wheel and bags of clay—or whatever other crafty thing she was into at the moment—weird health bars half unwrapped in the door pocket or stuck to the bottom of your shoe. Midwifery paraphernalia so puzzling and gross you did not even want to ask. Jackets, shoes, old junk mail. You always had to move stuff to sit down.

Lila waited until they pulled into their driveway to break the silence. "Just don't tell me you're going to change your name."

Emma got out of the car and shut the door hard behind her. If she hadn't wanted to change her name before, she sure did now.

Of all the lies he'd ever told, the one Ray probably regretted most was the one about losing his virginity. It wasn't necessarily the worst one. It didn't really do anyone harm. But unlike most lies that slipped into the past and let you forget about them, this one kept coming back.

For example, every time he considered that he hadn't actually lost his virginity, the lie tapped on his shoulder. Every time he considered how he might actually lose his virginity, it sort of coughed skeptically. This amounted to a lot of times.

Like now, for instance, as he lay in this bed under the moon and burrowed into the sheets slept on by Sasha the very night before and tried to ignore his nose, his nerve endings, his brain, and also his entire body, so as not to think too much about her.

Stupidly, he'd told the lie to Parker, who didn't care that much either way. Parker continued to be a good and true friend, so the lie came annoyingly along with the friendship.

Why had he done that? Sometimes it seemed like the person who gave in to these stupid impulses and the person who suffered over the consequences of them were two separate people. Parker didn't particularly judge him or care. Parker had never even told him his own status, so what had been the need?

Partly it was because he had the juvenile idea that he could casually get rid of it whenever he wanted to. Violet had already done it in ninth grade, she'd informed him. He figured he could just do it with her and not have to make a big deal of it. Since the option was at hand like that, it was practically the same as already having done it.

He'd vowed late in the spring that he'd do it before the end of the summer, before starting his senior year. He'd just get it over with.

But now, for other reasons, because of pushing out the boundaries of his former idea of love, he knew he probably couldn't just get it over with Violet. He'd have to hang on to it even longer, because he had the idea it could be something important.

Anyway, he had said this. A person had to live with his lies. That was what they cost.

Mattie didn't want to look at herself in the mirror anymore. She first realized it yesterday, slipping through the front hall of the Wainscott house with her head turned. She'd always loved the front-hall mirror. She liked herself better in that mirror than in any of the others, but she couldn't look right now. She snuck right in past it, a girl with a fear and a secret.

Since the time she'd discovered she was notably pretty in fifth or sixth grade, Mattie had spent an embarrassing number of hours bobbing her face into the wide mirror that sat over the bureau in her bedroom. She had celebrated versions of herself in it from her bed: Mattie reading a book; Mattie talking on the phone, giggling pleasingly at a joke; Mattie doing her homework, a serious expression on her face. Today she skirted her reflection when she got home from work, sat restlessly at her desk, pulled curtains and turned off lights before she flopped into bed and stared at her phone.

Tonight she was supposed to be going to the new taco place in East Hampton with Megan Vise and two of her friends from UCLA who were in town, but she couldn't stand her face in her makeup mirror. She couldn't pick a dress to wear. She called Megan and told her she wasn't feeling well.

The very qualities she usually appreciated in herself spooked her now. Her fine yellow hair and round violet-blue eyes. Quinn had the dark, otherworldly eyes; Emma was an exotic head-turner with thick black hair down to her belly button; and Sasha, the most Indian in looks, was quietly the prettiest of all of them; but her dad was a well-known sucker for a blonde. He'd been raised by a blonde. He'd married two of them for better or for worse. Her father marveled at her. It made Mattie special to him, special to herself.

I kind of got all of it had been her smug sense for so long. She'd won the genetic jackpot. She'd inherited her dad's smarts and grit, his merit as an outsider, his righteousness as a self-maker, his check mark in the diversity box. And all this she had in Disney Princess colors. It sickened her to frame the thought right now. Like pushing hard on a bruise.

And his love. Most important of all, she got to have her father's love, and the natural confidence that came with being his girl.

Suddenly there were so many things she was scared of in that mirror: Who she'd see, who else she'd see, who she wouldn't see. What she'd lose, what she'd realize she never had. For the first time she hated her differences and she hated her smugness even more.

Who was Jonathan Dawes? What did he expect? Had he thought all these years that he had a daughter out there? Had he known where she was all this time? Had he thought about her and wondered what kind of girl she was?

It scared her to think of herself in relation to him, to what he might have thought or hoped for. What kind of daughter did he require? To him she was not one of many daughters, as she always thought of herself, but one strange figure in his life. Was she somehow responsible to him?

She thought of covering the mirror the way they had at her friend Ellie's house when they sat shiva for her mother. But she couldn't exactly cover all the mirrors in the house—and over the years she'd had relationships with all of them. The one in the front hall, reflecting her long-term favorite Mattie, the coming-and-going Mattie. The Mattie above the fireplace in the living room, with whom she'd only become acquainted once she was tall enough to see her. And the oval one in the den caught the Mattie who watched TV if you bent your neck a little. There was the well-lit Mattie in the sunroom mirror, who plucked her eyebrows because the light was good. There were even the framed family prints in the stairwell, where she found her face in the glass. She always saw a mobile version reflected back from the dark judicial robe of Great-Uncle Henry Harrison.

She got up. She couldn't stand to be alone with her thoughts in the dark. She couldn't stand to be with her reflection in the light.

She hated her smugness, and along those lines she hated her

supposed crusade for justice. There she was, Miss Junior Detective, discovering family truth, catching her mother in a lie, and grandly preparing to extend forgiveness after the appropriate confessing and suffering. By bringing the darkness into light, she'd help them all find closure and a family rebirth, preferably in time for a really great party.

The only person she'd caught was herself. The suffering would be hers, and the forgiveness would come from no one.

She went downstairs to the den and turned on the TV. She hunched into the sofa and flicked through stupid shows to the even stupider ones. She settled on a terrible rip-off of a terrible show involving a tanning bed and a lot of plastic surgery. It fit her need: she could watch people other than herself with loathing and bewilderment.

She heard a rattling in the kitchen. The suck of the refrigerator door. Soft steps through the living room and up three stairs. She hadn't realized Quinn was home. Quinn, who'd told her to be careful, who'd all but warned her she'd wreck her own happiness if she kept prying.

Quinn appeared in the doorway of the den, bathed in TV light. Mattie kept her head down, but Quinn read her mood in less than a second.

"What is it?"

Mattie shook her head. She always told Quinn things. It was impossible not to; most of the time, Quinn knew before you told her anyway. It usually felt so good to hand over problems to Quinn, who took them and carried them uncomplainingly.

Mattie pressed her mind to think if there was any part of it she could unburden. But she couldn't this time. It was too uncertain, too unsettled. She didn't really have anything, just a feeling of sick suspicion and the shame of having petulantly demanded information she wasn't ready to hear. It wasn't just admitting to Quinn she'd been right again. It went without saying that Quinn was right. To share it would make it more real than she could tolerate yet.

Quinn's large, lovely eyes filled with concern.

Mattie hunkered deeper, trying to evade those supernatural sister eyes. She kept her mouth small. If she tried to say something she would cry.

Quinn stood thoughtfully. Mattie knew Quinn had the ballpark of the problem and a name to put to it, but she didn't push. It was just another way she did not resemble her horrible sister Mattie. Instead she went around to the back of the sofa. She started French braiding Mattie's hair the way she used to do.

Mattie felt a shiver at her sister's touch and then let her shoulders and neck settle.

"Two braids or one?" Quinn asked.

Big tears were already falling. Mattie wondered if Quinn knew that, understanding she needed to cry without explanation. Mattie held up two fingers.

Quinn's competent fingers divided and wove, divided and wove. Mattie cried silently. Quinn braided and made it seem like she couldn't tell. Neither of them said anything else, but the comfort was more than words.

Hey, Little Ray,

Can I tell you something weird? (Something else weird.)

I think of myself in relation to your dad a lot. Even when I was really small I had this idea that because he was my sisters' father, he was sort of mine, too. I don't know the guy. I imagine he has an opinion of me, even though I know he doesn't. Because my sisters always told stories about him, I figured he was how a father should be and I didn't want to disappoint him. How crazy is that?

Big Sasha

BS,

It amazes me, it makes me laugh, and sometimes it actually scares me how parallel our lives run. Yes, I get what you say about my dad. Yes, I've had all those same thoughts, exact thoughts, about your mother. And to take it a step worse, I've wished Lila were my mom, thrown my own mother under the bus (figuratively) in my desire to be the same as our sisters—to be one of them and not half-a-one. I think of Lila as the "real" mom, the serious, strong-willed one who could stand up to my dad. I think of my own mom as some kind of understudy imposter. How horrible is that? (I can't believe I just wrote that.)

I should probably mention that though Robert is a character and a half, he's no picnic.

LR

172

LR,

Parallel is right, sadly. Lines that go along forever together and never meet.

On the understudy imposter front, Adam lost his teaching job at the end of last semester and doesn't own either of the houses we live in. He left two kids in California to marry my mom and he barely knows them anymore. When I was a little kid I spent too much time thinking about those kids, technically my half brother and sister, a whole country away: Is a dad allowed to just do that? How strong are these bonds, anyway?

I love my dad. I respect him in a lot of ways, but I don't want to be like him.

BS

16

HOW TO PLAY DIRTY POOL

"Can you just stay for a minute?"

Mattie's mother had the same furtive look she'd been wearing for the last few weeks as she fled the Wainscott kitchen with her cup of tea seconds behind Adam.

"Please?" Mattie stood up quickly from the table. She didn't try to keep her voice level.

Her mom stopped. She heard the need, at least. She hadn't given up her mom job altogether. "Is everything okay?"

"Well." Mattie considered. She had her mother, a little of her, for a few seconds, at least. She didn't want to scare her into the living room. "Sort of." It shouldn't have surprised her much that she started to cry.

Her mom cast a look after Adam, who was most of the way to the den. She ventured toward Mattie. "Honey, what?"

Mattie perched on the table, half sitting. Hot rays of late-morning sun pitched through the sliding-glass doors of the kitchen. It revealed the soft skin starting to bag on her mother's neck, the faint brown spots along her cheekbone.

Mattie took a breath and it started coming out. She couldn't turn back anymore. She went forward. "I don't even know who I am right now."

Her mother drew closer, put her hand on Mattie's hand. Lila was skittish, still standing, her legs poised to flee, but at least she was still there.

"I know about Jonathan Dawes, even though you don't want me to."

Fear, self-protection, mother love battled on her mother's strained face. Under her pajama top Mattie felt drops of sweat rolling from under her arms down her ribs.

"He didn't tell me, because he said it was your decision to tell me, but I know something happened with you and him." She was crying more now and her mother was hugging her more now, so she couldn't read her face anymore. And that was a relief. She'd rather talk wetly into her neck for the next thing she needed to say.

"I know I'm part of this. I don't want to think about it, but I can't help it. I can't help thinking that I look a lot more like him . . . than I look like Dad."

Her mother was holding her almost too tight. "That doesn't mean anything."

Mattie pulled forcefully away. "I don't want you to avoid me or lie to me." She wiped her eyes and nose with the sleeve of her pajamas. "I just want you to tell me the truth right now. That's all."

The fight on her mother's face raged on. It didn't make her pretty. She looked punished, shamed, defiant, but she didn't say anything.

"Is Dad my dad?"

Her mother was crying now too. "Your dad is your dad." She was still holding back.

Mattie would have liked to leave it at this, but she couldn't. She had her mother to herself in a quiet room finally; she had nineteen years of secrets. She wouldn't just let her out of it. "If I took a DNA test, what would it show?"

Her mother looked stung. "Mattie, why would you want to do that?"

"I wouldn't want to do that. At all. I just want you to tell me the truth."

Her mom was crying openly now. "Try not to judge too harshly, Mattie. When we're unhappy we do stupid things. We make bad choices. We look for reassurance in destructive ways. We hurt people we love."

"Is that what you did?"

"I was terribly unhappy then. So was your father. I was confused. Maybe you'll understand better when you're older, when you're a wife and mother."

Mattie felt sympathy and judgment growing together. They didn't cancel each other out. "I hope I don't."

Her mother took it. The defiance was mostly gone. She blew her nose on a piece of paper towel and offered Mattie the other half. She swatted at tiny fruit flies floating around a bunch of brown bananas.

"The only thing you need to know is that your father adores you and he has since the moment you were born. There's never been any question that you are his daughter."

And here came the hardest question of all, and Mattie hadn't even known she had it: "But does he know?"

Big S,

The thing I didn't say before, which is also true, is that I dismiss my mother and I also feel protective of her. She's already got three stepdaughters, and two of them are eager to write her off. I'm the one who has to stand up for her. I try to. She is a sincerely generous person. My worst disloyalty is probably in my thoughts.

LR

LR,

This reminds me of something I haven't been able to tell anyone. I went to surprise my dad to listen to his lecture last semester at Brooklyn Law, where he teaches. (Used to teach.) It was a hall big enough for a couple hundred students . . . and there were two. He went on lecturing like every seat was full. I stayed because it *seemed even worse to leave, but I felt bad for him. And then there was the awkwardness on the way home, with each of us trying to brush it off, not feel embarrassed for the sake of the other. When I need to go easier on my dad, I think of that. I'm not sure it helps.*

I think I was kind of an afterthought in my family, most likely a mistake. I'm the one final complication that makes people give up trying to keep track. By the time they got around to having me, Lila already had three children and Adam had already left two. Lila had just launched her new career. Adam was forty-five years old. I'm the "yeah, whatever" kid.

Grandma Hardy is convinced I am no relation of hers. "You are a nice boy. Who is your mother?" I've met my half sister Esther fewer than five times. Her husband thinks my name is Roy. When Mattie went to college my parents rented out the ground floor of our house, and I overheard my mom telling the neighbors it was because they were finally "empty-nesters."

I'm not complaining. It's a relief not to deal with all the scrutiny and pressure a lot of my friends get. It's just the feeling of disbanding, unwinding, downsizing that gets me down sometimes.

Lila occasionally tries to psychoanalyze me. It's pure torture. She tells me my attachment to summers at the beach house is my inability to let go of the past. But with her and my dad getting rid of everything else, I think it's more my inability to let go of the present and future.

Sorry for the soul-dump. Not sure what's with me today.

BS

BS,

It's the opposite with me. I am Evie's first and only kid, and she doesn't have much else to do, so they make a big deal about how we are a little family. Special vacations, special dinners. They both take an "active interest" in my education, which is a bummer in every way. When Mattie went to college, my parents got a new, bigger place.

I know it's lucky to have your parents care about you. I try to be grateful. But if I'm being totally honest, I'll admit that every time our sisters packed up to go home to Brooklyn, I wanted nothing more than to go with them. When they were gone, I practically stopped existing. I was like C-3PO: "I'll be shutting down now."

Please dump your soul with me anytime. It is safe here. And as you see, I will dump mine right back.

LR

"I don't want to do this party anymore." Mattie was on her lunch break, eating a sandwich in the shade of the barn while Dana minded the store.

Quinn paused at the door, put down the bags of compost

she was carrying. She could feel Mattie's fragility. Mattie was not just back to the old bomb throwing.

"Why?" Quinn sat down cross-legged on the grass opposite her.

"Our parents are impossible."

"We knew that."

"Mom basically told George and Esther not to bother coming all the way across the country for it. She said to wait for the wedding, if it gets that far. *If it gets that far.* She said that."

Quinn nodded.

"Dad is torn between his desires to impress the Hurns and punish Lila. Guess which is winning out?"

"Punishing Lila."

"Right."

"So he agreed to match whatever amount of money Mom put in. Guess how much Mom put in?"

"None."

"Right. Her contribution is a bean salad, she said. So Dad said fine, he'd also contribute a salad. Guess what kind?"

"Lobster."

"Right."

"We can do the rest of it," Quinn said. "It doesn't have to be fancy. And you know Evie will help."

"Who's going to buy the booze?"

Quinn shrugged. "We'll use what's in the house." Robert kept a fair amount of liquor and wine around, knowing Lila didn't drink. "And I have some money saved up."

"Why should *you* be paying for it? Why are they always such babies?"

Quinn looked at her carefully. "Mattie, I know that can't be the reason. This is exactly what we knew would happen. They're both brave enough to come and face each other on pretty short notice, and that in itself is some kind of miracle."

Mattie sighed. "Yeah. I guess."

"What's the real reason?"

Mattie left her sandwich in the grass. "I just . . . don't have the stomach for it anymore."

Quinn knew Mattie was struggling with something bigger than this. She had a strong intuition for what it was, but she also knew Mattie didn't want to tell her yet. "You want to cancel it?"

"I don't want to hurt Emma's feelings, and I'm worried the Hurns already bought the plane tickets. So I feel really bad about it. But I honestly don't know what I was thinking. How could I possibly have thought it was a good idea?" Mattie put her hands on the top of her head. "So I guess it's good nobody else is traveling for it. Wouldn't it just be a relief not to have to do it? The truth is, I think Emma would be relieved too."

Quinn felt the sun on the tops of her knees. It would be a relief. But relief was not what she was looking for. Relief was a poor guide if ever there was one.

You couldn't deny the pain and you couldn't avoid it. Embrace it. That was her mantra, and yet look what had been happening in her own family for almost her entire life. You let it have a voice if it needed one. What if it needed one?

"I think we should go ahead," Quinn said finally. "I'll do everything, if you want."

"Why?"

"Because we've avoided it too long. We need to move on. All of us."

"You sure?" Mattie gave her a look, skeptical, with a lot of history in it. Because Quinn never showed up anywhere when she was supposed to and never dressed properly for any occasion, and could not even sit through the SATs.

"Yes."

"It might be terrible."

"It might. But that's not the reason not to do it."

Sasha/Ray,

My alter-ego, my counterpart, my zero-sum. (I'll be zero because you are sum.) We are never in the same place at the same time. Do we cancel each other out? Can anyone prove there are two of us? Flip sides, dark and light, girl and boy, yin and yang.

So how about this for an idea: we are complementary rather than opposing, my friend. As contrary forces, we don't cancel each other out, we give rise to each other.

But what if, even once, I just want to be with you?

Ray/Sasha

P.S. Somewhat drunk when I wrote that. Please
apply 40 oz. discount.

"Did you drive that black Audi that's parked out back?"

Mattie was trying to carry two large buckets full of zinnias. She kept sloshing the cold water down her legs. "Yeah."

Matt Reese smiled. "I think old Dana just took a picture of it."

Mattie rolled her eyes with extra gusto.

"Daddy's car, I'm guessing?"

"No, my stepmother's. Some jerk ran over the front wheel of my bike when it was parked in front of Dreesen's. My dad told me to drive this till it's fixed."

Matthew took one of the buckets from her. "I'm surprised you don't have your own car."

She put the remaining bucket of flowers down on the counter. "What's that supposed to mean?"

"I don't know." He shrugged. "'Cause you're a daddy's girl."

"My daddy has four girls," Mattie said flatly, a challenge in her eyes.

"None like you. Quinn says you're the one who can get away with anything."

"Quinn said that?"

Matthew sat down in one of the two lawn chairs they kept behind the counter. It was always slow on Wednesday evenings after the picking and sorting was done. "Sure. It's not a bad thing. It's a great thing. It's a lucky thing." There was a weight behind his words that sounded personal.

She sat down heavily in the other chair, leaning against the stretchy green tubing that made the backrest. The strange Reeses' farm talking serum was working again. "I guess it's because I'm the receiver of most of the divorce guilt. Because I was so little. Because Emma didn't need it and Quinn didn't want it. Because Sasha didn't deserve it." *Because I'm not theirs.* She felt her eyes fill up.

"I'm sorry," he said.

She was trying to keep her face from looking tragic, but he noticed anyway.

"I didn't mean to make you sad."

"That's okay."

"Don't listen to me. I've got nothing to say about parents. I don't know anything about them." He did an admirable job of keeping his voice light. "I do have a thing or two to contribute about grandparents."

"And I don't have much to say about those. Except Grandpa Harrison bankrupted the family and then died and Grandma Hardy stashes silverware in her purse every time she comes to visit."

He laughed. "Did you know your grandma Hardy tried to hire my grandma to clean her house when they were both newly married? My grandma has not forgotten it."

Mattie opened her eyes wide. "Well, you should tell your grandma that the once-grand Gloria Hardy Harrison is stealing silverware now. The cheap stainless steel kind. That will make her feel better."

Matthew considered.

"Maybe I'll tell her myself," Mattie said.

The conversation dried up, but Matthew didn't get up to go. Mattie took a deep lungful of late-July air. "Quinn's right, you know. Everybody does go easy on me. It's true I get away with a lot." She brushed at her eyes. "But things are not always how they seem. Maybe I was a daddy's girl. Now I don't know what I am."

He nodded, as though listening for more.

Suddenly she wondered if everybody knew or at least suspected the whole time. Maybe it was a regular feature of town gossip. . . . *And poor Robert Thomas actually thinks the little blond one is his.* . . . What if all these years it had been obvious to everyone but her and her dad?

She dunked her hand in the cold water of the flower bucket, trawling for loose leaves. "Everything I thought I knew about myself, I don't know anymore," she said quietly.

Later that night Mattie sat on a chaise by the swimming pool. The surface of the water was layered with leaves because the pool maintenance company quit when her mother stopped paying her half of the bills. When her father saw the state of it, he would blow a gasket.

It was the same old thing: Robert hated a dirty pool. Lila didn't particularly care about a dirty pool. Robert hated bailing Lila out even more than he hated the dirty pool.

"I like it better like this," Quinn said when she came out of the house.

"It's more hospitable to frogs and dragonflies," Mattie offered.

"I like that."

"Dad won't."

Quinn nodded. She sat in the chair next to Mattie.

"He'll get out there with the net again," Mattie predicted. "You watch. He'll clean it up. And at the end of this weekend, he'll put all the leaves and crap right back in."

Quinn laughed.

"He doesn't realize Mom doesn't care."

They sat together in silence for a while.

"Do you know anything about Matthew Reese's dad?" Mattie asked.

Quinn shook her head slowly. "I don't think anyone does."

"He doesn't even know who it is?"

"If his mom knew, she never said. Matthew asked his grandfather once and he told him, 'Your father could be any damned man in this country.'"

Mattie let this sink in. "Cameron probably has a different dad," she mused.

"Probably."

They fell into silence again.

"I saw their mom once," Quinn said in a hushed voice.

"Really? I thought she was gone for good."

"Two summers ago I was tending the peaches late at night. She was sitting on the back steps of the farmhouse in the rain, waiting for somebody to let her in, but all the lights were off. She asked me if I had any money."

"What did you do?"

"I said I had a twenty and I gave it to her and she left. I don't know if she's been back since then."

"That's so sad."

Quinn nodded.

"She and Mom were friends when they were young."

Quinn nodded again. "Carly Reese broke her dad's heart. Poor Mr. Reese can hardly say her name. She broke everyone's heart, again and again."

Holy shit, co-person. This party is actually happening. We will be in the same place at the same time!

I'll see your face up close in August. Dress code is flak jackets and hazmat suits.

Sasha read Ray's email and read it again. She went downstairs and wandered around until she found her mother in the laundry room.

"Is the engagement party for Em and Jamie really happening? Did Dad say yes?"

Even in the laundry room in the company of her one blood relation, her mother was diplomatic. "Seems like it's a go," she said brightly.

"Why?"

"Because the girls asked him."

"It's that easy? All these years. Why didn't someone tell me?"

"Don't be sarcastic, Sasha. It's unbecoming."

Unbecoming. Her mother said it a lot. Sasha knew it was bad, but did not know what it actually meant. How exactly did it relate to becoming? Was becoming good to do? She stifled her desire to ask, because sarcasm is unbecoming.

"And Lila said yes? That's even harder to imagine."

Her mother went back to folding Sasha's father's underpants. "At first she said no. From what I understand. But then she changed her mind."

Would she really see Ray on the evening of August ninth? She tried to imagine shaking his hand or air-hugging or kissing his cheek. Was that what they would do? Would the world allow for that?

And what about their parents? Would they stand in the same room? Would they listen to each other's voices? Would they shake hands? Would the world allow for *that*?

"Does Jamie's family have any idea what they're getting into?"

"No need to be dramatic. We're all adults." Her mother had that tight look on her face, like an usher in church.

Sasha tried not to grumble audibly. "No need to pretend like our whole life isn't a series of gyrations so Dad can avoid Lila and vice versa."

Her mother stopped folding and glared at her.

Sasha looked innocent. "Or . . . maybe we *do* need to pretend that."

The glare ticked up to the next level of annoyance.

Sasha shrugged. "Okay, well, you are in charge of pretending, so just, you know, give me my orders."

Why, oh why did she always do this to her mother?

In anger her mother's face finally animated. "I don't get it, Sasha. Why are you sweet to everyone but me?"

Sasha felt ashamed. She was officially unbecomed. Unbecame. But this was the pattern with her. She provoked and provoked until her mother said one honest thing.

Holy shit, you're right. I am feeling a dreadful excitement. Like when a hurricane is coming and it's gonna level the place. It's not even Mattie who's pushing this thing now. It's Quinn. ????

Never easy to follow Quinn's thoughts but always fun to try. Like locating a prairie dog. She disappears and pops up somewhere totally different. But this time, I've lost her. WTF is she thinking?

I wish I could tell you. Nobody takes it harder, feels it stronger than her. Nobody wishes for peace and suffers more when it never comes.

Well put, sister. (I mean, not my sister. Quinn's sister.) I can't stop thinking about what you wrote. How true, how true. It's fucking looonacy isn't it?

17

CURLY FEET

We never talked about it. That was what her mother said when Mattie asked if her father knew.

Mattie sat at the end of the dock, dangling her feet into the pond. There was late-day, sweet sunlight. The sky and the pond were both perfectly pink and smooth as a pearl, except for her kicking it. Her dad and Evie and Sasha would arrive any minute. She wanted to know when they got there, but she wasn't quite ready to see them.

It was sick, but sadly believable. Her mother hatches a blond, blue-eyed baby after her affair with her Californian surfing instructor, and she and her Bengali-born husband, according to her, at least, *never talked about it.*

Did they ever talk about the affair? Did he know? Based on her dad's reaction to hearing Jonathan Dawes's name, it seemed he must have known something. But how much? She'd been figuring it was the cause of their split—the timing and the general feeling of outrageousness supported it—but now she was getting the sense it was just a part of the larger disaster.

Sometimes Mattie wondered if the absolute most important things were the things they never talked about.

She heard the car on the gravel. She could tell her father was driving, because the car was going too fast. Her heart thumped along, accelerating as the car slowed down and stopped.

She'd never been worried to see him before, never felt like she'd had a real secret from him. Not even when she'd come home from camp, bursting with self-conscious importance for having gotten her first period. He was mostly easy and fun with her. He teased, but not too much.

Maybe he really didn't know.

Then again, he was pretty good at not knowing the things he didn't want to know.

She sat there frozen, listening, her toes still in the still water. Cars doors slammed. Gravel crunched under shoes. Her father threw open the front door of the house with his usual ease of ownership. She imagined it more than she could hear it.

It didn't matter that it was a house bought by the grandfather of his bitterly hated ex-wife, renovated by the father of that ex-wife, and inhabited half the weeks of the year by the very woman herself with her newer husband. When her father was there he occupied the place fully, happily, and without compunction.

"Anybody here?" he called. "Mattie?" He knew Emma was with Jamie staying with friends on Shelter Island tonight and Quinn was working. All the sliding-glass doors were open; he knew someone was home.

She heard him in the kitchen. She couldn't make out the quiet footsteps of Evie or Sasha, but she could count on hearing every stomp of her father's shoes.

"Matt?"

She kept her eyes on the line where the pond met the ocean. Would he know when he saw her face? Would he sense something had changed?

How could she go in there? What would she say? Should she just stand up and walk inside? She couldn't, but what would they think if she didn't?

It turned out she didn't need to walk in there. There was her father throwing open the sticky screen door of the living room, stomping out onto the damp grass.

"Mattie, is that you out there?"

She felt like crying. She couldn't even figure out how to open her mouth. She turned around and nodded, not sure whether he could see her gesture in the falling light.

He walked to her, right onto the dock, out of place in his fancy London suit, his shiny work shoes, arms opening early. "Hey, honey. What are you doing out here?"

Nothing was amiss in his face, his walk, his voice. If there was in hers, he didn't seem to notice. He stomped out to the end of the dock and put his arms around her.

He would always come out and get you. He wasn't complicated; he didn't check you before he committed himself. He didn't hold back.

He was strikingly brave in this way. After all he had been through, all he'd lost and had to lose, she couldn't understand it.

Would it change if he knew? Would she lose this? She prided herself on her own rebellious spirit even when it turned reckless, but unlike him, she suspected she was really a coward if it meant losing.

Her heart ached at the mental picture at Ditch Plains, the treasonous thought.

He hugged her and then pretended to throw her off the dock. That was their old thing. It was easy to go right back to it. She squealed, she laughed, she tried to throw him in. He pretended to stagger off the end of the dock. But he was big and strong and clever, and she knew by now he never went in unless he wanted to.

He put his arm around her shoulder as they walked back toward the house. "We're making hamburgers on the grill. Evie got some kind of special spices. How's the farm? Did you bring home more yellow peaches?"

She rested her head against his shoulder as they walked. Tears leaked out of her eyes, but he didn't notice.

He was always easy on her. It was easy to love him, easy to be loved.

He didn't know, did he?

And how would it be if he did?

Within a week or so of the engagement, Jamie's mother had written eager notes of introduction and congratulations to both of Emma's parents, and the difference in their responses told an unhappy tale.

Lila still hadn't answered hers. "God, I shudder when I see a handwritten note on engraved stationery," she had erupted when Emma asked about it. "Bane of my childhood. And *Mrs. Stewart Hurn*? Seriously? Does she not have a name? Em, tell me the truth. Are they country club people?"

"You could still answer it," Emma pointed out darkly. "Before they get here for the party."

And then, on the other hand, there was her father, who'd not only sent a jubilant note in return but the case of champagne along with it.

Emma had worried about Lila's stubbornness out loud to Jamie, and he'd said, "Well, my mom's still chattering about the champagne."

But that was the thing. The contrast was the problem. People with married parents tended to have the reflexive idea that parents reinforced each other, contributed to some grand parental whole. Hers did the opposite. Robert's gestures always made him the hero, but as Emma got older she understood a less heroic underside to them: he always put Lila in the shade.

On Friday night:

"Is Jamie coming out?"

"Not tonight, Dad. He's working late. Tomorrow, I hope. He's going to try to make an early jitney."

"Well, we'll be glad to see him whenever he gets here."

Next morning: "We going to see Jamie tonight?"

"As soon as he gets out of the office."

"He works hard, doesn't he?"

And then at the actual dinner that night, revered Jamie in attendance, her dad continued to drive her bananas.

"Marriage is the most wonderful thing in the world." He put his arm around Evie, who had finally sat down after all the cooking and serving.

Emma wanted to keep her mouth shut, but she also wanted to throw up. She was in a strange mood, stirred up and raw. The constant challenge by Lila set against the smug complacency of her father, now parading the glory of his marriage to a woman who wasn't her mother. Neither of her parents seemed to see her at all.

"Dad, what are you talking about? Isn't that kind of an over-simplification? You and Mom despise each other."

Her dad withdrew his arm and sat up. He looked as surprised as if the fern on the table had stuck out a frond and pinched him. "And that's why your mother and I are not married," he replied stiffly.

"But you were. Obviously. Some marriages are wonderful. Some are clearly not."

Jamie looked desperately uncomfortable.

Her dad was not in the mood for a challenge or even a real

conversation. It was the end of the week, his stomach was full, he'd had a couple of glasses of wine. He was in one of his affirmation moods. "Yours and Jamie's will be wonderful," he said conclusively, almost like it was an edict.

God, with her parents it was always a two-front war. "Yeah. If we try hard to make it be," she said.

Later that night Emma and Jamie sat at the edge of the patio, outside the circle of light.

"Why are they doing this?" Emma wasn't overly suspicious or particularly intuitive, but she had a deep, emerging sadness that she and Jamie were sheltering something special and unusual, a tender sapling trying to get rooted with the promise of digging far and reaching up. And the poison in her past, still regularly mixed and batched by her parents, would kill it. All that promise would just be a thing she and Jamie imagined together once.

Jamie scooted behind her. He put his hands on her shoulders, kneading the strips and tangles, and she began to melt. "I think it's supposed to make us happy," he said.

"Happy in what way?" she asked. She dropped her chin to her chest. She breathed in the thick scent of cut grass, chlorine, and sunshine fading off the paving stones. She relished the warmth of his body around hers.

"Celebrating us, us getting married. Taking us seriously, in spite of the fact that we are young and we met in April and nobody actually does."

"We do."

"We do."

"That's what matters."

"That's all that does."

"So why do we have to do this party?"

He worked his thumbs down her spine. She couldn't keep up arguing with him much longer. "Maybe we don't."

"We don't?"

"Do we?"

She considered. Mattie wanted to. Quinn wanted to. Why did they want to? Mattie could want it for selfish reasons. To try out some new canapés, get a sexy dress, have some wine, stir up some drama. But not Quinn. Emma trusted Quinn in ways she wouldn't necessarily concede out loud. For Quinn, who hated parties, never got dressed up, and absorbed everybody's strife, it was a sacrifice, a slow-motion torture. So why did she want it?

"Maybe it's a trial," Emma said into her chest.

"That doesn't sound like much fun."

"Maybe it's the day where everybody is tried. If we get through it, we're strong."

"Strong enough for the wedding?"

"Strong enough for the marriage. And the wedding too. But I have a feeling if we get this out of the way, the wedding will be all right. You figure you have to be strong to make a marriage work in this place."

"In any place."

"More so in this one."

"You and I will make it through," he said boldly. "I'm not scared."

She flopped face-forward onto the grass. "You probably should be," she said, muffled.

Sasha needed to get something out of the way:

> Are you bringing your girlfriend to the party?

> *My girlfriend?? You mean Violet?*

> Yeah. Francis is a big fan.

> *Ah, Francis. I should maybe be annoyed or surprised by that, but I'm not. Mainly, I am not having a boyfriend-like response because she is not my girlfriend. And no, she's not coming to the party.*

Suddenly he had a more terrible thought.

> *Are you?*

> Bringing a girlfriend? No. Boyfriend either.

God, Ray was relieved. It hadn't occurred to him that she had a boyfriend or would bring a boyfriend, and when it suddenly did, it consumed him with misery and agitation. He was glad he only had to be consumed with misery and agitation for around twelve minutes.

Quinn saw her mother in the paper goods aisle of the Stop & Shop on Newtown Lane before her mother saw her. It allowed her an unclaimed moment, outside the circulation of their relationship, both of them strangers in a strange place.

In the space of a moment a story could pass. In front of the paper plates and napkins a world could reveal itself. It happened in her transformation from stranger to daughter in her mother's eyes.

Quinn looked wrong here; she didn't fit. She was a don't-want-to-believe-your-eyes kind of wrong, like a living whale exposed and drying on open sand, immobile on its side, taking in fate through one large, sentient eye. Or maybe that was just how she felt.

Lila didn't want an ordinary kid. That was the thing. She professed disbelief at captain-of-every-team Emma, organizing her books by color. "She's my rebel," Lila liked to say of Emma whenever anybody asked where she was going to college. Lila rolled her eyes at Mattie's fortune in hair products, pink feathered flip-flops, eye-popping micro outfits. Quinn was her hope in this way.

"What are you doing here?" Lila's pupils seemed to dilate.

"Shopping."

"I can see that. *Why?*"

Lila would have celebrated a vegan, a dreadlocked, faux-leather-wearing, weed-smoking, folk-festival-attending social-ist. A girl you could comfortably deploy in the war against your ex-husband. Quinn knew and felt these things. There were times when she wanted to be these things. But Quinn wasn't that girl. She didn't fit into Lila's version of original. She didn't fit into anyone's. Her friends were plants and old people; her strongest connections she made with strangers; her arc was non-continuous. She didn't belong in a school or an office building and certainly not in the Stop & Shop. Quinn was confounding to her father, probably embarrassing to her sisters. Even Lila, conflicted as she was, couldn't help that native mother-desire to have her kid fit into something.

"For the party," Quinn explained.

"The thing for Emma and Jamie?" Lila didn't need to say: *You?* In this place? For *that*?

Quinn stared down at the two columns of plastic cups roll-ing around her basket. "Yes." That was the story she'd seen for a moment in Lila's eyes, the fear of real difference, the genuine article, slouching toward Bethlehem.

"Quinn, why in the *world* have you gotten yourself mixed up in this mess?" She dropped her empty basket with a clatter.

"It's not a mess, it's a party."

"Okay, it's a party. Since when do you like parties? You hate parties. I can't imagine you turning up at this thing, let alone wanting to throw it."

Quinn stopped on the word, eerily apt. She did want to

throw it. She wanted to throw it against the wall, hard, if necessary, and watch it break open. Let it go to pieces if it had to. She couldn't shy away anymore.

Maybe it would be a mess.

And maybe after that they could clean it up.

Sasha didn't know how to worry about all the things there were to worry about, so she decided to worry about a dress.

In a strange burst of serendipity, Emma and Mattie were both home and wanted to go shopping with her. If they had tried to plan it, even weeks in advance, it never would have happened.

"You already have a dress, Em," Mattie pointed out as they got into Emma's car.

"I know. But I can still help Sasha." Emma gave Mattie a look. "And you."

"You think you can tame the skank sister for introduction to Jamie's parents," Mattie suggested.

Emma laughed, but not that hard.

Walking along Main Street, East Hampton, amid the Lamborghinis and the balding men with supermodel girl-friends, between two of her three big sisters, Sasha felt her old uncertainties step right along with her.

Emma and Mattie were tall and she was not. They strode on long legs and she stumbled along with her awkward gait, pain-fully aware of her wrongness, the turn of her foot. The more she thought about it, the more exaggerated it felt, until she was surprised she could walk at all.

Emma was always "tall for her age," until she was just plain tall. Mattie was the same. Even Quinn, built like a twelve-year-old boy, had at least two inches on her. Sasha remembered saying mournfully to Evie once, "I think I might not be tall for my age."

Her sisters endlessly ran, raced, and jumped; kicked things, threw things, and rode things. Sasha waited for her foot to go straight, which it eventually sort of did. Except on days like today, when it seemed to curl right back in.

Sasha wondered, not for the first time, did her sisters ever tease her about it? Not to her face, which was fair game and expected, but behind her back? Did they tell Ray how graceless she was? The old fear meant a new thing to her now.

They turned onto Newtown Lane and tried the trendy stores first, so brightly lit and brightly colored and brightly perfumed Sasha's whole head hurt.

"No," Emma said to the mini–halter dress Mattie pulled out.

"No," she said to the skintight dress, the alligator-print dress.

After a while Mattie and Sasha were just pulling out the most outrageous ones they could find for the fun of it.

"No hot pink, no spandex, no feathers, no chains," Emma stated.

"I think we have to shop at Talbots," Mattie complained.

Sasha laughed. "I could just wear my school uniform."

Emma was becoming less amused. "I have to be at work by one," she said. She steered them down the sidewalk and upstairs to an upscale secondhand place. "Less expensive and less slutty options," she declared.

Emma pulled a bunch of things and brought them to the

dressing room. Sasha took a navy-blue-and-white-striped maxidress to humor her.

"Does it come with a burqa?" Mattie asked through the curtain.

Emma and Mattie were both waiting for her to come out. Sasha felt sweaty and mottled as she tried it on, in that particular fitting-room way. She felt like all the parts of her body were sticking out too far, trying too hard.

"Well, look at you." Emma studied her cleavage admiringly, resettled the waist of the dress on her. "Out of four we got one proper girl."

Mattie nodded. "Our own fertility goddess. It will be C-sections for the rest of us."

"I think you're calling me fat," Sasha said.

"I'm calling you gorgeous," Mattie said sincerely. Sometimes Mattie made her feel bad for the extra flesh, but today she was in a more generous mood.

"Try the black one," Mattie said.

"Why aren't you trying on any? Why is it just me?"

"None are slutty enough," Mattie said, giving Emma a sideways smile.

Sasha dutifully tried the black one and came out, sweatily, for inspection.

Emma turned her around by her shoulders. "Look at your tiny waist. I would show this off if I had it."

"Me too," Mattie said.

"If Mattie had your body she would never wear another stitch of clothing," Emma proclaimed.

"Just if it was cold," Mattie agreed.

The three of them gazed at her in the mirror. Sasha fidgeted with discomfort.

It was hard to do this in front of them. For once, she really did care. August 9 was possibly the only day in her foreseeable life when she would see Ray face to face, in the flesh, and he would see her.

She wanted to look pretty. She wanted him to think she was pretty. Would he? Would he ever think of her like that? Would he be astounded, horrified to know she thought of him like that? Because she suspected she did. In the midst of everything else, she was almost sure she did.

She wanted it to be sexy, but not too sexy. She wanted attention, but only some attention and not from just anyone. She wanted a dog whistle of a dress, a frequency heard only by him. An inside joke, intimate but not funny.

"Who are you dressing up for?" Emma asked.

Sasha stopped breathing. She felt her face heat up in mortification. In the mirror she watched the redness crawl up her neck. "What?" Could Emma possibly know?

"I always ask myself that," Emma continued philosophically. "It was actually Myrna Chapman who brought it up once. She said, 'When you really dress up, you're almost always dressing up for someone in particular.'"

Mattie was clowning around with a turquoise feather boa, but Emma had clearly tuned in to something. She arranged the hem of the black dress. "See, in my case I'm obviously dressing up for Jamie, but also for his mom, who I don't even know.

When I was picking out the dress, I realized I was really thinking about her."

Sasha swallowed. "What about you, Matt?"

Mattie looked up. "Matt," she answered.

"Yourself?"

"No, the other one. Matt Reese."

Emma let out a huff of breath. "Aren't we all," she said.

"Seriously. I dress or fail to dress for him every day, but he doesn't seem to notice."

Emma rolled her eyes. "How could he not notice? I'm sure he notices."

Mattie considered. "Then maybe it would be more accurate to say he doesn't enjoy or appreciate my efforts."

"Then he might be the only one," Sasha pointed out. "Cameron sure enjoys them."

Mattie made a face of disgust.

Emma turned back to Sasha. "You still didn't answer."

Sasha devoted her attention to a rack of clothing on wheels at the front of the dressing area. She seized on a beautiful color—something between celery and mint—and pulled it from the rack. She held it up. It was a slip dress in raw silk, three-quarter length and cut on the bias. It was ethereal but totally simple.

She went back into the fitting room and pulled it over her head.

She loved the feeling of it falling over her body, skimming her outlines but not pulling or sticking anywhere. Sheepishly she opened the curtain. She pushed her hot, heavy hair off her neck.

Her two sisters stared.

"I gawk," Mattie said.

"Wow, Sasha," Emma said. "That's the one."

Sasha turned, her skin prickling with the excitement of it. "Not too low-cut?"

"No, just right," Mattie said. "You've got to lose the bra, though."

They stared for another moment.

"Sash, it is not lost on me that you refuse to tell us who you are dressing up for. But whoever it is," Emma proclaimed, "will absolutely fall in love."

"So I hope it's not Jamie's mother," Mattie added.

18

THE TRUTH AND TWO LAWN MOWERS

As far as Mattie was concerned, it was not a good time for Jonathan Dawes to pull into the dusty parking lot of Reeses' Farm Stand.

Maybe it was a good time.

The engagement party, the great convergence of their lives, was less than forty-eight hours in the future, and what Mattie hoped would be an ennobling event turned out was not.

At the house the lawn was unkempt and overgrown. When her dad got to the house on Sunday his hair would fly off his head. And Mattie could not sweet-talk or even bribe any of the local lawn service companies to come fix it. They'd all been burned in the battle of her parents at one time or another. Same story with the swimming pool company. And again with the outfit that was supposed to remove the tree that had fallen into the driveway. Most times Mattie didn't particularly care about these things. But for this one day, she did.

"We like getting paid. We don't like affidavits," said Mike of Hamptons Hedges.

Fair enough.

Not even the valet parker wanted to do business with them. "We've heard stories," the guy said. "A house owned by enemies."

When Jonathan Dawes drove in, Mattie was sitting with her phone on her lap behind the counter under the shade of the oaks bunching cilantro, trying to locate the place where her father had rented a mower.

She hadn't really known she was mad at him until Jonathan Dawes swung shut the door of his rhubarb-red Prius and strode toward the farm stand. If he wasn't surprised to see her, he was a pretty good actor.

"Mattie," he said, half like a question, his eyebrows elevating.

She stood as he approached. She was glad there was a counter separating the space between them. She was relieved nobody else was around—no other customers or any Reeses for the moment. She didn't reach out to hug him. She lifted her arms and hugged herself.

"You work here?" he asked.

"Only for the last four years." Yes, she was angry. She felt it in her mouth.

He winced. "I guess I don't stop here too often."

"I guess you don't."

He tipped his head slightly. The air was awkward. "Everything . . . all right?" he asked.

She was tempted to just say yes, fine, and send him on his way with some tomatoes and corn or whatever, but the anger was still in her mouth. "Apart from my confusing loss of identity, yeah. It's all good."

His eyebrows stayed up, but the rest of his face fell. It took him a while to regroup. "Because of . . . what I said at Ditch Plains?"

"It had an impact, you might say."

"Of course," he said slowly. He rubbed his hands over his face. "I've replayed that conversation a hundred times in my mind. You must know I thought you knew. Or I thought you at least suspected. I thought that was why you came to see me."

Even now Mattie couldn't close the deal in her mind. A perverse part of her wanted to. Knew *what*? Suspected *what*? Another part really didn't.

"I came because you invited me," she said. "And the thing I wonder is, why did you invite me? Why did you approach me at all? Why did you start this?"

Whether he'd meant to or not, Jonathan Dawes had thrown a grenade into the middle of her life. It had wrecked her equilibrium, her confidence, and the damn thing hadn't even finished exploding yet.

His body looked both tired and more erect. He put his hands on the counter between them. "Listen. There's a lot to explain. This goes back a long way." He shifted uncomfortably. "I thought about you very often over the years. As you grew up I saw you and your sisters around town a few times, but I never made contact. I waited until you were an adult, capable of making your own choices about what you wanted to know about yourself."

"I didn't know there was anything to know," she broke in. "It was a lot easier that way."

He sighed. "When I approached you at the Black Horse, I figured I'd say hello and that would be the end of it. It was you who chose to come to Ditch Plains. This is not what I expected to happen."

Mattie stood up tall, almost as tall as him. She let her arms fall to her sides. "But is it what you wanted to happen?"

He looked down. When he met her eyes again, his estimation of her had changed.

"Because you really made a hash of things for me," she went on in a rush. "And for my parents. My mom, of course, but the real trouble lies with my dad. And you must have known that."

"I didn't . . ."

Mattie was past the point of caution, and for once it was in the service of honesty. "You may not have thought it through," she said. "I'm not saying I know what your intentions were. But you can't act like you were just an observer in everything that happened between my parents."

Here he stopped. After a while he nodded. "You're right. I can't."

"You were probably hurt by it too," she said, surprised by her own forwardness.

He was clearly struck. He considered her face for a long time, trying to gauge how much to say. He wasn't as young as he tried to appear. "I was. You're right about that, too."

He looked around. The place was quiet. Distant cars caught the light beyond the fields. "Is there a place we could sit down and talk?"

"We can talk here," she said. She thought fleetingly of the miraculous Reese farm talking magic.

"All right." He looked up at the sky. He looked down at the dusty ground. "I will be completely rash and tell you the truth. I loved your mother. At that time, I hated your father. And I hated that I couldn't be with her and with you."

Check another box. Mattie now knew where the rashness came from. But for some reason at this moment, she herself felt the opposite of it: infinitely old, capable of all secrets and possibilities. "Why couldn't you be?"

He shook his head. "It was a total catastrophe. I don't know how much of it you know."

"Not much."

"How much do you want to know?"

"More. Why couldn't you and my mom be together? After they split up?" Even her voice had a slow-motion calm, a purposeful unfolding.

"After you were born your parents' marriage came apart. And then Lila wanted out, but Robert wouldn't let her go. That was a terrible time." He looked up, as though at a memory.

"Your sister Quinn saw us together once, your mother and me. I always felt terrible about that. She was so little, I don't think she'd remember, but those eyes of hers . . ."

Mattie nodded. She knew those eyes well, and she doubted they forgot anything.

"Anyway, it made Robert crazy that Lila wanted to leave him. It was like he thought he owned her. He was already making big money then. He got his lawyers involved. He wanted to punish her. He called in a domestic violence complaint to my apartment when he knew Lila and I were together."

"God."

"Three officers burst into my bedroom. I was taken to the Montauk police station based on Robert's false information. Rumors circulated around the East End. Lila wore her scarlet letter."

"I didn't know any of that."

"That was just the beginning. Lila would have worn the shame. It was you girls. He threatened to take you away from her. He did take you. For six days he kept you all in a hotel in Manhattan, and your mother was frantic, not knowing where you were. A judge finally ordered him to bring you back to Wainscott. It was summertime. The judge ordered that you girls stay in the house while your parents took turns week to week."

That explained a few things. Did Emma remember any of that? Did Quinn?

Jonathan Dawes paused. He rubbed his eyes. His face seemed to get older as he traveled back in time. "And I did something stupid. I tried to claim you. Of course, your parents were married when you were born. Your father would have pulled the sky apart before even considering that you were not his. I had no legal standing, but I was angry. I couldn't accept it then. Even your mother begged me to drop it for your sake. That was what finally drove us apart."

Mattie nodded. She breathed. Breathed more. She looked at his face and felt sorry for him. Her world made more and less sense.

It was almost dark by the time Jonathan Dawes finished talking. Whatever produce he'd come for he no longer needed.

"Well." He sighed. He seemed to want to move toward her, but he wasn't going to presume anything anymore. "Forgive me," he said quietly. He turned and walked back to his car. "May the truth set you free, Mattie."

Slowly, diligently, Mattie closed up the farm stand for the night and walked her bike all the way home. She needed to stay as long as she could in the in-between.

In her mind she considered Jonathan Dawes's sun-lined face, his effortfully young body, his tired surfer's affect. He was stuck, just like everybody else, wasn't he? *May it set us all free,* she thought.

On the day before the party Quinn stopped at Myrna's with cherries, and Myrna was still in her bathrobe. "Are you okay?"

"I am fine, my darling. I just have a cold. Standard-issue."

Quinn went over and put a hand on Myrna's soft and yielding cheek.

Myrna studied her with shrewd eyes. "You are looking a bit run-down yourself, Quinn."

Quinn shrugged. "I'm fine. I'll make you tea. And these cherries are good for vitamin C."

"Tea would be lovely."

Quinn filled the kettle at the sink.

"But I'm afraid I won't be able to come to the party tomorrow."

Quinn put down the kettle. "Oh. Really? What if I pick you up in the car?"

"No need."

"How about I'll come check on you after lunch to see if you're up for it."

"No, darling. Really. You take care of yourself and don't be troubled. Just bring me a piece of your cake when it's all done."

The changeover was at noon like always, and Emma and Jamie's engagement party was at four. For the first time in Ray's life, he was going to leave his house an occupant and return to it four hours later a guest.

The place looked like crap. That was the thing that worried him. He wasn't Martha Stewart, but he did have basic standards. His mind flashed on a picture of his bedroom in Brooklyn. Okay, very basic.

The thing that woke him up at four a.m. was the idea of Robert and Evie (and Sasha!) arriving at a house left in disarray by Lila with less than four hours to fix it. He kept picturing

Robert's disappointed face, even though he didn't even know Robert's face, disappointed or otherwise.

Which was why Ray was cruising along atop a John Deere forty-two-inch zero-radius mower he'd rented from Power Equipment Plus in East Hampton, mowing the hell out of the lawn.

He couldn't do the edging like the professional guys, but it was better than nothing.

His mom and Adam were gone before he'd gotten back with the mower, which was frankly a relief to all four of her children. She and Adam weren't going all the way back to Brooklyn. They were having lunch with Grandma Hardy in Oyster Bay and then bringing her back for the party.

Ray planned to shower and change at his friend Frasier's place before returning for the party, but now he was worried he wouldn't finish mowing in time.

He'd never stayed past the changeover before. He'd always sort of imagined that the house disappeared into the air at noon every Sunday and then shimmeringly re-formed from the air as a slightly different house.

And it was the same old troubling thing of having to hustle away like an outlaw while his sisters got to stay and watch the metamorphosis. He imagined they were part of the magic too. At the stroke of noon, they became part of a different family.

What if he just kept mowing through noon when the other family arrived? He could pretend he was the guy from the lawn service company. They didn't know him, wouldn't recognize him. At least, Robert and Evie didn't.

He saw Mattie emerge from the front door of the house in her pajamas as he rounded the driveway. "What are you doing?" she yelled over the sound of the mower.

"Mowing the lawn."

"I see that. That's great. Where'd you get the mower?"

Ray braked and dropped the engine into neutral. "I rented it."

"Seriously?"

He made to look insulted. "I have a job."

"How'd you get it here?"

"They rented me a trailer."

"To attach to what?"

He was starting to feel less proud and more stupid. "To the car I rented from a different place." He threw the engine back into gear and drove off before she could ask him any more questions. The whole thing had, in truth, cost him more money than he made at the Black Horse in a week.

Later when he paused at the pool fence, wiping his face of sweat, Quinn fluttered across the grass and hopped onto the back of the mower. He was pretty sure this wasn't a two-person vehicle, but she folded herself weightlessly, like a cicada, to perch facing backward. He rode from pond to pool, patio to forest.

He liked her companionship. He turned to look at her. He smiled. It was too noisy to say anything. She held a piece of sprouted grass in her teeth like an old-time farmer, as they drove back and forth, back and forth.

Occasionally she elbowed him in the back. "Not that. That's clover," and he veered around.

At the end she hopped off. The silence was more silent after all the noise. The humid, thick smell of grass filled his nose.

"Wait. Why do you have that look?" he asked her.

"What look?"

There was mischief. No question. "That look."

"Fine," she said. "Come with me."

He followed her across the grass to the shed where they kept old bikes and the garden tools. She pushed open the door and he peered into the gloom. His eyes barely needed adjustment to see, so shiny and new it was. A John Deere fifty-four-inch zero-radius mower.

"Shit."

"My dad had it delivered this morning," Quinn explained with a smile and a shrug. "It came while you were out."

19

SOW THE WIND....

Okay, Little Ray. Here goes nothing.

Sasha saw Ray's text as she heard the door opening downstairs for the first guests, and her heart kicked up another notch.

She stood at the top of the stairs, looking down. You couldn't call them guests exactly. As arranged, they had come first, fellow hosts, to gather before the Hurns arrived from the airport.

"Hello?" Lila called, opening the front door. You couldn't really expect her to knock at her own house, could you? Her own great-grandfather's house. Not with how everything felt right now.

Sasha drew in her breath and took a step backward on the landing, hoping she hadn't been seen yet. She wanted a moment to observe, to fill her eyes, without having to be looked at.

Lila was first in, looking tall and imperious. But Sasha could already make out faint sweat stains under the arms of her pale linen dress. Her blond-gray hair was a straight, fine bob and her shoes were pointy beige pumps. She wore sheer stockings, and Sasha was oddly riveted by the faded orange freckles that covered her calves and feet and hands and other parts of her skin you could see. For all the times Sasha had imagined Lila, she hadn't imagined the freckles.

Sasha felt dark in comparison, a dark stranger to freckles.

Next came Adam. He was smaller than she had pictured. Not short, exactly, but he took up less space. His hair was wiry and gray and curled around his ears. He wore a blue blazer and round wire-rimmed glasses like Leon Trotsky.

Then came Ray. She had to steady herself to look at him. He was half a head taller than his dad but didn't share Lila's expression. He was bemused, nervous, a little wary. She felt the fast tick under her rib cage. She tried to see him for the separate person he was, tried to see him with calm eyes in clear outlines, but it wasn't easy. How could he fit all the things she'd felt about him into his one person?

He glanced upward like he knew she was there. He didn't say anything. Just looked at her, smiled, shrugged a little. He didn't call her out for spying, but she knew it was time to come downstairs. She kept her eyes on him, smiled knowingly, wary to match his wariness. As nervous as she was, she didn't take her eyes away.

Sasha came down the stairs just as her dad and mom appeared from the living room. She was aware of the pale green silk of her dress rustling around her knees, the subdued silver of her shoes.

Here we go.

She glanced again at Ray. It was a comfort, having a counterpart. Though she'd had almost no proximity to his flesh, his body, she felt as if the two of them were watching their parents from behind the same eyes.

Robert made the first move. First he shook Adam's hand, then Ray's. Meanwhile, Lila reached to shake Evie's hand, then Sasha's. Were other hands as sweaty and cold as hers felt? "Hello's" and "Nice to see you's" went around.

She was sorely conscious of how red the red of her mother's dress pulsed next to Lila's beige, how red her mother's lips looked compared to Lila's plain gloss. Again she felt the warring feelings, the cowardice and shame battling. Would Lila approve of her own dress? She would, wouldn't she? Would she approve of Evie's? No. She might even laugh about it later.

Even worse, she felt the undeniable force of Lila's confidence, Lila's basic sense of belonging. Evie's dress probably cost ten times as much, but Lila was the one who knew how to do this: how to look, how to act. In her posture alone you could feel that it was still her house, still fundamentally her family, however Robert tried to spin it otherwise.

When they all pulled back and it came time for Robert and Lila to greet each other, they didn't. Time got slow and thick. Lila cocked her head, pressed her lips together. Robert's jaw was clamped. He put an arm around Evie. Sasha felt his other hand land on her angel bone, not solidly possessive, as she would expect, but slightly shaky. That rattled her too.

Sasha was nervous to keep looking at him. With Lila in the room, she saw him through different eyes, and she wasn't sure she wanted to.

Robert placed his large frame at the place where the foyer opened up to the rest of the house, like it was his and he was the gatekeeper. Lila's entrance was inexorable, but he was acting like he got to say when.

Sasha cast an eye at Ray and saw her trepidation mirrored there. So united were they, she suddenly remembered they forgot they hadn't met. As momentous an occasion as this was, nobody appeared to be paying much attention to them. She turned and took a step toward him, put her hand out. "Hi, Ray," she said.

"Can I get anyone a drink?" Robert boomed. He turned and walked down the three stairs into the living room. And that was that. Robert said when.

How would they greet each other? They wouldn't greet each other. That was the answer.

All the parents moved through the foyer and into the living room. Ray held her hand for an extra second. "Hi, Sasha," he said just to her.

Quinn came out from the kitchen. She was wearing an aqua-colored Indian print tunic, her fine, wispy hair neater than usual, with a sprig of jasmine tucked above her ear. A silver dot sparkled in her nose, in spite of her dad's demand that she not wear it. But her face was troubled, complicated. Her eyes were so far away it looked like they saw a different house, a different party.

She hugged Sasha, even though she'd seen her ten minutes earlier. And then Sasha watched Quinn hug Ray.

When she was little, she'd been jealous when Quinn talked about Ray. She was tormented by envy when Quinn left their old apartment on Eighty-First Street to go back to Brooklyn. She knew Ray was there, and that her loss was always his gain. She knew Quinn loved him. She knew it, and now for the first time she saw it: for a moment Quinn's troubled, distant face was remade by her tenderness, her comfort with him, and Ray's face lit up in return. Looking at it from here, Sasha didn't feel jealous anymore.

She saw from the outside what she had, and she felt lucky that in a family like theirs they had it—they both had it. In a family where there was always too much, there was never enough, Quinn was their shared miracle. Her influence over the two of them was as quietly powerful as any. It was because of her that Sasha and Ray understood each other as they did.

It was strange, it was wonderful to have a counterpart.

Ray couldn't remember what Sasha looked like even minutes after he'd seen her. That was why it hit him so hard this time. He was flappable. He was flapped. He worried if he so much as turned a corner, he'd lose her again.

Last time, casually clothed in a darkish hallway, the shape of her seemed partly a function of his heated imagination. Back then she was still a stranger with a stranger's possibilities.

This time he just gaped, a violent deadlock of desires and inhibitions. Her delicacy and roundness and slenderness were a story justly told by her pale green dress—told better than his overheating brain could muster.

She was talking to Jamie's sister. He could barely look at her, but he couldn't look anywhere else.

The inhibitions were not quite holding up their end, were they? He tried to concentrate on what he was saying to Mr. Folkes, their neighbor on Eel Cove Road, but he kept losing track. Mr. Folkes was largely senile, so they, at least, were decently matched.

Sasha/Ray, is that really you? Can the yin of my yang really look like that? Make me feel like that?

An eerie breeze blew across the patio, across the pond. Robert walked by and looked him up and down, and Ray's inhibitions got back in the game.

Just before the party started, Emma had tentatively begun to eschew the whole idea of the trial. She'd had a perilously delusional thought: *What if this is actually fun?*

She'd felt confident in her peach-pink dress. Jamie had kissed her passionately behind the hedge just before his family arrived. She'd thought, well, maybe it really was their party: to control, to enjoy.

Her sisters had gone all out to make everything look pretty. Jamie's parents seemed wholesome and friendly. At first.

"Can you say something to the bartender? Don't let him give

my mother another gin and tonic, okay?" Jamie whispered to her urgently as he was drawn past by Grandma Hardy.

Emma looked around. Susan Hurn was standing a few feet from the makeshift bar, tall lime-topped glass in hand, talking animatedly with Evie. Jamie's father was standing by the pool with her father discussing golf or fishing or home repair or something. Her dad kept gesturing a large movement with his arm.

The clouds to the west were distinctly gray, and an erratic breeze was starting to blow. Party guests were anchoring paper plates and napkins under glasses and bottles.

Emma caught sight of her own mother standing near the house with an untouched plate of food, barely holding it together. Adam was in careful attendance. He felt the danger too, she knew.

It worried her that the Hurns seemed to be snubbing Lila. Was it because of the stupid note on engraved stationery? Had Lila never responded? They must have sensed her hostility to the whole thing. "She'll come around to it," she'd overheard Jamie saying to his mother on the phone the night before.

Emma dipped into the house and saw Quinn assembling her flower cake in the kitchen. Mattie, dressed like a pilgrim, relatively speaking, and uncharacteristically shy, was fixing up the buffet. The small contingent of Princeton friends had walked down to the pond.

I wish this was over.

She watched Jamie's mother take a step toward the bar and order yet another drink from the pimply neighbor kid playing bartender.

What was Emma supposed to do? Was she supposed to take the drink from her mother-in-law-to-be's clenched hand? A woman with whom she'd so far exchanged all of five sentences? It seemed early in the relationship for intervention and tough love. *Why didn't he mention his mother was a lush?* she thought uncharitably. There had been clues though, hadn't there? If she'd been paying attention. If she'd wanted to ask. Had he wanted her to?

Emma had always been an uncharitable person, fine, yet she'd never had an uncharitable thought about Jamie before this.

She heard the dreaded clinking of fork on glass. Her father was keeping track of the sky too. This was uncomfortable, but a necessary step in getting the party over with. She cast a wary eye at Jamie. *Here goes.*

Her father positioned himself in the center of the patio with Evie nearby. He clinked his glass again and guests began to drift over. Jamie set Grandma Hardy up in a sturdy chair and went over to check on his mother. His father had already found a seat for her. Jamie's sister, Grace, looked apprehensive.

You're supposed to be the normal ones, Emma mused.

Lila was still backed up against the house, a semi-willing participant. No one wanted to eat her bean salad.

Mattie emerged from the house and steered a wide path around Lila. Quinn came out the sliding-glass kitchen doors carrying her cake, framed in wildflowers, the loveliest offering of all, and placed it on the buffet table. Sasha stood uncomfortably by Evie; Ray stood with Mr. and Mrs. Reese under the shade of the arbor.

Jamie appeared at Emma's side and reached for her hand. She saw the sweat stains down the back of his shirt and felt a wave of tenderness.

"First, Evie and I would like to welcome our guests," her father began in a loud, public voice. He reached over to wrap his arm around Evie.

Emma cast an uneasy look at her mother. It didn't help, her father putting it like that.

"Especially the Hurns, who've come all the way from Ohio to be with us," he went on. Her father didn't seem nervous, exactly, but he did seem stiff. He talked on about how proud he was of her and Jamie for their commitment to each other and to the great institution of marriage blah blah.

A bit of polite clapping came mostly from the old people in the group.

"Emma, you are a beautiful and accomplished young woman." He lifted his glass and she lifted hers in return. "Jamie, you are a credit to your family and a credit to our firm."

"Thank you, sir."

Usually Emma enjoyed praise of any kind, but this she could do without. Intimate praise for public ears never felt right to her. Anyway, it wasn't for her and Jamie. It was mostly for himself and for the Hurns.

"I raise my glass to you both."

There was a lot of clapping and glass raising and corny "hear, hear" kinds of things.

Jamie's father, Stewart, moved next to Robert. He cleared his throat, waited for quiet. "Susan and I would like to thank

Robert and Evie for opening their beautiful home to us."

Emma waited for him to thank Lila and Adam, but he didn't. He droned on for a while longer and finished with another groaner:

"And we'd like to thank Robert for giving Jamie this great opportunity at Califax and an even greater opportunity to marry his daughter."

Robert laughed heartily in appreciation and a few other people laughed lightly in embarrassment. Emma could not even look at her mother. God, this was painful.

Did the Hurns not understand the state of things here? That there was plenty of hostility between the two sides of her family without them getting in the middle and stoking it? Emma cast a desperate glance at Quinn.

Quinn took a couple of brave steps toward the center of the group. "Excuse me, Mr. Hurn, I'm sorry to interrupt. But before you go on, I wanted to say that it's also my—"

Now it was too late. Lila put her wineglass down so hard on the table it smashed. All eyes switched to her. It was more effective than just clinking a fork.

Lila didn't even glance down at the pieces. "Stewart, you are mistaken," she said, moving a few feet out from the wall. Emma couldn't tell if Lila meant to be talking to just Stewart and Robert or to the whole assembly. "About several things." She stood tall and her voice carried well enough to be heard. She was the witch come to curse the wedding. And yet Emma's sympathy went with the witch at the moment.

Jamie held tight to Emma's hand. She felt frozen in place.

"I'm not sure what Jamie told you, but this is not Robert's house. My grandfather built it on land bought by his father. Yes, you are his guest, but you are also mine. Robert doesn't own this house and he doesn't own Emma."

Jamie tried to say something, but Robert shut him down.

Her dad was seething now, on the slim edge of control. It scared Emma to see him like this. "I'd like to explain," he kept saying. He wouldn't even look at Lila; he kept addressing himself to poor Stewart Hurn. Emma could feel the social distress around the patio as her dad started telling Mr. Hurn how he'd bought the house from Lila's lout of a father before he defaulted and lost it to the bank. Were these poor guests supposed to be listening anymore?

Emma barely heard the content of her father's words. She heard the pent-up force of his anger, as though he'd been waiting twenty years to release it.

Even Lila seemed to blench in the face of it, but she wasn't going to bow out. "We were still married then. We bought it from him together."

Emma could not believe they were having this out here. Could they not control themselves at all? It was exactly what she'd feared and at the same time it was ridiculous and unimaginable.

Now her father did turn to Lila, and Emma had to look away. The rhythm of her heart got behind and couldn't catch up. There was bitterness and disgust in his manner, to be expected, but there were other parts too that proud public Robert couldn't have wanted anyone to see. "Were we married? Really?

You didn't act like it." Emma heard for the first time an unformed, naive kind of pain under his voice.

Most of the guests were politely slipping away, Emma realized numbly. They were trailing down to the dock or into the house. It was too raw, too excruciating to watch.

"Dad," Sasha said quietly.

Lila had both her hands on her throat. Her skin wasn't the right color. "Why are you doing this here?"

Jamie stepped into the charged space between her parents. Emma probably would have held him back if she'd been able to think right.

His voice was controlled and quiet. "Let's put this aside for now," he asked, "in honor of what we hope will be a happy occasion in the future." For Jamie, she knew, the impulse was always to do the right thing, and when that wasn't clear, to do something.

Emma looked to her mother's face for a little bit of sanity, but she didn't see it.

"Please stay out of it, Jamie," Lila said in a hard voice.

Sasha watched the thing in acute distress, looking up every so often at the suspenseful sky.

She'd wanted to get away long before, but Evie was squeezing her hand so tight, she'd lost almost all feeling.

Squeeze my fingers as hard as it hurts, she remembered Evie telling Sasha when she was little and had to get stitches or shots.

She saw Jamie look from Lila's implacable face to Robert's

boiling one, his posture rigid. And then Jamie turned his head to his mother getting up from her seat a few yards from where Sasha was standing. He just sagged.

Sasha could only see part of Susan Hurn's face, but could tell she was unsteady and furious. Jamie's mother muttered a few heated things at Lila, and then one thing came through loud and piercing. "And don't you *dare* tell my son what to do."

"Susan," her husband muttered.

"Fuck," Jamie said under his breath.

Now Jamie's mother was fully up, waving her arm, accusing Lila of a lot of objectionable things. "Do you *hear* me?"

Oh my God. Sasha cast another furtive look at Ray.

Lila was too stunned to respond. Her dad's anger was finally punctured, but it was too late. Sasha could have sworn she saw in Robert's face a spark of compunction toward Lila. They'd reaped the whirlwind, all right.

In that moment, Sasha hated them and pitied them. But Emma she loved. For Emma she felt worse.

"Drunk bitch."

Sasha drew in a sharp breath. She heard silverware clatter to the ground. She couldn't see who'd said it at first, but of course it was Mattie. Mattie, who had clearly been crying.

Oh my God. Sasha put her free hand over her mouth.

Jamie's sister, Grace, was pulling on her mother's arm. She was also crying.

Susan Hurn shook Grace off, took a step back, and then shoved the entire buffet table over. China, glass, silver exploded onto the flagstones of the terrace. Party shrapnel flew. Pounds of lobster salad collapsed into heaps of bean salad. Rolls rolled and melon chunks skittered.

Seconds and impressions tangled, but somehow Sasha and Ray had the same thought at the same time. Quinn's cake with the flowers: cultivated flowers she had grown from seed and wildflowers she had carefully collected, arranged around and on top of the cake, fragile petals torn lovingly into batter. It had Quinn's special magic in it. It was on the table and the table was going over.

The cake seemed to fall upward into the air as the two of them ran to it from different sides of the table. Sasha had the discordant, slow-motion observation that the cake was not perfectly whole. It was missing one clean triangle of a piece.

Sasha and Ray reached for it at the same time. But neither was fast enough to save it. Sasha watched in despair as the cake turned and fell; air and magic, sugar and butter deflated slowly onto the stones.

Is this happening?

Please don't let this be happening.

Ray was too angry at his mother to be sympathetic to her. For the first time, Robert was trivial to him. He didn't care about Jamie's fucking psycho mother or the food on the floor or the broken glass all over the patio. Though if Jamie's dad took one step closer to Lila, Ray would personally punch him in the face.

He did care about Sasha's faltering attempts at comfort. He

cared about Quinn's brave attempts to put herself between their idiot parents, so much better than they deserved.

His spirit anguished over Quinn's beautiful cake, now crushed under thoughtless fleeing feet, tracked to the four corners of the patio and beyond.

Fine if their parents were working out some primal bitterness, but what had Quinn done? Why did Sasha have to watch this? Why did he?

There was a fiery look of combat still burning on his mother's face. He could catch fire himself and she wouldn't notice. But Sasha's lovely young body drooped with sadness. Why was it the people who had no beef suffered the most? Like all slow and terrible wars, it was fought and borne by those who had no grievance, the most innocent enduring the worst.

Because we are the ones who want peace among the grown-ups, and they still want war.

Why did it still have to matter so much to them? To him and his sisters and Sasha? Why did they have to keep loving these people, in spite of their selfishness and their flair for destruction? It would be better if they could just give up. Why did they have to count on them, even now? Would they have to go forward carrying on the same corrosive grudges?

He looked at Sasha helplessly, the toppled buffet table still between them. She was holding Evie's purse for some reason, standing bewildered and forlorn next to an overturned chair. Dark liquid stained a sash across her mint-green dress. Would she blame him for being on the other side of this disaster? He closed his eyes.

He opened them in time to watch with relief as the Hurns exited around the side of the house. Jamie's father hunched under some mixture of anger and shame; his mother's steps were unsteady. Grace's face was puffy with sorrow.

Jamie made a final huddle with Emma, whispering in her ear before he left to follow his family. His family had to be settled somewhere. There was so much talking down to be done.

How did you tuck all the pieces in so you could pack this into the past? They'd gone far beyond the place where you could try to pretend it hadn't happened.

Emma was picking shards of glass from the patio and collecting them into a wide wooden salad bowl. When she stood he could see the tears written in black mascara. What a fucking mess.

But where was Quinn?

Robert stood with arms thuggishly crossed by the front door, apparently waiting for Lila and Adam to go through it.

Ray heard shouting on the front lawn. At this point he didn't know or care whose it was. Cars scrambled across the gravel, down the driveway, escaping onto the smooth town road. Who wouldn't choose to get out of here?

Except they, the children, even grown, didn't get to choose. That was the part that was most unfair.

But no, they wouldn't carry the grudges. Sasha looked up and met his eyes. She didn't and wouldn't blame him. He knew that.

Of all the people in the world, he knew how she felt. She knew how he felt. They didn't need to say anything to know it. In a strange way, they'd never had to.

He wasn't really thinking when he walked over to her. He had no clear intention in his mind when he stepped around the fallen table, over chairs and plates to be nearer to her. Her physical presence was still strange to him, but he reached his hand toward hers and she took hold of it. The two of them stood there in the middle of it, hands clasped, observing what was left of the kingdom.

He didn't really care who saw at this point. What were they protecting their parents from? Harmony, God forbid. Compassion and an unusual kind of love.

Their parents didn't deserve to be forgiven, and yet they would be. Where was the cure for that?

20

I WASN'T CRYING, BUT I COULDN'T STOP.

The clouds finally decided to open to rain. It was a relief more than anything. It came down hard and heavy.

Quinn watched the rain beat sideways into the pond, into the swimming pool. The steam rose from the ground and the sky came down to meet it.

The rain washed the fallen food on the patio into a single creeping muck. Rain and tears united and returned to puddle, pool, and pond.

Her bare feet sank into velvet wet ground. Her head went hollow when the fat drops splattered down on it. She turned her face up to the sky and let the rainwater bless her eyelids.

Let the pain in. Give it a voice if it needs one.

Now it had one. It was ugly but it spoke. Maybe none of them could feel the change in the air, but she could. Maybe now they could all get on with it.

Mostly everyone had gone now. None of the words or images lingered on the warm stones. She let them all wash away except one: the picture of mint silk Sasha and sport coat Ray standing together in the center of the mess. Small and big, dark and light, left and right. Behind them, she saw that they held hands. All the opposites, everything at once came together. The despair washed away, and that was the thing that stayed. There was the past and there was the future. It felt whole.

How hopeful we were and are. How can we be any other way?

She sat in the wet grass and watched the rain tap the surface of the pond thousands of times. In her mind she saw their two clasped hands.

She could stay like this until the sun dipped down and probably until it came up again. She could repair herself here for a while. But there was still something she needed to do. What must she do? It seemed faint to her now.

And then she remembered she owed Myrna a piece of cake.

Sasha's father was already in the car, her mother told her. Please come *now,* she mouthed dramatically, twice.

Sasha had tried to keep some order among her impressions, fears, feelings, until they were simply too much. With the press of Ray's hand against her hand all systems sizzled, shorted, and went blank.

By now her mind was a canvas over which fleeting sensations scratched like rodents: The sting of a blister chewed into her heel by the strap of her new silver shoe. The clutch of Susan Hurn's white fingers on the table. The flower cake rising gently into a dark gray sky.

Before she could get into the car, Sasha needed to find Quinn. She needed to see her face to know it would be okay. Mattie said she'd seen her. She said Quinn was lying in the grass by the pond.

Rain splashed down as Sasha tripped barefoot across the grass. Soft mud burped under her toes, her heavy sodden dress sticking to her legs, tangling her stride. Dusk had begun to fall. Her perfect green dress took light from light. Now it just looked black.

Quinn wasn't there. Sasha stumbled back up to the house. She could sense her father in the car, windows closed against the rain, steam clotting the outside world, the air inside so pressurized by indignation the whole thing could blow like a special effect in a Vin Diesel movie. She imagined bits of her father's Mercedes spread from Manorville to Montauk.

Emma had left in her own car minutes earlier. That was what Mattie had said. And yes, she seemed calm enough to drive. Mattie was going with Lila and Adam. And Ray had been designated driver of Mattie's car to return Grandma Hardy to her old person home in Oyster Bay.

Briefly Sasha saw Lila in the passenger seat of a car through a window streaming with rain. *You are not what I thought. I imagined you better.*

She could already feel the urge to reconstruct her father and Lila and all the mythology that depended on them. And yet she knew it wasn't the right thing to do. They didn't deserve it. *Maybe it's for us that we hold them up, not for them.*

We're a bunch of fantasists, she thought. Reality horned in once in a while and they all tripped over each other trying to get away from it.

Except maybe Quinn. She wasn't afraid.

Sasha stepped out the front door. Her mother buzzed the window down impatiently. "Get what you need and come on! We'll meet you at the end of the driveway."

Who would want to remain at the site of this disaster? Nobody. *Run for the exits, put it farther away, let it be somebody else's problem a little more than yours.*

Except Quinn. Where was she?

Sasha found her injuring silver shoes she'd kicked off by the patio. She found her phone and her bag in the kitchen.

On the way across the gravel out front, she finally found Quinn. Quinn sat astride her bike, still in her long tunic, soaked with rain and muddy at the hem. Her hair dripped; the dot in her nose sparkled. A cherry-red canvas bag hung over her shoulder.

"Are you okay?"

"Yes. I'm coming back. I just need to take care of one thing," Quinn called, starting off pedaling into the darkening air.

There was something else Sasha needed to ask, but she

couldn't think what. Heavy leaves weighted branches on either side of the driveway to form a gothic arch over Quinn's head.

Even now her sister did stand-up pedaling like she was in fourth grade, and it was just another thing that made Sasha feel teary.

Whatever they had all wanted, it was too late. Maybe it wasn't too late.

Sitting in traffic in Queens, a mile back from the Midtown Tunnel, Sasha's father's phone rang. He was driving. He was still too angry to talk to his wife or daughter, much less his phone. It stayed in his pocket.

It rang again. He got madder at it. Cursed and ignored it.

And then it rang again.

Sasha sat up straight, her heart accelerating heavily.

"Darling, you should pick it up," Evie said. "What if there's an emergency?"

"My God, Evie. What more could go wrong today?" Robert growled.

His words coincided with the onset of the fourth ring, and stabbed fear into Sasha's heart. In her private religion that was the kind of thing you were never allowed to say.

He lifted out of his seat to fish the phone from the bottom of his pocket.

"Dammit," he muttered. "I missed it." He tossed the phone at Evie like he was beyond disappointment or fear.

"It's a six-three-one number. I don't recognize it," she said.

"All of them?"

"Four calls." Evie waited until he came to a stop to show him the phone. "Do you recognize it?"

Robert squinted at the screen, shook his head. "Play the voice mail."

Instinctively Sasha put both feet on the floor of the car, put her hands flat on the seat on either side of her. She realized the vibration in her stomach was not just agitation, but her own phone buzzing. She let it go, intent on hearing the voice mail.

Evie pressed Robert's phone to her head so only faint sounds leaked out. "Robert, pull over," she said.

Never had Evie given an order to Robert. Never would Robert have complied with one had her voice not sounded like that. Robert spun the wheel roughly to the right through two lanes of traffic and pulled to a stop on the shoulder. Two lanes worth of cars honked at him.

His hands still clutched the wheel even though he'd stopped driving. "Who?"

"It's a woman from the trauma center at Brookhaven."

Her father's jaw was set; his eyes were closed. She was scared for him. Why for him? Why did she imagine it would be his news and not hers?

Evie loosed a strange animal noise followed by five words, quickly: "Quinn was in an accident."

Real tragedies didn't happen gradually. They didn't build you up with foreshadowing like in books and movies. They didn't culminate with lessons learned or rebalance the moral ledger.

Real tragedies happened in five seconds, in five words. They waited until you were getting herded into the stupid Midtown Tunnel and smashed you in the head. They took what you loved away and left you with nothing.

Sasha heard an unrecognizable voice come out of her own mouth. "Is she okay?"

From Evie's face, Sasha was both frantic to know and did not want Evie to answer. Sasha put both hands to her head, like a punch-drunk boxer awaiting the haymaker, protecting her ears from taking in more words.

Her father was a black hole of fear, gravitationally collapsed, too terrible to look at.

"They say we should go to the hospital."

No, no. We are too far down. We aren't ready, Sasha thought.

21

AFTER THAT YOU CLEAN IT UP.

Ray's parents stayed in their darkened room in the Brooklyn house. Every so often he heard a terrible keening sound from his mother and then silence again.

Emma and Mattie had fallen asleep on the living room couches.

A doctor at Brookhaven had provided a bottle of sleeping pills, and by that means he suspected his sisters had taken a route to temporary oblivion.

How long had they been at the hospital that day? Late afternoon had passed into night, and still it had seemed so abrupt as to make him wonder if he'd imagined it. They'd gone to take care of Quinn and heal her. But by the time they got there it was too late. She was already gone. There was no one there to hold or comfort. There was no one to hold and comfort them. *How could you, Quinn?*

It was just two mute halves of a damaged, disoriented family staring at each other across the abyss. *How are we supposed to do without you?*

There were matters for the parents to settle. He wasn't sure how or when those things happened. He gave sway to his confusion and didn't dare try to get to the bottom of it. They went to find Quinn and she wasn't there and wasn't anywhere. What did you do then? You went home.

He'd considered swallowing a pill or two himself. It was agony being conscious, but if he went under he'd have to wake up again and let the truth of what happened pounce on him in a weak and bleary state. He knew he needed to stay with the truth, keep a wary eye on it as long as he could.

So, no, he would not sleep. He was far too agitated to sit down. He couldn't be inside and he couldn't be outside. He couldn't *be.*

He walked up and down Carroll Street, noticing the rain but not feeling it. An occasional flash of lightning woke him up and then woke him down again.

He descended all the way to the stench of the Gowanus Canal before he realized where he needed to go, and then he walked up to the Atlantic Avenue station and caught the night's last train bound for Montauk.

He walked up and down the aisles. There seemed to be only

a few people in each of the cars. Yes, he was annoying, but he couldn't make his legs bend him into sitting.

He sent a text from the train. It was hard to imagine that the words from his phone would go up into space and come down in her phone. But maybe they would. And maybe she was feeling as alone as he was.

The town names were a strange childhood poem to his ears, but on this night they took on a ghastly aspect. *Wantagh, Seaford, Amityville, Babylon, Islip, Speonk.*

His mind flashed on a story Quinn once told him about a skunk from Speonk. He could feel his face folding and he cried through the back three cars of the train. He wondered if Sasha knew that story.

He pictured Sasha's eyes meeting his across the waiting room at the hospital hours before. He couldn't hold the picture for long.

How could this be?

He had the instinct not to see or do any more than was necessary, because every experience would mix with this night, this horror, and would be infected by proximity. And every experience tomorrow and tomorrow. And maybe every experience for the rest of his life would be poisoned by happening in the world without Quinn in it.

He got off at East Hampton. The station was empty. There was one cab outside and the driver was asleep. He started to walk.

The wind got stronger as he made his way south toward the ocean. After a while he couldn't feel his feet anymore. He wondered if the numbness would climb all the way up his body.

He promised himself to keep an eye on the truth, but it was hard. What if it wasn't really her? What if she wasn't really gone? What if she could still come to?

What if he'd just imagined that it happened and some realer reality could come along and save them from this one?

His mind kept rolling back time. What if she hadn't gotten on her bike? What if she'd left a few minutes earlier or later? What if it hadn't been raining? What if she'd taken a different way?

What if the driver hadn't been a fucking idiot? What if he hadn't drunk margaritas at a garden party? The cops declared him under the legal limit, but still.

What if she had fallen into the grass instead of the street? How could she have fallen onto the street?

And then he had to get his eye back on the truth, because if it got away, if it crept behind him, it could take him down and maybe he wouldn't be able to get up again.

Sasha didn't tell her parents she was leaving. She'd had the idea even before she'd seen Ray's words appear on the screen of her phone. She just snuck out. Not like her parents would notice at this hour, on this day.

She couldn't look at her dad again tonight. She was scared for him. *He doesn't know how to do a thing like this,* she found herself thinking.

Not that she did. But she knew she loved Quinn beyond

reason. She understood that Quinn was their secret special magic. Quinn was the story and the storyteller. Without her they would just float around not making sense anymore. They would go empty. Their tanks might still feel full of her now, but they would drain quickly and without her they wouldn't be filled again.

In her grieving heart Sasha knew her father had yet to realize all that. He'd been caught up in pierced noses and Indian handloom, erratic hours and uneven grades. He mistook those things for what mattered. "Parents of teenagers and young adults get hung up on the absolute dumbest things," she'd overheard a teacher say once, and she'd thought of it often. Her dad obsessed over Quinn's nose to get a little distance, maybe. So he could try to love her a little less as she grew up and away from him.

And now all there was left for him to do was fall and fall and fall, each collision a new trauma, while Sasha was already waiting for him at the bottom.

She hurried down to the street and let herself out quietly. There was nothing of Quinn in this house. She had climbed the stairs and crept the halls, craving something, but there was nothing. Quinn had her own room here, but in the two years since Robert and Evie had bought the house, she had never slept in it. Quinn would have sooner slept in the park on a bench. She probably had. Quinn had eaten dinner in the dining room maybe a handful of times and never looked comfortable during one of them.

Whatever was left of Quinn from their old apartment on

Eighty-First Street had been replaced, reupholstered, upgraded. Sasha needed to hold on to what there was. Whatever smells and tastes and sounds still held some of her sister, she needed to absorb them before they released the last traces.

The final Long Island Railroad train of the night had already left, so she took the car out of the garage. The attendant looked surprised, but asked no questions. She drove through the rainy streets like just what she was: a New York City girl who'd had her license for less than a year.

Her father would have a heart attack if he knew what she was doing, but there was not much left to attack on either side.

She more or less knew how to go. Maybe she'd planned this escape before. She tapped the destination into the navigation system. She'd done that for her dad on different trips. He had an unreliable sense of direction.

She let it guide her over the Fifty-Ninth Street bridge. She couldn't pass through the Midtown Tunnel again.

She wasn't wearing shoes, she realized. She must have taken off the mint-green dress at some point after they got back from the hospital and put on leggings and a flannel shirt, but she had no memory of doing it.

It felt good to drive. Because she was poor at it, it soaked up most of her autonomic attention. There was hardly another car on the dreaded Montauk Highway.

She was hell-bent on getting there, and as soon as she pulled into the driveway, she was overwhelmed by despair and had no idea what to do. She draped over the steering wheel and went boneless.

When she got out she found the front door was locked, so she picked her way across the stones and followed them around to the back.

Ray heard a car pull in. His mind wasn't working right, so it didn't alarm him or interest him as it might have. It couldn't be her. His entire being was clenched into a raisin at the base of his head. It didn't possess curiosity or hope or conventional fear.

He paced the grass. His legs were worn stumps barely connected to his torso. It occurred to him, vaguely, that he was still wearing his new shoes he'd gotten for the party and that they were tearing his feet to shreds. He felt dizzy pulling them off. His feet were blistered beyond feeling. His toenails would invariably turn black and fall off. He didn't mind that so much. Mainly he just couldn't stop moving, because then and if and if and then. He didn't know if he could keep going, but if he collapsed then the truth would get its chance to sneak up when he wasn't ready. He knew it would.

He trudged down to the bank of the pond and cooled his feet. He picked up a flat, mossy stone and threw it as far as he could. That felt all right. He picked up another and then another. His arm was so loose in the joint he half expected it would detach from his body and fly into the pond too.

A time to cast away stones.

What was that from? From the Bible. He'd heard it at a funeral. His grandfather Harrison's funeral.

He threw another. He threw it so hard he imagined it soaring all the way across and pinging the house on the other side. He heard it plunk in the water like the others.

Even in the dark Sasha saw the shapes of ruin all around the patio. She hadn't forgotten, but it had gotten buried under a thick layer of ash. The memories started like an orchestra tuning up. They didn't turn into music but got uglier and more cacophonous.

She stumbled over a wineglass. She picked up the two pieces and stared at them. And then she threw them down into a hundred pieces. She took a deep breath.

Next in her path was a white china plate. She picked that up and threw it too, flat down with two hands for a sparkling blast. Another plate winked at her like a big white eye. She picked it up and smashed it. Glass bits bounced off her legs. She took a step and some of those same glass bits burrowed into her bare feet. The plates were at her mercy, her feet at theirs.

She was ready. What else?

Ray heard the shattering of glass in the direction of the house. He heard more. His legs drew him up the hill toward the sounds.

The raisin inside his skull was not curious or conventionally afraid or capable of surprise. Was it her? It took him a few seconds to arrange the facts. Sasha, sum to his zero, was here at this house in the dark and she was beating the shit out of the china. The raisin was capable of enthrallment.

It made so much sense. It was the only thing there was to do. He stumped over to the patio and picked up the first plate he saw. He threw it down with a thrilling vengeance. Shards flew so high he felt them ding his forehead.

Sasha froze, cake plate in hand. She stared at him. He stared at her. By the faint solar lights he took her in from fierce face down to bare white feet.

A proud acknowledgment passed between them. His agony rose and reached out for hers. The set of her chin showed signs of struggle. His own face started to fold. He couldn't let it go yet.

He smashed another plate instead. She let loose a lemonade pitcher against the house like she was Clayton Kershaw. They moved around each other in a strange ballet of demolition, conversing in crashes.

The sun finally peered up from under the horizon and saw what they had done. They stopped. The rain was over. Everything that had been whole was broken.

Wordlessly she found the big trash bags in the pool house. He got the heavy-duty broom and went about sweeping like a man possessed. By the first sun he'd seen the blood all over the patio from their feet, and he couldn't bear to watch her walk on it anymore.

For the next stretch of time the ballet continued, silently, in reverse. Piles of broken glass, chunks of lobster, sodden paper goods went into heavy lawn bags. Tables and chairs turned back upright. With the hose on full he washed away the rest of the blood and the food.

Together they stacked the bags neatly in the garbage shed. He admired her work ethic as he had done many times at the Black Horse Market.

He followed her across the grass to the little rise overlooking the pond under Quinn's favorite linden tree. You could still see remnants of her old tree fort if you looked up at the right angle.

She stopped and so did he. Even though he was only a raisin he found himself taking her hands. Courageously she looked up at him and then he was lost. He saw the grief in her face and he couldn't hold back any longer. Her face crumbled and so did his. His anguish came out so raw he didn't want her to see.

He lost his legs and found himself kneeling on the ground. She put her arms around him, buried his head in her chest. He held her waist and wept.

At some point she got down and they eased onto the grass. They lay there holding on to each other for a long time. Her sobs made a counterpoint to his.

Eventually they both got quiet. She turned over and he felt her heart beating under his hands. Her lovely body curled against his. He pressed his face into her neck, just behind her ear. That smell, her safe, soft smell, which he'd only gotten in faint, secondhand doses and yearned for year after year, now passed into and around him, shrouding him in mercy.

He let consciousness scatter and muscles go. The truth could sneak up and clout him, even fatally, upon waking, but he would be here with her.

Sasha's eyes opened. She surfaced out of sleep carefully, slowly, knowing to fear what she would find when she broke through.

Her head was on the grass. Ray's arms were around her, his face against her neck. This was Ray. She could tell by his heaviness he was still asleep. She kept very still. She took inventory of his parts and hers. Her feet were wound through his calves and they burned.

Slowly, carefully, she connected the pieces that had brought them here. She didn't let the coldest fact get to her in words right away. But the feelings she couldn't keep away. Her eyes filled and spilled over again and again. She tried to keep very still. Tears dripped over the bridge of her nose down into the grass. She tried not to shake.

The sun was halfway up the sky and birds were growing rowdy. Her parents would be panicked. In the frankness of morning she knew she couldn't add to their pain.

Very gently she rotated her body to face Ray's. He stirred in sleep and pulled her closer. She hugged him tenderly and hard. She tried to memorize him.

She dared lay a kiss on his jaw, another next to his ear. "I'm sorry I have to go," she whispered as she extricated her limbs from his.

"Please," he murmured, and so she held him patiently through the gauntlet of waking up.

Later he was a bit awkward getting to his feet. He wanted to walk her to her car. They both hobbled. They didn't try to talk about anything, which was a relief.

He watched her pull out of the driveway. He brushed at his eyes.

She felt a cord that stretched between them pulling taut. She left him there, hands in his pockets, hair going in all directions.

The cord stretched and stretched, until it vibrated like a banjo string as she drove on. It pulled hard on her heart, but it did not snap.

22

"THERE'S RUE FOR YOU, AND HERE'S SOME FOR ME.... O, YOU MUST WEAR YOUR RUE WITH A DIFFERENCE."

"I can't get married anymore."

Emma had been ruminating over it through her many hours of half sleep, going in and out of consciousness, in and out of dreams with no shape and days with no time. There was something she and Jamie had been trying to protect, trying desperately to hold on to, but she couldn't do it anymore. She couldn't even remember what it was.

She'd told Jamie not to come over, and he waited a few days. He sent groceries from Fresh Direct. He sent a giant box of fruit from Dean & Deluca. Then finally he sent himself. He held her on the couch in the living room of the house on Carroll Street.

"We don't have to think about that," he said to her.

"I don't want to see you for a while. I just want to stay home and lie in my bed."

"Okay. I understand."

"I don't want to think about the future or anyone in it."

"Okay."

He was holding her closer than ever and it felt good. But it also felt confusing and forward-leaning and reminded her of things she didn't want to have to think about.

"That means you untangling from me and leaving," she said.

"Right now?"

"Yeah."

"Can I come tomorrow?"

"No."

"Next week?"

"No. I don't know. I can't think about it. I don't want to make any decisions. I just know I need a break and I need you to listen to me."

"Okay." He put his forehead against her cheek. "I don't want to but I will."

"Thanks."

"The thing that's hard is that my mind is here with you all the time. I want to help."

"I know, but you can't right now."

He sighed. "Okay. I'll stay away until you're ready for me to come back."

"That's good."

"In the meantime will you promise to call if there's anything you need? If there's anything I can do? Anything at all, no matter how big or small."

"I promise I will."

"Okay."

"So now you have to take your arms away," she said. She was crying again and so was he.

"All right. I will." He did. "Em?"

"What?" she asked. He wasn't moving.

"You have to take your arms from around me too."

In and out of her long hours and days of dreaming, Emma thought about the tiny apple tree given to her father by her mother on the last birthday he had while they were still married. It was late October, so they left it in its box in the shed for the winter, to plant in the spring.

But sometime after that was when things started coming apart between her parents. Spring and summer came and went and nobody opened the box. It just sat month after month. "Well, it's long dead by now," her father said when another winter passed, but she noticed he didn't throw it away.

Emma was probably five or six at the time. She imagined how her mother felt each time she went for a rake or shovel and saw the tall skinny brown box unopened. It was another bitter stalemate between her parents with another innocent victim languishing inside.

Quinn was the one who finally dragged the box out of the

shed. Emma helped her open it. They both shut their eyes, scared to see the sad remains. The sapling did look scraggly and hopeless, but Quinn wouldn't let them throw it away. She got Adam to help dig a hole at the edge of the woods. They undid the roots very carefully and put it in the ground, even though they knew it was dead.

Are we planting or burying? she remembered asking Quinn.

Same thing, Quinn said, and she sat with the little scrap of tree for hours and talked to it.

Maybe it was then that Quinn embarked on her peculiar belief system about growing. Every day they ran out to check on the small tree first thing and last thing.

Within six days two tiny green tendrils pushed out of the ends of two skinny brown twigs. She remembered the damp quiet of the morning air, the sound of their breathing, hers and Quinn's, the wonder. The next day there were more. By the end of the second week pale green leaves sprouted from every dry brown stick.

After a month they brought their father out, each holding a hand. "That's not the old bare root apple tree," he said.

They nodded solemnly.

"Can't be."

"It is."

He walked away from it shaking his head, chalking it up to some childhood vagueness.

At the end of the summer Lila saw it too. "Your father finally planted it?"

Emma looked at Quinn, half frozen, and Quinn nodded faintly. It was the only wisp of a lie she'd ever known Quinn to tell.

* * *

Several times a day for several days in a row Emma walked down the dark hall and listened attentively at her mother's door. Sometimes the sobs scared her away. Sometimes the silence scared her more. Today she heard a sigh, and it sounded like an invitation.

"Mom?" She pushed the door open a little of the way.

"Emma?"

"Yes."

"Come in."

Her mother sat up in bed. The shades were pulled down, but not the whole way down today. Lila wore a faded T-shirt and yoga pants. Her blond hair was going in the direction of dreadlocks.

Emma got in bed next to her. "Can I rub your back?" It was what Lila always said to them—when they slept late and she crawled in, when they stayed home sick from school.

"Okay," Lila said, and turned onto her stomach, her arms pinned under her.

Emma glided her hand back and forth, using her mother's most comforting technique.

"What's it like out in the world?" her mom asked faintly.

"Same as it was. Mostly. For other people. Less than it was for us."

Lila nodded into her pillow. "It will always be less. But will it be something?"

"It will be something."

"She was so easy to love. I took her for granted."

"We all did." Emma began to cry.

"She was the reason I became a midwife, you know."

"I know," Emma said.

"She was born in my bed. In this very bed. Can you believe that?"

Emma knew these stories, but she could sense it gave her mother solace to tell them again.

"There was an amazing, beautiful snowstorm the night she was born. Your father was desperately trying to shovel out the car. He wanted to call an ambulance, but I told him no. What could be less conducive to labor than an ambulance?"

Emma didn't know.

"So instead he found Monica, who lived on Union Street at the time."

Emma knew this was the Monica who also delivered Mattie and Ray, and became Lila's mentor and eventually her partner.

"Quinn was born in her caul. It was like a shimmering veil over her head and face. Monica had never seen a caulbearer with her own eyes before. She said it was a sign."

"Of what?"

"Of a special destiny."

"It was."

"It was."

Lila's breathing got slower. They lay together for a long time in silence until she thought her mother might be sleeping.

"How is Jamie?" Lila asked softly. She wasn't sleeping.

"I don't know. I haven't seen him in a while."

"Because of me?"

"Because of everything."

Lila turned back over so she could face her. "You really love him, don't you?"

"Yes."

"I can tell."

"I wish you'd noticed that before."

"Let me tell you, so do I." Lila closed her eyes. Tears spilled out of them, onto the sheets.

Emma propped her head up on her elbow. "Yesterday I said to Mattie, 'I like myself better when I'm with him.' And you know what Mattie said?"

Lila shook her head.

"She said, 'I like you better when you're with him too.'"

Lila smiled the ghost of a smile.

"It's true. I admit I am a softer, calmer person when he's around."

"You should tell him that. You need to be with him."

Emma sighed. "That's a little funny, coming from you."

Lila propped her head up too. "God, I know." The tears resumed. "I recant. I regret. So many things. Day after day I lie here and that's what I do."

There was so much in those words, feelings just laid bare, that Emma started to cry too. Her mother wasn't even trying to protect herself anymore. "Oh, Mom."

"I know, sweetheart. I know." Lila patted Emma's hair, smoothed it back from her face.

It was what Emma wanted, for her mother to finally lay down arms, but in another way, it was scarier still.

23

TENDER AND CROUCHING

"I'm sure you don't need to go to work," Ray's mother told him as he came into the kitchen of the Wainscott house, finally shaved and wearing something other than his Batman pajama pants. He knew Lila wanted to keep holding on to them for as long as she could.

"I know, but I want to. Emma went. Mattie went."

"They're crazy," Lila said.

They'd spent nine days in a dark house in Brooklyn before his mother could face going to Wainscott. There had been calls, letters, flowers, food deliveries, and a few visitors, including George Riggs, who'd briefly stopped in from California to pay respects. Then they'd spent four days in a bright house in Wain-scott, during which Lila left the house exactly once: to visit Myrna. It was a brave act and made such a sad picture in Ray's mind he couldn't even ask how she was.

Now it was Monday, ten in the morning, the first day and hour to rise out of the murk. He needed to get away from his parents.

"They need to do something. I do too. I need a change of scenery and something to do with my hands."

At work, Francis and the others offered awkward condolences. It seemed like no one around town could quite look at him, like they were unsure how to confront a sadness of that size.

Ray was listless in the stockroom. He smoked a cigarette by the dumpsters with Julio. It was awful and probably the best part of his day.

Eventually he got home and made it upstairs without talking to anyone. He held his breath as he opened the door to his room. Every time he walked in he smelled her smell and felt her presence.

I don't know what to do, he told her silently.

There was a pitiless yearning in his heart. A constant ache. It came in waves, and some were unbearable. So black and mysterious were the events of August 9, he'd begun to doubt they had actually happened. He only knew Quinn was gone and so was Sasha.

He couldn't distinguish the missing Quinn from the missing Sasha, but it felt slightly more hopeful to miss Sasha. He couldn't distinguish between his pain and Sasha's. It was the same pain, the same loss. Thinking of her both compounded it and offered a strange comfort.

He turned on the shower. He got in and turned it hot, preferring the thick steam and the sting of it on his back.

He thought of Sasha in the shower. He thought of Sasha everywhere. Her hands turned this same stubborn cold knob. Her torn-up toes stood on the same slippery ceramic as his torn-up toes. He had a lot of complicated feelings. A few unbidden ones were admittedly lustful, but not all.

He sensed they were both prisoners: of their grief and of their families and of their families' grief. He guessed she, like he, had parents who could not let her out of their sight. He wondered about guilt sometimes too. He got out and stood in front of the mirror. This mirror got to see Sasha; why not him?

He reached out his index finger and wrote words in the condensation. He opened the door to the cool air of their bedroom and watched the words disappear.

The sky had turned an eerie yellow color over the Reeses' farm and the wind kept changing direction. Mattie had already moved all the produce and baskets under the shelter of the awnings.

"Do you want me to put everything into the storeroom for tonight?" she called to Matthew.

Matthew was hurrying from the barn with two giant rolls of tarp. He had an anxious look on his face.

She fell into step with him. "What's going on? It feels like a big storm, doesn't it?"

His face was still cloaked. They could still barely look at each other. "Supposed to be hail. Which is a fucking disaster."

"What are you going to do?"

"I'm going to cover everything I can."

"By yourself?"

He threw the two rolls down by the pumpkin patch.

Mattie knew Matthew wasn't older than Emma—they were born the same month, in fact. She'd seen the picture of the two tired mommies with their two fat babies. Lila once said Carly stayed around long enough to sit for that picture and not much longer. But sometimes Matthew looked like he was forty years old, if not a hundred, and that made her sad.

She knew he was alone. Patsy and lame Dana had already left for the summer.

Mattie remembered a night a few years before when Quinn hadn't come home from the farm. Dinner came and went. It was past midnight and her father was pacing the floors when she finally came back from the Reeses', soaked and exhilarated, telling the story of what you do on a truck farm in the case of hail.

"Can I help?" Mattie asked.

"You weren't supposed to come at all today," Matthew said.

She knew Matthew had been trying to protect her in her grief. It was Mrs. Reese who'd called and asked her to come to work. Mrs. Reese didn't say it, but Mattie knew he was knocked back too. He was struggling badly. They all were.

"I don't mind."

He was shaking his head, walking back to the barn. "It's heavy, messy, endless work."

She kept following him. *Please don't let me off easy for once.* She trailed him back to the barn to get more sheeting and back out to the orchard. "I know I'm not Quinn," she said in a wavery voice.

He stopped finally and turned to her. She didn't know his face was capable of such open despair. He nodded. "You can help if you want," he said.

Mattie just kept following him around for the first part, trying to get the idea of it. She might have been annoying, she recognized, but she might have been more annoying pelting him with a hundred questions. She carefully watched him cover and stake the first row of melons. He let her help on the second. On the third he let her do one side and end while he did the others.

The rain began teasingly. It started as warm slaps and quickly got cold. On the next run to the barn he brought her a jacket that smelled like him. As she pulled it on he looked skeptically at her feet. Metallic flip-flops and aqua-blue toenails. "What size?"

This was a figure she had never spoken aloud since she was fourteen. Not to her friends, not to her sisters, not even to her mother, and certainly not to the most handsome young man she ever knew. She looked up at the sky. What was there to fear when the worst things happened anyway? "Eleven."

"Awesome," he said in perfect sincerity, running back to the barn again. "You can take a pair of mine."

Mattie kept her head down and worked. Her arms ached and her feet hurt. The skin of her hands was raw. Under that lurked a pain somewhere deeper than her muscles, and it was caused by all the preening she'd done among the zinnias and the blueberries for the last four summers, being delightful at the front where the customers came.

She posed at a job, posed at earning money, battled it out with stupid Dana for who could dress cuter and flirt more. *I hate myself.* No wonder Matthew shook his head and walked the other way. This was Matthew's life work, his family's work, his livelihood. She suffered a visceral self-chastisement, a long-overdue reorientation, as she worked beside him.

When he was ready to trust her with the low crops, he ran to the orchard. She sensed he was most worried about that.

The rain came hard and turned the ground to mud. She slid from row to row, twice falling so extravagantly she splatted in mud up to her forehead. It was a small farm, she knew, but God, it felt big tonight. Eggplants, cauliflowers, sweet corn, cucumbers, summer squash. Quinn's tender babies, nurtured by Quinn's mystical hands, now helpless and crouching under the fast-moving sky. Mattie's heart went out to them, and to herself a little too. *We miss you. We need you. How could you leave us?*

She had become Matthew's shadow, his alter ego, his twin in a matching coat and work boots, racing back and forth between the barn and the fields. Row after row after row: grape tomatoes, peppers, potatoes, blueberries, blackberries, more melons. Pushing in the stakes to secure the covers got harder as the ground got softer.

There were still four rows of blueberry bushes in front of her. She felt a frenzied, desperate energy powering a deep concentration. She had no sense of time anymore. She couldn't bear the idea of a single berry, a single stalk going unprotected. She could go faster, and she did. The wild inefficiency of her regular mind gathered behind one simple purpose.

She began to doubt the ice would come and then the ice came. Just little pits and sparks whizzing by at first, almost playful. The next time Matthew ran out of the barn he carried a bicycle helmet and he thrust it at her.

"Seriously?" she said. It was just as well he didn't hear her. She buckled the strap under her chin.

Oh, if Dana could see her now.

She couldn't feel her body anymore. Just the plastic cover stretching under her fingers. She resented the sharp little pings of ice. How would that feel to a blueberry?

When she couldn't finish the last row she stopped and huddled three young bushes under her body and waited. She was so intense she scared herself a little, but that self and this new blueberry-mother were wide apart.

I don't know who I am anymore, she'd said to Matthew. Were truer words ever spoken? The sound of ice clumps falling from the sky thunking against a borrowed bicycle helmet in the middle of a field, with mud up to her eyebrows and her body stretched over blueberry bushes, was a novelty indeed.

Matthew found Mattie there sometime later. "I think the worst of it is over," he said cautiously.

She nodded, untangled herself from the bushes, straightened

her helmet. She tried not to weave or stagger as she walked toward him. You couldn't cede your dignity altogether.

"Are you okay?"

She nodded.

He looked over the fields with a look approaching disbelief. "You did an *unbelievable* job."

She started to shiver.

"I don't even know what to say."

She nodded again.

"If I'd had two of myself tonight I wouldn't have done it as well."

She shrugged. With shaking hands she took off the helmet. It was hard to make any words come. She finally got hold of some and forced them out. "Y-you didn't know I could do it."

His whole face opened again and he looked no older than the twenty-two years he was. He covered the few feet between them in one large step and put both of his arms around her. He held her shivering body and buried his tired face in her hair. "I didn't know you at all."

24

THE DEEPER MAGIC

It was hard to come back here. They all felt it.

It had been almost three weeks. After the first frantic night, Sasha had promised her parents she would stay put, and she had.

Summer was over. Lila and her family had already come back here the week before. So that was maybe why they needed to do it too.

Her dad slumped around the edges of rooms like an extra in a movie. His posture had changed since it happened. He said his body didn't digest food right anymore. His stomach wasn't at all fat now. It was the vacuum into which the other parts of him began to sink.

Evie was as nervous as an insect. "He'll get through this. We all will," she tended to say nervously, which tended to make Sasha fear the opposite.

The only structure holding up their lives was the family memorial they planned for late September.

Early that morning Sasha had overheard her father trying to arrange the details with Evie over his untouched oatmeal, as though it could be just them doing it. And suddenly zing, through the muck of Sasha's mind, sliced the sharp imperative: haven't we gotten anywhere?

Sasha pulled to a stop in front of the kitchen table. "You have to call Lila and plan it with her," she told him.

He looked up at her in confusion. No fight left, just the dust still swirling after defeat.

Later that morning, as her father walked the edges of rooms, she saw a gradual dawning in him. At noon she overheard her father's hushed phone conversation with Lila. Sasha listened for bitterness and recrimination in his voice, but he just sounded tired. Together they agreed on the particulars.

It was hard for Sasha to walk into her bedroom and confusing to stay there.

Ray had tried to make the bed. It was almost certainly the first time in their joint tenancy he had done that. Rusty smile muscles worked at her mouth. The bed looked like the work of a five-year-old.

She was scared to think about him. She was scared to remember the feeling of their bodies curled together for those few hours of sleep on the grass. Because what if it was the fruit of a bargain she hadn't meant to make? What if she'd unknowingly traded her greatest dread for her oldest wish?

Her cheap, stunted, nonmystical religion required that she offer up her happiness in return for a little less disappointment, a little less fear. Suffering was how you put money in the karmic bank. There were always more bills to be paid. No joy was allowed to come out of this.

But Quinn had a different religion. A brave and expansive one. Don't be scared of the pain, she would have said. Don't avoid the ways you feel. Don't bargain away your happiness. Let joy come out of this.

Sasha now sat gingerly on the bed, their bed, breathing deep late-summer air, feeling Quinn's presence and allowing thoughts of him to come. "I wish we didn't keep dividing," Quinn had said to her the day of the accident. She wouldn't let Quinn's death be another reason to divide.

Sasha went into the bathroom. Sometimes a shower made her thoughts go straight. Sometimes a shower gave her a new look at the day.

She turned on the faucets and let the water get hot. She was stepping into the shower when she saw the words magically appear out of steam on the mirror:

I WISH I COULD SEE YOU

"How does Jamie seem?" Emma asked not long after she arrived in Wainscott late in the week. She didn't want to ask, but she had to. She couldn't help it.

Her father was sitting by the pool dangling his feet in the cold water, his pants rolled up. He didn't seem to notice anymore that it was full of leaves and frogs. He cocked his head at her. "Why do you ask me?"

So he wasn't going to make it easy. "Because I know you went to the office for a few hours on Wednesday. Evie told me."

He patted the space next to him for her to sit, and she sat. "I did go to the office, but I didn't see him, because he doesn't work there anymore. I thought you would know that."

She turned to him, eyes wide. "I didn't know that. I haven't talked to him in a few weeks. We're taking a break . . . because . . . after everything . . ." Her simple goal of the day was to get through without crying and she'd only made it to four p.m.

Her dad put his arm around her. "Oh, my dear. I understand. Of course I do."

She wiped her nose flagrantly on her sleeve. "When did he leave? Did he say why?"

"He gave notice last Friday. He gave a respectable explanation to the partners. To me personally he called and explained it would be easier for the two of you. He never wanted you to think his job compromised his commitment to you."

"He said that? We're not even together."

"Exactly. That's why I was surprised before."

She nodded and sighed. "I don't think he's thinking of our break as a breakup."

"Are you?"

She shook her head. "No. He's in my mind all day. I miss him terribly. I just don't think I can be with anybody right now."

"I understand," he said again, and his voice was heavy with emotion. He took a few breaths. He kicked up the water and watched the drops fall. "I have a feeling he'll be patient."

"He says so."

"He was absolutely decent about it, as you would expect."

She smiled. She leaned her head against his shoulder. Sometimes she and her father had their best conversations when they were sideways.

"I said I hoped he knew I didn't hold him responsible in any way for the unpleasantness at that party. You know I had already apologized personally to him and to his parents."

Emma was reminded that she hadn't been able to bring herself to open the thick cream-colored envelope that held the letter of condolence from Jamie's parents.

The way her dad spoke, it occurred to Emma that they were jointly rewriting that day. In light of the real tragedy that had followed, the engagement party had begun to feel like farce to them.

Emma nodded again. "What did he say?"

"He said he understood and accepted my words in their most generous spirit. He said he bore no ill will, only compassion, and he wasn't leaving the firm because of the past, but because he wanted a clean slate for his future with you."

Her eyebrows went up. "And what did you say?"

He shrugged. "What could I say? I said to him, and I quote: 'You are a good man, James Hurn, and you are right to love my daughter more than this job, because she is infinitely more important than it will ever be.'"

*　*　*

Ray decided he had to talk to his mother.

He found her sitting at the table of the small cluttered Brooklyn kitchen in front of a mug of tea. Out the back window she watched Hank, the downstairs tenant, watering the garden.

When he sat down across from her Lila gave him a wan and distracted smile.

"Hey, Mom?"

"Yeah, sweetie." Her face was white these days.

"You know how you were saying to Adam that the memorial is happening on our weekend and should we offer Robert to stay in the house Friday night and we'll stay Saturday?" He needed to say it pretty fast to get it out.

"Yes."

"Well." He took a breath. "I think that's the wrong way to think about it."

She put her hands around her mug. She tipped her head. "What do you mean?"

He bounced his heels. He was always fidgety at this table. "The house belongs to all of us. I think we should share it."

She nodded slowly. "I know. I agree. That's what I was saying."

"No, but not the regular way, like you take Friday, we'll take Saturday, but like actually share it."

His mother stared at him. Her expression wasn't so much defensive or disagreeable, but more like a computer that didn't quite understand her programming.

"Like we could all stay there together for the weekend," he explained.

Lila's computer was still not computing.

"You know, like all of us staying in the house at the same time."

Suddenly her circuits came to life, pinging and zapping. "Stay in the house together? *At the same time?*"

"Yes."

"But—"

"What?"

Her eyes were getting a little frantic. "I don't—"

"Mom, there's plenty of space. It's not like you don't all have the privacy of your own bedrooms and bathrooms. It's a big house. And I'm not suggesting a permanent change or anything. Just for this one time." He let Quinn's image come to him, but only in flashes. "I think it would befit the occasion. I really do."

Lila raised both hands on her face. She still couldn't make full sense of it. But he could see she was trying. She was beginning to grasp the idea underlying it. She looked out the window. Hank had finished with the hose.

Her eyes were full when she turned back to him. "But do you think—" Her voice came out a little shaky. "Robert and Evie—"

"I think you should call Robert and suggest the idea."

Lila considered this, her wet eyes large and unfocused. Her circuit board emitted one last fizzle. "Where would Sasha sleep?"

*　*　*

Ray finally wrote to Sasha.

> *I don't know what to say. It's too hard a world.*
> *I just want to make sure you are still in it.*

> *I am still here. I'm pretty sure.*
> *I bought us a new kalanchoe plant. You don't have*
> *to water it or anything. I got it because it has the exact*
> *same little orange flowers our old one had.*

Sasha thought for a long time about what to say.

> *I wish I could see you too.*

Same bikini. Same blond hair. Same big feet. Same Ditch Plains. But nonetheless, Mattie knew it was all different this time.

Jonathan Dawes was surprised to see her. He dropped his board instantly, excused himself from his conversation with another grizzled surfer. He came over and hugged her.

"I am so sorry, Mattie."

"I know. Thank you. Thank you for the note you sent."

He'd written her three lovely pages of his old memories of Quinn, wild little sprite, and she'd wept over each of them.

He nodded. "How are you doing?"

After everything that had passed between them, she wanted to answer honestly and not just say fine. "At first it was pure sadness. Now it's more like I'm . . . uncomfortable . . . a lot of the time. But that's not always a bad thing."

He touched her hand. "Wise girl you are. How is your mom?"

Mattie let out her breath. "I think she's starting to come back to life. A little."

His face twisted with empathy. "I can't even begin to imagine."

"She was in her room for a long time. Yesterday morning she made us breakfast."

"Green shoots," he said.

"I hope so," she replied. "None of us will ever be how we were."

"I know."

"I miss her all the time." Her eyes began their daily quotient of leaking. She realized she trusted him. He'd told her the truth. She would keep telling him the truth.

He looked like he was going to cry too. He was quiet for a while, but his face was moving, trying to formulate thoughts. "I've worried so many times I did the wrong thing, telling you about what happened back then . . . and then when Quinn . . . If I've added to your burden I am sorry for it."

She kicked the sand around with her large foot. "No." She felt the warmth of the sun on top of her head. "Don't be sorry for it."

She'd asked herself: Was it wrong? Was she angry at him for it? It wasn't. She wasn't.

"It wasn't wrong," she said. She looked at him carefully. "I'm grateful to you for taking me seriously enough to tell me the truth and for . . . waking me up, I guess. It's made me rethink some ways I am—some ways we are—that weren't doing me or any of us much good. . . ." She took a breath. "It's hard to explain."

He nodded.

She took another big breath. "I also wanted to say that in spite of everything I know now, and for all his faults, I already have a father."

He nodded again. He sort of tipped his head. "I already have a daughter."

She glanced up. "You do?"

"Yes, her name is Julia. From my first marriage. She's twenty-seven and she lives in LA. I think you'd like her."

"Wow." Another potential sister, partial sister. How very strange. And strangely liberating. She'd imagined emptiness and regret for him, but Jonathan Dawes had that base covered before she was even born. "I'd like to meet her sometime."

"I'd like that too."

They fell to silence for a few moments, a companionable silence.

Why was it there were some things you could have multiples of, like daughters and sisters, and other things you didn't, like fathers and husbands?

"Hey, Mattie?"

"Yeah?"

"I respect that you are not looking for another father. And I am not looking for a daughter. But I am open to friendship if you are. Now that we've gotten everything on the table. I'd perfectly understand if not. But I'd like to know you if you'd like to be known, if you'd like to know me. No pressure. No obligations, no labels."

She studied him. She wasn't mad at him anymore. She liked him. He did have large feet. "I think that sounds good," she said.

When Ray saw the orange kalanchoe plant he wanted to hug it. He felt kind of fatherly toward it. He could see it from where he lay down on the bed and he found himself worrying for its well-being.

When he couldn't sleep he wrote to Sasha:

> I've sort of got the hang of waking up in the morning, but it's not easy. I fight with falling asleep at night. Some nights it feels impossible.
> If I could hold you again, I think I could do it.

Awake in her room in New York, Sasha wanted to say something clever, to add something important. But mostly she just wanted to cry.

> If I could hold you again, I think I could sleep too.

* * *

"Where are you?" Emma asked into her phone.

"I'm on Carroll Street. Right outside your house."

"Why?"

"Because I have ice cream. Only Chubby Hubby and chocolate chip cookie dough, though."

"Jamie."

"I know. But I have here a person who loves you and some ice cream. So why should I stay away?"

"Because I told you to."

"Well, that's true. But you need me a little, at least. And ice cream."

She missed him so much her ribs ached. What could she do? "Oh, fine."

Once inside, they sat on the floor of the living room with two spoons and ate ice cream directly out of the cartons. She got him to tell the story of his departure from Califax Capital.

"Some of the partners were pretty pissed," he explained. "At my exit meeting, they threatened to claw back money and enforce a noncompete so I couldn't work in the industry for the next three years."

"That's terrible."

"I know."

"That's what you get for being indispensable. That sucks. If you'd done a worse job they would have packed you off no problem."

"But wait. The story gets better. Because then your dad heard about it from my direct boss, Gary. Gary was not happy either. Your dad called a meeting of the partners. He came in for it on Monday. According to Gary he roared like a lion. He said you always stay loyal to the hard workers. If you're good to them when they leave, they may come back. If you retaliate, they'll only want to crush you. He told them to lay off me—no claw backs, no noncompetes—and he himself would pen a stellar letter of recommendation."

Emma laughed. "I am sure he will. I'd like to get a look at that letter."

"He didn't tell you about all that?"

"No."

Jamie breathed out. "Your dad is an amazing person."

"I know. He is." She laughed. "If it doesn't work out with us, I think you and my dad should get married."

25

BROKEN OPEN

It seemed to Sasha they had all entered the afterlife. They had somehow snuck through in disguise, in altered versions of themselves, searching for her. Trying to be worthy of her.

We would do anything to find you, Quinn.

Her father would not only countenance Lila, Quinn's mother, but embrace her. He would stand next to her, waist-deep in the cold autumn pond, as the eight of them scattered Quinn's ashes. Who else understood the love and the pain of it?

Of course Sasha's eyes had gone to Ray. Who else understood? It was good, it was miraculous, that someone did.

They would all stand in the water, holding hands in a circle, as though they'd never done things any other way. Evie holding Lila's hand, Robert between Lila and Adam. Robert, her father, would wear the kurta Quinn had bought him years ago, looking like a proper Bengali gentleman. Mattie would tuck a sprig of sweet jasmine above her ear, just like Quinn had worn on her last day. They would cry.

We are with you, a little bit, Quinn, aren't we?

Quinn would have loved it. That was the best and the worst part. The best, that it had happened. The worst, that it had happened without her.

But you are here, aren't you? I know you are. This is because of you.

Quinn's magic was at its high mark. Strange and undeniable. Their tanks had gone empty, but she'd left them the means to help each other fill up.

Did you do this? Is this what you wanted to happen?

No one loved harmony and wholeness as Quinn did. No one suffered more from the discord. But she didn't turn away from it. She embraced it and endured it. That was her particular courage.

Sasha's heart was as full as it had ever been as she lay in her bed replaying all the pictures of the day, watching for the moon to cross the exact center of the skylight.

How could you even think the thought of Lila and Robert, Adam and Evie, sleeping under the roof of this house together? Up until August 9 it would have been purely unimaginable, as so many things these last few weeks had been, and mostly for the horror of them. But this was something different. She imagined all eight of them wide-eyed in their beds at the strangeness of this night.

And then she imagined they were all still suspended in the pond together, reaching slowly through strange valences of feeling, like pockets of warm and cold water. It was a quiet and rapturous suspense. But eventually you had to climb out.

Could they stay in it for a while longer, though? Could they make breakfast together as they had dinner last night—all careful and overpolite but agreeable? Would her dad put on an apron again and find something to put on the grill? Would he and Lila reminisce again, haltingly at first but not discordantly, about the snowy night Quinn was born in their bed?

Would Lila squeeze Sasha's hand out of the blue again and say, "You remind me so much of my girls I feel like I know you."

Would her dad and Ray take another look at the faulty air compressor together, nodding their heads in a manly way, her father standing up a little straighter again?

Would she and Ray continue their glazed looks across the table, trying to make it appear that they were lightest of acquaintances, while she yearned to grab him and touch him and feel how all his parts felt against hers?

Would Emma say, clueless, to the two of them, "You know, I actually think you guys might get along"?

It was strange water they were spinning in.

The only problem was Ray sleeping in an unfamiliar room at the other end of the hallway. She felt half of her was missing, wandering around the house like a zombie.

She'd offered to take the guest room, but he'd insisted as a gentleman that he'd do it. She hated that on such a night she got to be here and he didn't. She didn't want to be zero-sum anymore. She wanted to be together.

There would be no sleep on this bed tonight. It was hard enough to surrender to sleep as it was, but now there was Sasha less than fifty feet away.

There was the invincible strangeness and sweetness of the day. And in honor of Quinn he tried to welcome it all in: the bad and the good, the puzzling, the weird.

Still. This was the opposite of where he wanted to be. This generic, unlived-in room with its scratchy carpet smelled like Union Street Cleaners. The bedspread was stiff and covered with stupid blue flowers. It didn't smell at all like Sasha. He hated that about it.

He might as well have been at a Holiday Inn while miracles were taking place under the roof of his own house.

He got up and marched around on the carpet. His feet were nearly healed. His feet were less grudging than the rest of him. Yesterday he'd left his nearly new party shoes in the Goodwill box at the church.

He would rather sleep on the couch in the den than in this horrible room.

He'd rather sleep in the grass out back.

He'd probably rather sleep on the gravel in Grandpa Harrison's old dog run.

He'd really, really rather sleep in his bed. In Sasha's bed. In their bed. *Their* bed. With a view of the moon and *their* kalanchoe plant.

They were in the same house! They were in the same place at the same time. At night! That wasn't supposed to be possible.

Sasha is in my bed and I'm not. It was unbearable.

He stared out the window at darkness. There were faint solar lights dotting the entrance to the dock. As he looked longer he saw other dots of light, moving sparking light, and of course they were fireflies.

He crept out of the Holiday Inn and past the big room across the hall where Robert and Evie slept. That room had not been occupied a single night that he'd been in the house. He'd barely ever walked in it; it was a foreign country. It was like the Vatican City inside Rome, the sole part of the house that belonged exclusively to "the other family." He turned the bend in the hall back into the familiarity of home. He passed Emma's and Mattie's rooms. At Quinn's door he made himself stop and take a breath.

Let it all in, he told himself. That was what Quinn would do. Feel everything.

He walked past the door of the bedroom where his parents slept. He hadn't bothered to wonder before why his parents got the master bedroom and Robert and Evie didn't. He approached the door of his room. Sasha's room.

There was suddenly something captivating about his otherwise ordinary door: it wasn't shut. It was very slightly open.

Was she really in there? It seemed fantastical. He wasn't in there, which did lend credence to the idea.

Had she left it open a little on purpose? His breathing got very shallow very quickly. He tried to settle down, annoyed at himself. *What are you, twelve?*

Could he knock? Should he? No, someone else would hear. Not Robert, unless he had bionic ears, and not Adam, because he was slightly deaf, but very possibly Lila.

His palms were sweating. His almost-healed feet were sweating. He pushed a little on the door and it opened. He pushed most of his body through, not sure if he meant to or not.

Now he was this far. Was this a good idea? It didn't matter. He couldn't not do it.

He pushed the door shut behind him. Holding his breath, he turned to look at the bed. The room was dark, but faint moonlight poured through the skylight and onto her, as it had done onto him so many nights. She was there as though he'd dreamed her. She was even wearing the silky nightgown kind of thing he'd smelled an embarrassing number of times.

He took a step closer. He was so transfixed by the sight of her that he forgot for a moment that he was there. And then her eyes popped open and she was staring at him. So he was there, that meant.

She sat up.

How would he explain this? Was it too late to ask if he could come in? He felt so tenderly toward her. He could barely hold himself together. "There's a girl sleeping in my bed," he whispered. He lifted his hands in wonder. "How did you get here?"

She laughed. She didn't look mad or sorry. She pushed over to the side of the bed.

"Come," she said. She made room for him.

It was only right and fitting that it happen here, in their bed. One bed for two people turned two people into one: breathing, pulsing, folding together, and finally complete. He saw his expressions in her face, felt her desire in his chest, heard his emotions in her voice. All of it mixed up, shared around. He couldn't distinguish himself from her and didn't want to.

It was a very quiet avalanche. It had to be quiet because all their parents were down the hall. Every one of the million moments he'd thought of her over these years, every molecule of her smell that he'd smelled in all that time seemed to amplify the force of it. The sheer momentum allowed for no stumbling.

He didn't know a body could undergo these extravagances. He marveled at the strange wonder of the whole enterprise. That he could feel like that. That she could be like that, look like that, move like that. Her body, the shapes, the smells, the taste of her. How could that even be?

After the roar subsided and the calmer part set in, he felt the weight of her head on his bare chest, her damp body along his. She turned her face up to him and he had to look away for a moment. He didn't want to leave any glimpse of her, any crumb of sensation, on the table, but he couldn't take it. Too much pleasure. Too much ache curled alongside it. That was always how it would be, two sides of the same devotion.

Strange miracles abounded. Mattie and her mother and Evie baked a cake in the kitchen. Mattie's throat swelled at their good-natured but cautious patter: the deference over sticks of butter, number of eggs, the robust agreement on the virtue of vanilla, the desire under their words to say more than they were saying. Adam was at his desk in the bedroom working on his book. Her dad was fishing on the dock. Emma walked on the beach where the cell service was best, telling Jamie about everything that happened. Ray and Sasha went together into town to get groceries. It was really something. What would Quinn have thought of this?

You are here, aren't you? What do you think?

It all felt dazzlingly fragile, and she was afraid if she breathed too hard it would crumple and fly away like gold leaf. But then Mattie made herself breathe hard. What was there to be afraid of anymore?

Today was Sunday, and tonight, after a final dinner to honor Quinn, they would all go back to their regular lives. Tomorrow they'd go back to school, back to work, back to the old week-to-week rotation.

This might be the last time Mattie ever had both her parents in the house again. Amicable and generous as they were being, she didn't expect they'd make a habit of it. The divisions would return. Of course they would. Grass would grow. Leaves would fall. Bills would fail to be paid.

With a potent mix of thrill and disquiet she pictured Sasha and Ray walking toward the car together. Some things would be changed forever.

She went out to keep her dad company.

"Hi, sweetie," he said. He wore his classic paisley print bathing suit, a peach cabled sweater, his signature Ray-Bans flipped up onto his head. His outfit glowed with tradition and optimism. His face was still a heartbreak.

"Hi, Dad. Anything biting?" She peered into his hopeful bucket.

"Not yet," he said.

She sat by him on the dock and dangled her feet in the water as she used to do so often when she was small. He leaned over and tousled her hair.

The air was autumn cool. The trees around the pond pulsed with color.

"I like having both my parents in this house," she said. "I admit it. I love both of you. I love both my families. I love this house." She felt it so strongly and gratefully, even with everything she knew.

He nodded. His face didn't forbid anything, so she kept going.

"Have I ever had this before? Did you and Mom ever stay here together after I was born?" she asked. She wasn't sure how much she was going for.

"Not for long. Maybe two months. Just long enough for you to start to smile."

"Did I?"

"Oh, yes. Gloriously. Always." He smiled quite sincerely at the memory. "It's what kept us all going."

"Really?"

"On my hardest days, it still does."

She saw his tears. She wasn't scared of them anymore. If anything, she was getting used to them. She put her chin down and cried too. Tears dotted her legs.

She knew that this was a time of strange enchantment, when mysterious pathways hung open in the air. Soon they would close again. The old boundaries and restrictions would snap back into place. She needed to be brave and push through them while she could.

"Was my being born enough to finally push you and Mom apart?" she asked.

He looked at her, aghast. "No. That wasn't it."

And more brave. "I didn't look like the other babies. I know I didn't. I still don't. I know I'm different." It was hard to say it.

He took in her words. He realized what she meant. He put down his fishing rod. He regrouped. She saw it as it happened. She could almost hear him pushing into the reeds, getting out the machete, ready to combat the serious undergrowth. He was the brave one. Because of course he knew. He'd always known.

He turned to her and took her hands, her white-pink hands in his brown ones. His gaze was unflinching. "You know that I was raised and loved by two people to whom I bore no physical resemblance. You know that, right?"

She nodded.

"You've seen pictures of my dear mother, Matilda, for whom you are named."

She nodded again.

"My mother and father gave me everything they had, everything I am."

She cried openly. She tried to keep her face from crumbling.

"They loved me and cared for me, so they are my parents. There are no other parents. It is simply that way."

"Is it?"

He pulled her toward him and hugged her. "I love you and I care for you. I always have and I always will."

Jamie came up on the jitney late Sunday morning. Emma wanted him to see Brigadoon before it disappeared. She picked him up at the bus stop and they made a plan on the short drive to the house, which they decided to announce when they got there.

"Get ready," she prepared him.

Because it really was like walking into a dream, seeing them all amicably settled around the kitchen table eating french toast. Jamie had the look of a man hallucinating.

"Welcome," Lila said, getting up, pulling more chairs over, as if she'd never been anything other than welcoming.

Jamie looked from Robert to Lila, from Adam to Evie, from Ray to Sasha in disbelief. To Mattie he shrugged.

"We're going to elope in November," Emma announced to the group without preamble. "You can all come."

There was general approval, congratulations, not much surprise. Ray did his taxi whistle.

"Why not a wedding?" Lila asked. "We'll behave this time." She glanced at Robert and her face turned more serious. "*I* will behave this time."

Robert looked at Lila. The look wasn't affectionate, exactly, but it was without bitterness. "I will too."

"I'll make another bean salad," Lila offered.

Emma spun toward her. "No bean salad."

"I was kidding." It was a remarkable feat that Lila had advanced to kidding.

Emma and Jamie shared a look. "Well, for once, you all aren't even the problem," Emma explained.

Jamie looked pained but unbroken. "We can go to city hall together."

Can you see this, Quinn? I really hope you can.

ANN BRASHARES

is the #1 *New York Times* bestselling author of the Sisterhood of the Traveling Pants series, *The Here and Now, 3 Willows, The Last Summer (of You & Me),* and *My Name Is Memory.* She lives in New York City with her family.